"We both know *he* was here, and you accepted his gift—"

"No, Gabriel, you're wrong. I didn't accept—"

"Don't lie to me!"

I'd never seen him so angry, and I knew it was a waste of time trying to explain what had happened. Even if Gabriel allowed me to speak, he was in no mood to listen. His hand clutched the string of opals in a grip so tight I saw his knuckles blanch. Would the precious stones caught in his palm be pulverized to dust from the pressure of his fist? He came toward me and reached for my hand with his free one, turning it palm up. Opening his fingers, he pooled the smooth stones in my palm, closing my fingers over them when he was done.

"I've told you before to never lie to me." His disappointment stung.

"Gabriel—please! I'm not lying! I didn't—"

"Shhh." He placed a finger against my mouth. "If you had refused . . . you could not hold the stones in your hand."

Also by Carla Susan Smith

A Vampire's Promise

A Vampire's Soul

A Vampire's Honor

A Vampire's Hunger

Carla Susan Smith

LYRICAL PRESS
Kensington Publishing Corp.
www.kensingtonbooks.com

LYRICAL PRESS BOOKS are published by

Kensington Publishing Corp.
119 West 40th Street
New York, NY 10018

All Kensington titles, imprints, and distributed lines are available at special quantity discounts for bulk purchases for sales promotion, premiums, fund-raising, educational, or institutional use.

Special book excerpts or customized printings can also be created to fit specific needs. For details, write or phone the office of the Kensington Sales Manager: Kensington Publishing Corp., 119 West 40th Street, New York, NY 10018. Attn. Sales Department. Phone: 1-800-221-2647.

Lyrical Press and Lyrical Press logo Reg. U.S. Pat. & TM Off.

First Electronic Edition: October 2016
eISBN-13: 978-1-60183-960-2
eISBN-10: 1-60183-960-X

First Print Edition: October 2016
ISBN-13: 978-1-60183-961-9
ISBN-10: 1-60183-961-8

Printed in the United States of America

I owe a debt of thanks to some wonderful people who helped to bring this book to life.
Jack, Joseph and Cayden just for being who you are.
Ruth Guillot for being my first reader.
Lynne Harter for making sure I'm as grammatically correct as possible.
My friend, and fellow author, L.G. O'Connor, who showed me Las Vegas and proved it is possible to have too much of a good thing.
My editor, Alicia Condon, and the wonderful team at Kensington Publishing who make all my dreams a reality.
And most especially to you, my readers, for agreeing to take this wonderful, crazy ride with me. Without you none of this would have ever happened. Thank you.

Chapter 1

The candle was as thick and as long as Ryiel's forearm. After lighting it, he placed it in the iron sconce on the stone wall, where the flame made a game of chasing shadows. In truth, the vampire had no need of artificial illumination to help him with his task, but he enjoyed the ambience the candlelight afforded. And this room, with its multitude of fixtures, had been made for light. Once it had reverberated with prayers to a deity now long forgotten, and every now and then, when the wind found a way in through an open window or an unattended door, Ryiel fancied he heard the ghostly echo of chanting voices.

"Doubtful," Stavros told him. The vampire's raised brow invited clarification. "There's no evidence of a fireplace or any other type of heat source," the sentinel explained, "and as cold as it is this high up the mountain, it would have taken them all day to recite the Lord's Prayer with chattering teeth."

"Enough bodies in a single chamber would surely generate sufficient warmth."

"You're a vampire," the sentinel pointed out. "You can't feel how cold it actually is."

"How cold is it?"

For a moment Stavros thought he was being teased, that Ryiel was actually making a joke. But there was no hidden humor lurking in the vampire's expression, only mild curiosity. The sentinel ran a hand over his bald head. "Too cold to be reciting prayers with chattering teeth." He paused and looked thoughtful for a moment. "Nah, I'd bet my last silver coin they were a silent order. Most of these religious groups are, you know."

"And your reasoning for such an astute observation?"

"If you can't speak, then you can't complain."

"What would they have to complain about, surrounded by such magnificence?" The spread of Ryiel's arms was meant to encompass not only the room, but the mountain itself.

Stavros grinned. "You mean apart from the freeze-your-balls-off cold? Lack of female companionship would be high on my list. I imagine any number of them probably went bat-shit crazy if all they could fuck was each other."

"That has never seemed to bother you," Ryiel pointed out.

"True, but I'm not a human male." Stavros gave the vampire a knowing look. "They have a lot of insecurities, especially when it comes to fornicating."

Ryiel gave his sentinel a curious stare. Stavros was not usually so talkative, which made him the perfect guardian for a vampire who preferred to keep himself isolated as much as possible from the rest of the world. "So you prefer women?" he asked, deciding to indulge the sentinel for however long he chose to be loquacious.

"Given a choice? Absolutely."

One of the first things Stavros had done upon their arrival was to establish contact with the closest village to the abandoned monastery. It was a humble settlement, located a few thousand feet down the mountainside, and tucked away in a hidden valley Ryiel doubted few outsiders knew existed. The population numbered almost a thousand, and as if to compensate for the apparently low procreation rate, longevity was impressive.

The village elders had welcomed the sentinel. He estimated the group, made up of both sexes, to have an average age of a hundred and fifty years, with no frailty, either physical or mental, detected amongst them. But though they treated Stavros with great respect, they politely refused to consider his request, asking that he return at dusk, and bring his master with him. They might be insulated from the modern world, but they knew the manner of creature who sought to walk among them.

Ryiel found the entire village waiting for him. Dressed in their finest clothes, they were all eager for a chance to glimpse the silver-eyed vampire who had chosen to be a part of their community. He did not disappoint. Wearing dark pants tucked into boots boasting a mirror shine, he came bare-chested, as was his fashion. Long hair, black as a raven's wing, shimmered in the moonlight. It hung in a single, thick braid between the livid scars marring each shoulder blade. He presented himself to the elders, waiting as they noted the glyphs tattooed on his chest before he addressed them. They showed neither alarm nor surprise at hearing the vampire speak to them in their own tongue, and they invited him to sit and share a pipe with them. After receiving his personal assurance his needs required no human sacrifice, the villagers were more than happy to provide for him and his sentinel.

It was agreed the elders would choose the female for the vampire to feed from when so needed, and he in turn would keep their secret and protect them from the outside world. Stavros negotiated the terms of his own compact. The village would have the use of his broad back and strong legs for spring planting and the subsequent harvest. And after the first year, when the annual yield was considerably more than anticipated, the villagers realized the vampire who lived high above them on the mountain was not the only supernatural being in their midst. The sentinel had gifts of his own. Gifts that were of the earth. Gifts he chose to share. Because of his generosity, Stavros was also offered a female, but his needs were satisfied a little more frequently, and in a much different way. And it definitely stopped him from going bat-shit crazy.

The elders knew nothing about those who had built the temple. For reasons of their own, the occupants had chosen to keep to themselves. Whether or not they were silent remained unknown. Ryiel had never understood the compulsion of such a restriction, but he had stopped looking for reasons to explain human behavior long ago. Still, the choice to remain mute was something that had always puzzled him. Tongues were designed to be used in many ways, and it was not the nature of human beings to remain silent. So why embrace such an unnatural constraint of one's free will? He did not know, but then he was certain there were aspects of vampire life that would be just as bewildering to human comprehension.

It had taken only a few centuries for the vampire to conclude that any endeavor to bring the human race to its knees was a futile one. Although the petition to the Dark Realm by the lesser beasts for a superior predator had been granted with the most spectacular interpretation of their wish, it was not enough. Relying on physical supremacy, the lesser beasts had, through no fault of their own, dismissed certain traits possessed by those they wished to subjugate—the most unexpected being the human will to survive.

And there was another factor. Breeding for most animals occurred at a designated time within the arc of the seasons. Human beings were bound by no such constraints. Their ability to reproduce at any time, coupled with self-imposed restrictions from the vampires themselves, hampered any effort to use population control as a way to hold the species in check. No matter how many humans were dispatched, their ranks did not thin. Frustrated, the leader of the Original Vampires had turned to Ryiel, the most learned of them all, seeking an answer. Ryiel had steeled himself before responding, anticipating Gabriel's reaction to his proposal.

"We must completely eradicate an entire generation," he said. "It is the only way to curb them. Take those not yet old enough to procreate, and severely limit the ability of those left behind."

It was barbaric.

It was brutal.

It was brilliant.

And it was never going to happen.

Gabriel's own edict that the young should not be harmed effectively tied the vampires' hands, turning them into mice on a wheel that went around and around, arriving nowhere. The only difference was that the mice had no idea their journey was a pointless one.

The other miscalculation of the lesser beasts had been the number of humans that could be turned into vampires. The more humans they killed, the fewer were found with the necessary dormant gene. It was almost as if nature itself was conspiring against them, burying the latent code so deep within the human DNA, it became almost impossible to detect. Of those that were turned, fewer than half survived the transition, and less than half of those made it through the perilous first year.

Realizing the impossible situation that presented itself, Gabriel had called his brothers together and sought to redefine their role in the world. If vampires were to survive, they had to adapt to change. They owed it to those they had turned as well as those who had called them into being. And they owed it to themselves.

It was a sobering reminder that the reason for vampires' existence was to prevent domination by a race now grown so arrogant it no longer saw the necessity of sharing resources with those it considered of lesser worth. A species whose greatest threat came from itself. If the risk of extinction did not also include the destruction of every other living, breathing creature, the rest of the food chain would have been perfectly willing to stand back and let the human race destroy itself. But the concept of codependency had been a gift from the Creator, and who were they to question His design?

And so the role of hunter and prey was reassessed. Vampires would still hunt humans, only now they would concentrate on those who were capable of doing the greatest harm. For Ryiel, this new attitude brought a certain freedom that allowed him to take a step back and view the world and its inhabitants in a different light. But though the light was brighter, what was revealed pleased him little. So he sequestered himself with his treasure in this place deep inside the Himalayas.

Now every room in the abandoned monastery, save those necessary for the preparation of meals, bathing, and sleeping, had been altered for the sole purpose of holding the contents of what had once been the greatest scholarly resource in the known world. The Library at Alexandria. Human history said the library had burned. And it had. More than once. But the last time it was set ablaze, Ryiel had felt compelled to take action. Recognizing the ferocity of the impending inferno, he had swept through the impressive building, gathering as many scrolls as he could, and transporting them to a place of safety. The irony did not escape him that his preternatural speed might have contributed to the spread of the flames.

No one knew how many scrolls were in the library. Some reports put the number as low as 40,000, others as high as 400,000. Ryiel wondered if modern human historians would be surprised to know that 400,000 was a conservative estimate. The library had contained three times that number, and most of the scrolls were now in his possession. Except it wasn't just human knowledge Ryiel had been saving. Hidden within the scrolls were others. Neither papyrus nor parchment, these were of a different medium and unknown to man. Meant to last through the ages, they were already ancient when the library was nothing but the musings of a Macedonian general.

These other scrolls were the historical accounts of Ryiel's kind, recording not only the lives of the Original Vampires, but also detailing what they once had been. As revealing as the tattoos each Original bore on his body, these archaic writings served as an invaluable source of information . . . if one knew how to read them.

Ryiel had taken it upon himself to rescue and preserve as much of the contents of the library as he possibly could, and now he perused the writings for another reason. He was searching for a key—one that would show him how to nullify a deal made with a demon. It was a tedious task, but somewhere in the back of his mind he carried a hazy recollection of having read such an incantation. A law that would invalidate any agreement made with a denizen of the Dark Realm.

A sudden dip of the candle flame told Ryiel he was no longer alone. "I'm not in the habit of talking to myself, Katja, so eavesdropping is a waste of time."

The disgraced female vampire, made by him in a moment of weakness, was now his prisoner. Obsessed with Gabriel, she had refused to accept that he would always be bonded to Rowan, who was both the love of his life and also his Promise. Katja's method of dealing with rejection had been to try to kill her rival, and she might have succeeded if not for the timely intervention of the angel Sebastian, who'd spirited Rowan away before anyone else could intervene. It was the only reason Katja's head was still attached to her elegant neck. Now she stepped through the stone arch, carrying the next batch of scrolls Ryiel had requested. Dressed in baggy jeans and an oversized T-shirt, she put the scrolls on the table.

"I don't need to eavesdrop," she told him in a sulky tone. "I can hear you snoring even when I'm not in my cell."

Ryiel grunted. He knew his sentinel and the prisoner were physically intimate. Stavros had confessed it was nice to bed a female and not worry about accidentally breaking a rib. Ryiel supposed it was a combination of curiosity, frustration, and boredom that made Katja return to the sentinel's bed.

He had no idea whether the female vampire knew how close she had come to her own demise at his hands. Had she succeeded in taking Rowan's life, he would have been left with no choice but to take her head. She seemed to accept the conditions of her punishment with no complaint, and Ryiel had taken advantage of her quick mind to catalog the Alexandria scrolls he had yet to sort. She knew what he was looking for, and he took measures to ensure she did not sabotage his efforts to find an answer to Rowan's problem. She had not done so. Yet. He sighed. The workings of the female mind, either human or vampire, were complicated. He had no doubt Katja's feelings for Gabriel were still strong, but whether she wanted to fuck him or kill him he couldn't say.

Probably both. At the same time.

"Do you have another list?" She held out her hand. The ligature marks on her wrist, though fading, were still livid against the paleness of her skin.

He found a piece of paper and handed it to her, his fingers closing around her wrist as she took it from him. "What happened?"

"I tried to give your sentinel the ultimate sexual experience."

"In what way?"

"By slipping a knife between his ribs as he was coming." She shrugged and rubbed her wrist as he released it. "He didn't appreciate my efforts."

Stavros might have to be more careful when having sex with one of the women from the village, but he never had to worry that any of them wanted to kill him in the act. Ryiel suspected the female vampire would have to submit to a pat-down along with a body-cavity search before being allowed to slip between his sentinel's sheets from now on. He dismissed her and returned to his task.

The papyrus was an ancient text, and an extraordinary amount of care was required to unroll it and explore its secrets. Last read by scholars who had perished almost two centuries before, the words seemed to jump off the page. Ryiel stared at the script with a glazed look in his eyes until his mind rearranged the formation of lines and symbols to form a language he was familiar with. It was not what he was looking for. But as he began to carefully roll up the document, marks on the lower edge of the papyrus caught his eye.

Written in an entirely different language, the words made no sense in the context of the scroll. It was like coming across a copy of Hamlet's soliloquy written in Shakespeare's own hand, only to find he'd also included the opening lines to *A Christmas Carol*.

To sleep, perchance to Dream; aye, there's the rub,
Marley was dead, to begin with. There is no doubt whatever
about that,
For in that sleep of death, what dreams may come . . .

It made absolutely no sense at all . . . unless you were an Original Vampire.

Opening the scroll once more, Ryiel anchored each corner with one of the many polished stones he used as paperweights. The line of misplaced script was a directive on how to release the hidden writing contained within. Recognizing the presence of one who could unlock their knowledge, the glyphs and symbols now began to pulse and glow with a life of their own, impatient to reveal their secrets.

A soft click and Ryiel's fangs slid smoothly past his lower lip. He held his wrist to his mouth and broke the skin, piercing the vein closest to the surface. Blood welled up, and he turned his arm so it would drip onto the ancient papyrus. There was a mild hiss as the liquid quickly spread across the surface, covering the original lettering with a thick, crimson flow. Static electricity pulled at his long hair, making it stand out until it resembled the exotic headdress of a Mayan god. A strange odor filled the air, something Ryiel had not smelled in a long time—a peculiar sweetness coupled with the underlying scent of decay. It was the perfume of corruption, and it sealed all such writings.

The vampire's senses, already superior, now became even more acute. He could hear the soft swoosh of his blood as it flowed through the chambers of his massive heart, the echo of each muscle expanding and contracting with its appointed task. His olfactory sense was quickly becoming overwhelmed by the stench of the tainted papyrus, but it was not so compromised that he couldn't distinguish the mouse droppings that had escaped Stavros's broom. The electrifying tingle he got from rubbing the pad of his thumb across the tips of his fingers told him his sense of touch was now hyper-receptive. But it was his vision that amazed him most of all. Staring at the unfurled scroll, he could actually separate the overlapping pigments in the ink, as well as the strands of fibrous pith comprising the papyrus sheet.

He watched as his blood spread, covering the meaningless text before turning black and hardening like the carapace of an animal long since extinct. Beneath the obsidian shell, Ryiel knew the document's true purpose was manifesting itself. Intuition made him take a step back, throwing a forearm up to shield his eyes as the dark, glossy covering exploded. His blood had been transformed into a hard substance that filled the air with a sound reminiscent of wind chimes, as the razor-sharp slivers bounced on the ground.

Did the words exist to break the agreement Rowan had made in the Dark Realm? Ryiel was certain of it, for no compact or accord was ever proclaimed that did not contain such an escape. All he had to do was find it, and thankfully Rowan had been clever enough to negotiate the time he needed. He waited until all he could hear was the sound of his own breathing before he lowered his arm. His senses had returned to their normal state of vampire awareness, but Ryiel found himself suffering a mild twinge of disappointment at the loss of such heightened awareness. There was a definite advantage in being able to hear a functioning heart so clearly.

The language was one forgotten long before he was brought into existence, and he had never been more thankful than he was now for the twist of fate that had piqued his interest in studying such antediluvian forms of communication. When he was finished, he sat in the large, high-backed chair that was, apart from the table, the only furniture in the room. Resting his hands on his knees, he leaned back and closed his silver eyes, allowing his mind to make sense of the text's discord. He did not stir again until the candle he had placed in the wall sconce earlier had burned down to three-quarters of its original size.

Rising from the chair, Ryiel returned to the table and read the document again—and then once more, just to be certain he had made no mistake with his translation. Carefully he deciphered each word, exploring all possible definitions, but no matter how many times he read the text, no matter how many ways he restructured the sentences, he knew he was not mistaken.

The answer to breaking Rowan's deal with her demon had been in her hands the moment she was cast out of the Dark Realm. She just didn't know it, which was, Ryiel suspected, the very thing this particular demon was counting on.

Chapter 2

The hand that had been cradling my head was now fondling my breast. I should have been slapping it away and making some sort of protest at the forwardness of such a gesture, but I was so overjoyed to know it was actually capable of movement, I refused to worry about something as mundane as copping a feel.

Vaguely I recalled the sound of popping—the type of sound that comes when you burst really big bubble wrap, the kind used to protect piano legs and such. Aleksei let out a groan with each explosion of noise, and it took me a moment before I understood why. What I was hearing were the bones in his hand being realigned so they could reset and heal. By my reckoning, at least three fingers had been broken. I'd recently had all four fingers of one hand broken, and that hurt like a son of a bitch. But I hadn't had to suffer this kind of healing process because Gabriel had taken me into his sarcophagus, where I hadn't felt a thing.

But these were vampire bones, and they no longer possessed the same structure and composition as regular human bones. Once the hand had healed itself and regained its flexibility, it moved to my chest. Maybe it was a vampire thing.

Now I was distracted by a pinprick at the side of my neck—one of many that had occurred since I'd assumed a horizontal position on the floor of my new apartment. I hadn't had much say in the matter. Aleksei had collapsed on me, and there was no way I could hold up close to three hundred pounds of vampire on my own. I was just grateful he'd had the presence of mind to cradle the back of my head as we went down. I'm not sure I could afford to lose many more brain cells.

Aleksei had done a lot of feeding in a relatively short period of time, but he was still too weak to strike with any authority, so multiple puncture marks were the result. My neck must look like a vampire pincushion.

He had shown up on my doorstep, beaten, battered, and with the Grim Reaper on his heels. That he could still stand was a miracle in itself. That he knew to come to me was something I didn't even think to question. There was no way I was going to turn him away in his condition, even if it did mean we were both breaking a vampire cardinal rule. The human-vampire bond is not only complicated, it's also fiercely protected. A bonded human only ever feeds the vampire he or she is joined to, and the vampire does not look to feed from a different human. I was hoping something like imminent death would prove to be a mitigating factor. If not, we were both royally screwed.

Aleksei had, until only a few hours previously, been bonded to Anasztaizia. I didn't know or fully understand what was involved with breaking a bond, but I was certain he'd done it to protect her. A vampire planning to actually marry a human doesn't simply walk away. Aleksei loved Anasztaizia, but because she didn't possess the necessary gene to make her a vampire, he had already elicited Gabriel's promise to take his life when the beautiful Magyar's three score years and ten deal was over. I thought it was one of the most fucked-up miscarriages of fairness I've ever come across.

As for me, my connection to Gabriel goes far beyond the normal human-vampire relationship. For one thing he's an Original Vampire, and we're joined by an archaic ritual that makes me his Promise—the keeper of his soul—an agreement I willingly entered into when I first saw him impaled on the thorns of a rowan tree. It was also the moment I fell in love with him . . . I think. Recently, I'd been having some weird dreams that might actually have been old memories trying to resurface, and they'd got me thinking that perhaps I had fallen in love with Gabriel even before that moment.

Before he became a vampire . . . when he was still an angel.

There was something all too familiar about the sword he was gifted with so he could fulfill his role as an avenging angel. I knew I'd seen it before. Just like I knew there was a nick in the handle that, if it was held the wrong way, would leave a wicked bruise on your palm.

The hand on my breast was beginning a slow massage. You would think that as I was a healthy female with a normal sex drive, such an action would have evoked some type of physical response from me. But even though the well-muscled body lying on top of me was there at my invitation, I didn't react. And it wasn't because he was a vampire. It was because he was the wrong vampire. Only Gabriel could liquefy my spine with his voice, awaken a hunger deep inside me with a single look, and make my body ache for him with the touch of his hand. But this wasn't Gabriel, and my reason for my feeding a vampire I wasn't bonded to had nothing to do with sex.

It was the only way I could keep Aleksei alive.

Vampires aren't easy to kill. I know because I've asked how to do it. I was relieved to find out the whole stake-through-the-heart thing was a myth. It always seemed too chancy for my liking. I think you've got to have really good aim and exceptionally steady hands to get the equivalent of a large tent peg between someone's ribs. Decapitation and incineration by sunlight make a lot more sense. Only now it seemed there was a third way to effectively kill a vampire. One I managed to figure out for myself from looking at Aleksei before he fell through my door.

Massive trauma to the body.

Part of the vampire myth involving immortality is the fact that they're pretty much indestructible compared to humans. Bigger and stronger, their bodies also have the ability to heal with an efficiency that's frightening. Unless, it would seem, the trauma is so extensive it overwhelms the body's ability to repair itself. Which was what I figured was happening to Aleksei. Contusions and broken bones I could see, but I had no idea what kind of internal injuries he might have. All I knew was that if there was any chance of helping his own body kick-start the healing process, he needed to replace the blood he'd lost with a transfusion. It's amazing to think how this one procedure can be a lifesaver to both our species—the only difference being vampires bypass the necessity for an IV line, preferring a more direct approach.

When Gabriel feeds from me, I can tap into his emotions, and as my lover usually enjoys feeding while having sex, I get to share the intensity of his orgasms. Knowing I'm the reason he feels this way is more than an ego boost, but sometimes a head full of vampire emotions isn't always so pleasant.

When Katja decided to rip open my neck in an effort to make me bleed out, she inadvertently shared scenes from her childhood with me. The life she had endured was horrific. I didn't care if it was a couple of hundred years ago; no child should be made to go through what she did. With her hair curled and beribboned, and dressed in the finest silks, she became a living doll who was also used as a sexual plaything for degenerate aristocrats. It was no surprise she lacked empathy or compassion and had the morals of an alley cat. All of which actually made her the stereotypical evil vampire.

Kartel, another of the Original Vampires, had taken a sip of blood from my wrist, and I couldn't say why I didn't get any feedback from him. Then again, I was so worried about how seeing him at my wrist was affecting Gabriel, I probably shut out any emotional images he may have been sending me. For all I know, I could have locked away inside my head a video of the blue-haired vampire dancing naked in Times Square and not realize it.

And now I was giving my blood to another vampire. But this was different. This was by my choice and something I was doing willingly.

Thankfully, Aleksei wasn't even remotely aroused, which wasn't that much of a surprise, given his present condition. The Russian vampire had a way to go before an erection was part of his future. At least I wasn't getting any erotic flashes from him. Which was a good thing because the affection I have for the big guy is more sibling in nature. From the first time I saw Aleksei, I thought he was devastatingly handsome, even with his scarred face, but I never had any inclination to act on those feelings.

After hearing how Aleksei's family had been murdered in front of him by a butchering member of the Russian aristocracy, I was braced for snapshots of these horrors as he took my blood. But I didn't get any. What Aleksei gave me was nothing but his overwhelming gratitude. Grateful I had not turned him away, grateful I gave him my blood, and grateful I understood why he couldn't go to anyone else.

Which still made his hand fondling my breast kind of weird.

"It's going to take a lot more than that to turn me on, big guy," I murmured as I felt the fingers squeeze and relax once more.

His response was something garbled in his native tongue. I don't speak Russian, and even if I did, I don't speak Aleksei-Russian. Language is constantly evolving and changing. How many people do you know who use the same vernacular, the same slang, as their grandparents? Aleksei's verbal process was over three hundred years old. Even if I could speak Russian, I still wouldn't know what he was saying.

"I have no idea what you just said," I told him as he continued to mumble.

"Feel... heartbeat..." he managed to get out in a voice that sounded cracked and strained, and begged not to have to repeat itself.

"Oh... okay then."

I had no way of knowing how much blood I had given up, but if keeping tabs on my cardiovascular function made him happy, who was I to argue? It wasn't like he could kill me. I wouldn't die until Gabriel did, thanks to the demonic deal I'd made, but I don't recall any mention of what type of condition I had to be in. I could be in a vegetative state and still be alive. It would be too ironic if helping Aleksei meant I succumbed to hemorrhagic shock or something equally devastating to my physical well-being. If squeezing my boob was Aleksei's way of making sure I didn't turn into a rutabaga, I was fine with that.

I'd been rubbing his back with my hand, making what I hoped were soothing circles when I felt his entire upper body suddenly tense and become rigid. His hips ground into me, which if he'd had an erection would have been quite alarming. As it was I felt a strong pressure between my legs, and the noise this time was much louder than exploding bubble wrap. It sounded like a friggin' cannon going off next to my ear and was so loud it nearly smothered Aleksei's moan of pain.

Something was going on below hip level. Another bone being twisted and slotted back into place so it could be repaired, and from the sweat now breaking out on the big guy's upper lip and forehead, I guessed it was most likely his femur. Instinctively I clamped my thighs together, holding the limb being pushed between my legs as still as possible. I had no idea if I was helping or hurting. What I knew about mending broken bones involved a cast and immobility for a set period of time; I had no idea if such things were necessary for a vampire.

The sudden rush of warm air fanning the side of my neck said the stabilizing action of my thighs was appreciated. Apparently vampire bones also needed to be kept still while they healed. I was glad my muscles were strong enough to hold onto Aleksei's leg. An unexpected benefit of marathon sex sessions with Gabriel.

My heart was pounding furiously in my chest, and the breath I sucked in between my clenched teeth made an odd whistling sound. I forced myself to be calm, to slow my accelerated heartbeat to a more normal rhythm. The last thing I needed was to pass out under the big guy. The hand on my chest moved from breast to breastbone. Two fingers began to tap lightly against my sternum in a slow, steady beat, and I felt my heart respond, mimicking the tapping fingers until it had regulated itself. My mouth curved into a smile as Aleksei's fingers returned to my breast.

Checking your heartbeat, my ass!

Raising his head, Aleksei looked at me. It was the first time he had made eye contact since taking me down to the floor. Without thinking, I fluttered my fingertips over the scar on the side of his face. Stretching from temple to jaw, it puckered angrily as if resentful it couldn't be healed along with the rest of his injuries.

"Still . . . handsome?" The big guy croaked at me.

"Still handsome," I agreed.

It was hard to tell which of us had the raspier voice.

His face did look better than before, now that the awful gray pallor was gone, replaced by something that fell between zombie blush and crypt-keeper white—a considerable improvement. But it was still a mess. The abrasion on his forehead now looked more like an angry sunburn, which considering that Aleksei is a vampire, I found kind of funny. The bruising on his cheek had almost faded, but his one eye still wouldn't open. Taking into account how the rest of his body was managing to heal itself, I couldn't begin to imagine the trauma this particular orb had suffered. On the plus side, his other eye was no longer filled with blood, and as the closed lid appeared to be covering something solid, I was fairly confident the damaged eyeball hadn't been gouged out. His nose practically straightened itself while we looked at each other, and all that remained of the split in his lower lip was a faint, pale line.

Aleksei opened his mouth to speak, but no words came out. The good eye closed, and I saw his thick, dark lashes become glossy as moisture trickled down the side of the just-repaired nose. He sucked in a shuddering breath and opened his mouth again, but I put my fingers against his lips.

"Don't," I told him, my voice as raw as my throat felt. "It's okay . . . just don't."

Deciding he no longer needed to function as an EKG monitor, Aleksei wrapped my fingers inside his hand and rocked his hips slightly as he settled his head on my shoulder. He tucked his hand, still holding mine, beneath his chin, and I could feel him relax as sleep overcame him. Perhaps I was stronger than I realized, or maybe I was used to having a vampire on top of me, but even though it felt like a baby grand was on my chest, I didn't mind. Carefully I rolled and resettled my hips. The leg wedged between my thighs flexed in response to the movement. I took that as another good sign.

Either the worst part of his healing was done, or the big guy was too exhausted to deal with whatever else his body had to go through. With my free hand, I carefully explored his head, checking for any lumps, bumps, or things that shouldn't be there. Surprisingly, his head appeared to be okay, although there were patches where dried blood had turned his buzz cut into a wire brush. But he didn't wince or complain about my roving fingers, and the steady, rhythmic inhale-exhale told me he was headed for dreamland. I wished him well. God knows he deserved it.

Sleep was the last thing on my mind, though I was exhausted both mentally and physically. Acutely aware of Aleksei's body healing itself, I could feel every remaining break, fracture, and dislocation sliding into place and becoming whole again. I knew the moment his lacerated liver had repaired itself. I could sense when both kidneys were functioning normally again so he wouldn't piss blood, and I knew when every bruised muscle and torn ligament was restored to wellness. And all of it was happening because of my blood.

My blood.

A shadow moved in the hallway beyond the still-open front door. I didn't need to see to know who it was or what it wanted.

"Fuck off—you can't have him," I rasped. "Not now, not tonight. He's mine, and I won't let you take him from me."

I'm willing to bet I'm not the first person to have been hissed at by the Grim Reaper and lived to tell the tale. Only I wonder how many realized the same thing I did. The bitch is a sore loser.

Chapter 3

At some point I either fell asleep or passed out. I'm not sure which, and I don't think it made much of a difference. Surfacing back to the land of semi-consciousness, I became aware of three things. I was no longer on the floor, I was completely naked, and the vampire holding me was very much the right one. I took in a breath, and the scent of snow and pine trees and that other elusive *something* that was uniquely Gabriel flooded through me.

"Shhh," he murmured, pressing his lips against my forehead. "Go back to sleep."

"What . . . time . . . ?" I mumbled.

"Almost midnight."

I smoothed my hand across the wide expanse of his chest, my palm brushing over a nipple that immediately hardened at the contact. Gabriel sucked in a breath, and I felt the ridge of muscles in his abdomen tighten before he slowly exhaled as my hand moved. I let my fingers drift down his rib cage to his waist and then over his hip, curling my hand in the pocket of warmth above his thigh. His erection kicked against my belly. I felt warm, safe, aroused—and guilty.

"Where's Aleksei?"

I went to push myself upright, using the hand I had on Gabriel's hip for leverage, but it slipped, and I almost squashed his balls. The sound my lover made was one I hope to never hear again. At least not from his lips. It was a cross between a wheeze, a grunt, and an almost girly shriek of pain. To prevent any further chance of accidental emasculation, long fingers closed firmly around my wrist.

"He's resting," Gabriel told me. "I put him in your father's room. It was the only other one with a bed. I hope you don't mind."

It was my father's room only because a few of his old work shirts were hanging in the closet, and some personal items were on the dresser—all things I couldn't yet bear to get rid of. The shirts were for comfort. If I was feeling particularly melancholy, as I usually did on the anniversary of his death, I would slip one on and go lie on the bed in his room and cry myself to sleep. At least that's what I did in the house where we had both lived. The house that now belonged to my best friend and her family. And because I had moved in with Gabriel, all my dad's belongings had been packed in a cardboard box and put in a storage unit. This year I'd had no shirt to slip on. Instead Gabriel let me hold onto him until I cried myself to sleep. And that was part of the reason he had bought me the apartment. He hated the idea of my dad's belongings being kept in a concrete-floored, ten-by-twenty steel-walled box almost as much as I did.

And now a vampire was resting in my father's room. Thankfully, it wasn't the bed my dad had slept in. I'm sentimental, not stupid, so no, I wasn't upset Gabriel had put Aleksei in there. It was the only logical choice because otherwise it would have meant having the Russian vampire in the king-size bed along with me and . . .

"What are you doing here?" I winced at the sharpness of my tone.

"What do you mean?"

I couldn't say if Gabriel was surprised by my tartness, or if the question itself was what caught him off guard. Either way, the look he gave me was decidedly wary.

"I mean, you were on your way to California, and now you're here." I pulled my hand free of his hold and gestured to the room. "How did you get here, inside the apartment?"

Gabriel hadn't physically been inside the apartment since I'd signed the necessary papers to put the deed in my name. And Aleksei hadn't been able to cross the threshold without my invitation. So how was it my lover was now naked and horny and lying in the bed he and I hadn't even christened yet?

"There are places a vampire doesn't need an invitation to enter," he said, looking strangely guilty.

This I knew. Places with public access, such as libraries, banks, supermarkets, and movie theaters. And apartment buildings. I understood he could walk into the lobby downstairs, but that didn't mean he could automatically cross the threshold of any apartment in the same building unless . . . unless . . . he already had permission to do so. I stared at him and saw his expression change the moment he realized I knew exactly what he'd done.

"Son of a bitch! You didn't just buy this apartment, did you? You bought the whole friggin' building as well."

"It's a good investment," he murmured, catching hold of my hand.

"And did you buy it before or after I agreed to the apartment?"

"After."

Of course it was after. I knew I ought to be making some sort of a protest about this place of my own only being an illusion. The fact that Gabriel could come and go as he pleased meant it was never truly "mine" to begin with. But I think a part of me accepted all along that he would always find a way to circumvent any restriction seeking to keep him from me. So who was I really pissed off with? Gabriel for being true to his nature, or me for not anticipating he would be?

I'll take stupid human females for $400, Alex.

"Rowan, I will always respect your privacy, and I promise never to come here unless you invite me." He pressed his lips to my fingers.

"Hate to point out the obvious, but that's a promise you've already broken."

"You weren't exactly in a position to issue an invite, love, and did you truly expect me to wait until you became conscious again?"

I shook my head. It wasn't hard to imagine the state he'd been in when he saw me passed out on the floor with an equally semi-comatose Aleksei on top of me. I just hope I hadn't been smiling. Of course I was glad he had come to me. It was a relief knowing I was able to share the responsibility for Aleksei. Speaking of which . . .

"Is Aleksei going to be all right?"

"Well, I think he may have to cut down on his workouts for a day or two, but he'll get through this."

My sigh was heartfelt. Knowing the big guy was going to pull through gave me the strength to deal with the next difficulty in my path. And it was one I fully intended to take sole responsibility for.

"Gabriel . . . I gave Aleksei my blood." I paused, waiting for some sort of nuclear fallout. There was nothing. "He fed from me. A lot," I added in case he didn't quite grasp my meaning.

"Uh-huh."

I looked at him. He seemed perfectly calm, serene almost. His body was relaxed, each breath well regulated. Even his erection, though twitching a little impatiently, seemed perfectly at ease with my confession.

It hadn't sunk in. It couldn't have, because Gabriel was taking this far better than he ought to. I know how possessive vampires are, especially of those they feed from. And I was bound not to just any vampire, but an Original Vampire. I was his Promise. It was a bonding that went beyond sacrosanct. And yet I had given myself to another vampire. I hadn't been tricked or coerced or threatened with something horrible if I didn't comply. I had willingly given my blood to another. A sin worse than adultery—and Gabriel was all right with this?

"Are you sure you understood me?" I asked hesitantly. "You realize what I'm telling you I did?"

"Yes, I know. You gave Aleksei your blood." He reached up and stroked the side of my neck, skimming his fingers over the multiple puncture holes that were starting to scab over. Obviously, my own loss of blood was slowing the healing process. "You look worried." *No shit, Sherlock!* "Did something else happen?"

I swallowed and licked my lips. Apparently volunteering as an all-you-can-eat vampire entrée was no cause for concern. "Uh, I'm pretty sure I told someone to fuck off," I confessed. "It might have been the Grim Reaper," I added as an afterthought.

"Ah well, no doubt I'll hear about it."

"You speak with . . . ?"

"We've crossed paths, but I have to admit the conversation tends to be one-sided."

Now it was my turn to say, "Uh-huh."

"Rowan, I'm sure everything will be all right."

"So you're not angry with me?"

"For what? Mouthing off to the Specter of Death? Trust me, it's not the first time she's been told to fuck off"—he paused and smiled at me—"and I can guarantee it won't be the last."

"No!" I snapped irritably. "About giving Aleksei my blood!"

He moved quickly—

Damn! Would I ever get used to that?

—and took me in his arms. His mouth found mine and he kissed me. Slowly at first, as if reacquainting himself with the feel of my lips or checking to see if I tasted different now, and then he became more demanding. His tongue slid over my teeth before pushing its way into my mouth, where it stroked and teased. Pulling back and thrusting forward, it created a delicious friction my lover used to arouse me.

My arms slid around his neck, and my fingers curled in his hair as I pressed myself against him. I wasn't sure how it happened, but we were both up on our knees, and as one of Gabriel's hands cradled the back of my head, the other cupped my butt cheek. My breasts pillowed against the hard muscles of his chest, and I felt his cock, erect and massive, pressing against the softness of my belly.

I broke the connection between our mouths and took in a gasping rush of air. I watched his pupils contract and dilate as he stared into my face. "Tell me you're not angry," I panted. If I had to rely on body language alone, then Gabriel was answering me in a way that was hard to ignore, but I needed to hear the words. My fingers tightened in his hair. "Tell me!" I insisted.

"Sweetheart—who do you think sent Aleksei to you in the first place?"

Aw shit! Why hadn't I realized that? Then again, why would it? I loosened my fingers from his hair and pulled my arms from around his neck. A frown tugged at my brows, forming a furrow in my forehead. Gabriel had sent Aleksei to me? How was that possible? The last time I'd seen my lover, he was headed for Death Valley to prevent Aleksei from turning Nikolayev Petrov into a crispy piece of bacon. On the face of it, staking out that piece of shit wasn't such a bad idea, but only an Original Vampire can take the life of another vampire. Aleksei's need to play judge, jury, and executioner was not going to go over well, even if his reasons for wanting to commit vampiricide were understandable.

Whether or not Petrov was the big guy's half brother was still up for speculation in my book, but there was no doubt the bastard had murdered Aleksei's family. Who cared if it had happened over three hundred years ago? He'd killed them all in front of Aleksei, and it was hardly the sort of thing you forgot. Or forgave. Wanting revenge was not only reasonable, it was highly therapeutic. Of course, I might be a tiny bit biased considering the nasty little fuck had also tried to kill me.

Petrov is a slimy little shit, and by the time Gabriel and I realized

Aleksei was walking into a trap, the wheels had already been put in motion. Gabriel had no other choice but to go after Aleksei, although ultimately his concern wasn't so much with preventing vampire murder as with something quite different.

None of us had reckoned with a certain blue-haired Original Vampire. In addition to Kartel being Petrov's maker, there was a history between him and Gabriel. Hah! I imagine some sort of history existed between all the Originals simply because of how long they've been around, but this was history of the not-so-good kind. Whatever had happened in the past, it was enough to make Gabriel distrust the other Original Vampire—something Kartel's unexpected visit only intensified.

"So what happened?" My voice was pitched a little higher than normal. "I thought you were going after Kartel?"

"I was, until I realized Aleksei had never left town."

"How did you know he hadn't left?" My stomach lurched and I felt nauseous. I knew the moment I saw Aleksei barely holding himself up outside my door, he'd been set up.

Gabriel's thumb brushed across my lower lip. "He's the only vampire I've ever made." It was all he needed to say.

A shudder ran through me, and Gabriel pulled me close. The heat from his body felt good as it sent a soothing glow radiating through me. Aleksei might have broken his bond with Anasztaizia, the woman he loved, but he could not do the same with Gabriel. Even if he wanted to.

"It was other vampires that got him, wasn't it?" It had to be. No one else would be able to get the drop on Aleksei. Gabriel nodded, confirming my suspicions. "But you found him."

"Yeah."

"Where was he?"

"In a fighting pit."

I had only a vague idea what he was talking about, and visions of Conan, Spartacus, and gladiators collided in my head in one massive testosterone-laden free-for-all. "Was it bad?"

His hand began to move in languid strokes down my back. "It could have been a lot worse. I don't think they expected Aleksei to last as long as he did."

"They underestimated him," I murmured, feeling fiercely protective and proud all at the same time.

Gabriel pressed his lips against my temple. "They certainly did."

I was almost too afraid to ask, but I did anyway. "How many vampires were there?"

He caught one of my curls and wrapped it around his forefinger. "I stopped counting at a hundred."

"Did you . . . did you kill them all?"

"Of course. I will always protect what is mine."

I knew Gabriel had killed people. He's a vampire, for God's sake, and I was confident, being the efficient predator he was, that he'd taken more than a hundred lives before. Even all at one time. However, the topic of murder and mayhem doesn't make the best pillow talk, so it's not something we've ever discussed. I don't think there's ever a "good" time to talk about such things, but I wanted him to know he *could* talk to me about them. And I could tell something had happened that still bothered him. Could it be that killing vampires was more troubling than killing humans?

"Was it difficult for you," I asked, "because they were vampires?"

He took my face in his hands and looked at me. His eyes, framed by dark sooty lashes, were an electrifying shade of neon-blue. "I have no problem killing vampires if I need to," he said in a calm, steady voice. "I just hated having to kill the bear."

"You killed . . . a bear?"

He nodded. "There was no other choice. It had been given something to make it hyper-aggressive. It could not be returned to its natural habitat."

The fingers of my hand curled around his wrist. "What was the bear supposed to do?"

"Kill Aleksei, I imagine. It's why he was in the pit."

"They were making him fight a bear?" Gabriel simply looked down at me, his fingers sweeping gently over my cheek. "Why would they do such a thing?"

He shrugged. "Because then none of them could be blamed for Aleksei's death."

"What a bunch of fucking cowards!"

No wonder Aleksei could barely stand. I couldn't even begin to imagine how he had managed to defend himself against a bear. And I was also furious because an innocent creature had been drugged and turned into a killing machine to achieve something those vampires weren't brave enough to do themselves. At least Aleksei was vampire enough to go after Petrov, prepared to stake the bastard out in the sun himself, and take the consequences.

The enormity of what the big guy had been through suddenly hit me all at once, and I began to tremble. Gabriel put his arms around me, holding me until it passed. I pressed my lips against his chest as a heat ignited inside me and began to lick its way up my belly. "Gabriel . . ." I murmured, barely recognized the huskiness of my own voice.

It's not often I make the first move and initiate our lovemaking. Usually Gabriel is so in tune with my emotions, he knows what I want before I know it myself. But this time was different. I could feel him hesitate even though his own body trumpeted to the world how much he wanted me.

"Rowan, this might not be the best time. You've been through a lot, you need time to recover, you need—"

"To feel you moving inside me," I interrupted. He stopped speaking, and I could see he was getting ready to find a different way to refuse me. "Please, Gabriel . . . I need this . . . I need you."

And then he rolled me beneath him, and there was no more talking, and no more thinking. Just his hands stroking my skin, his mouth kissing mine as his own need met mine, giving me some delicious moments when I wasn't sure I would ever breathe again.

Chapter 4

It was getting close to dawn when Gabriel murmured in my ear. Some quality time in his sarcophagus was needed, and though I was loath to let him go, I understood why he had to leave me. Propped up on one elbow, I watched as he dressed. It was a striptease in reverse, and the sight of Gabriel naked was enough to derail whatever train of thought I might be on. I gawped like a schoolgirl gazing at her first full-frontal centerfold, minus the always awkwardly placed staples, of course.

Knowing all too well the effect he had on me, Gabriel turned his back. Unable to help myself, I let out a whimper seeing his glutes tighten and relax. The ripple of his heavy thighs as he stepped into his jeans made me salivate, and the play of muscles in his arms and shoulders as he pulled on a T-shirt had my imagination doing sinfully wicked things to him with my tongue and a bowl of whipped cream. I swear I could watch him dress and undress a hundred times a day and never get tired of the show. And he knew it.

Throwing back the covers, I followed Gabriel's lead and got dressed myself. I doubt the show I put on was anywhere near as sexy or seductive as the one he gave me, especially not when I almost fell over putting my panties on. Still, it was nice to see the look of disappointment on Gabriel's face as I hooked up my bra. I don't think he'd mind one bit if I chose to go braless for the rest of my life. I, on the other hand, am not quite ready to be so bold. And besides, a C-cup needs support. I completed my ensemble with a pair of unimaginative gray sweat pants and a favorite NFL T-shirt.

"Is Aleksei going to be all right here?" I was concerned that whoever had jumped him might decide to try again, once they discovered he hadn't been eaten by Smokey the Bear. Of course, whatever carnage my lover had left behind might give them second thoughts.

"This is probably the safest place for him right now," Gabriel assured me, "but even if it wasn't, he's not going to want to leave. At least not for a day or two."

"Why not?"

Taking my hand, Gabriel sat on the edge of the bed and pulled me onto his lap. "You may notice some changes in Aleksei's behavior, especially in the way he relates to you. I promise it's only temporary, but until it passes, it's better if he stays here with you."

"Better for who?"

"Him definitely, but probably both of you."

This was starting to get weird. "What sort of changes?" I tried not to sound overly concerned.

"Um, well, he'll most likely want to maintain a connection to you."

"What sort of connection?"

"A physical one."

"Uh-huh. And what does that mean exactly?"

Puffing up his cheeks, Gabriel blew out a breath. "It'll probably be something fairly innocuous like wanting to hold your hand."

"Well, that doesn't sound so bad." To be honest, I had no idea what I'd been expecting.

"Um . . . all the time . . . for the next few days," Gabriel added.

All the time?

"What, even when I need to pee?" I gave a nervous laugh.

"I think if you're firm enough, he'll stay outside the bathroom, but it might be best to lock the door. Just in case."

I stared at Gabriel's face, waiting for the telltale twitch at the corner of his mouth that would tell me he was joking. There was no twitch, only an anxious crinkle at the corners of his eyes, making me ask, "You're serious, aren't you?" It was a stupid question, and even though Gabriel nodded, I didn't need him to answer. Nothing about this was funny. "But why would Aleksei want to hold my hand?"

"It's an emotional response to having your blood in his system."

"So is he going to want to hold your hand as well?"

My lover shook his head. "The amount of blood I gave was enough to make sure his body could complete the healing process started by you," Gabriel explained. "Right now he has more of your blood in him than his own. It will take a few days for his body to process it, and until then he's going to want to stay close to you." Pulling a curl free from my hurriedly pulled-together ponytail, Gabriel curled it around his finger. "Under the circumstances, it's a perfectly natural reaction."

"And when I feed him again?"

The finger playing with my curl stopped in mid-twist, and the arm around my waist tightened enough that I noticed. "That won't be necessary," Gabriel said huskily. I looked at him, seeing his eyes turn a dark slate color. "The amount of blood you have already given is more than sufficient to carry Aleksei through the next few days. By the time he needs to feed again, Anasztaizia will be able to take care of him."

Oh my God—Anasztaizia! I'd almost forgotten about the lovely Hungarian.

"Is that why Aleksei broke his bond with her? Because he knew she might be in danger?"

"That would be my guess. In order to keep her safe, and make sure she could not be used as coercion, all other vampires had to believe he was done with her. The reason why was not important, just the end result."

"But now he can reestablish their bond, right?"

"Yes, once he has overcome the effects of your blood."

For a few moments neither of us spoke as I tried to grasp all the possible ramifications my blood could be having as it coursed through the Russian vampire's body. It was obvious that Gabriel was keeping a hold on his temper. I caught him staring at the rumpled bed sheets, a fierce look on his face. Was he worried that Aleksei's out-of-whack emotional response might manifest itself in some sort of display of carnal lust?

You'd never be able to fight him off, my inner bitch declared in a horrified tone. *Hell, you couldn't even hold him up when he fell through your doorway!*

Thanking my inner bitch for the reminder, I told her to stow it or get locked in a box. If she was going to make comments, they needed to be constructive and useful. Tell me what I could do, not point out what I couldn't. She snorted disdainfully. Motivational Coach wasn't in her job description. But she did have a point about my inability to protect myself.

I put my palm on Gabriel's cheek, pulling him away from whatever dark thoughts he was having. "Is that all he's going to want to do? Hold my hand?"

Realizing what I was asking, and that I'd noticed his concern, Gabriel leaned forward and brushed his lips across my mouth. "He won't want anything more from you."

"You're certain?" It was a valid question. My lover was about to go across town and submit to a self-induced coma for possibly the next twelve hours or so. A hell of a lot could happen in that amount of time.

"If Aleksei wanted to be . . . intimate, he would have broken the door down while I was with you."

Recalling Gabriel's initial reluctance to have sex, I pulled out of his arms. "Please tell me that's not why you made love to me. To test him in some way."

He reached for me, pulling me back to him. "No. It was an afterthought only." Gabriel kissed me, his tongue pushing into my mouth in a way that could only be described as politely insistent. His fangs dropped, and I felt a prick as he pierced my lower lip. Unable to feed from me himself, he needed a taste of my blood. His tongue swiped over my lip, sealing the pinprick holes, before he let me go. "You've given your blood to another vampire, Rowan. I needed to reclaim what is mine."

"But you didn't seem to want to." It was the first time I had ever known him to be hesitant.

"Rowan, Rowan, Rowan!" He punctuated each repetition of my name with a little shake of my shoulders. "I *always* want you, but after what you've just been through, I needed to know you still wanted me. I needed to hear you say it."

He'd been worried my life-saving action might have caused a shift in my affection. It was gratifying to know there were times when he was vulnerable, that his confidence could be shaken. A warm glow erupted in the middle of my chest. I took his hand and linked my fingers with his. "So . . . hand-holding only?"

His dimple winked at me. "Why don't we go find out?"

Chapter 5

A leksei was taking up far too much space in the apartment's small kitchen. Hearing Gabriel and me, he turned to greet us with a carafe of cold water in one hand and a canister of coffee in the other. If I didn't know better, I'd think the expression on his face was some sort of commentary regarding my coffeemaker. Mr. Coffee may not be a top-of-the-line machine, but it gets the job done without having to show off and light up like the instrument panel of a 747 every time it's switched on. However, the look on Aleksei's face had nothing to do with kitchen appliance performance levels.

I doubted few people had ever seen the look of grim disquiet he now wore. Aleksei could no more influence or manipulate the effects of my blood running through him than he could walk outside at high noon. Clearly, it was not a condition he was comfortable with.

From the way Gabriel had been talking, I half expected the Russian vampire to take one look at me, rush to my side, and enfold me in one of his giant hugs while giving me an adoring, sappy-dog look. And it might have been true if he had made eye contact with me. But Aleksei was studiously ignoring me, keeping his eyes firmly fixed on Gabriel. The big guy might have more of my blood running through him right now, but it wasn't enough to make him forget who was the dominant presence in our little triangle.

Well, isn't this deliciously awkward?

It would seem my inner bitch didn't quite grasp the concept of constructive and useful. I sighed, wondering why I even bothered.

Atta girl.

There was a sudden shift in Aleksei's expression. The disquiet now changed to something veering toward apologetic. Did the Russian feel he needed to ask forgiveness for wanting to make coffee, or was he worried he should have asked permission first? Either way, he was addressing the wrong person, but given the noticeable swell in tension and testosterone, I wasn't about to have my new apartment wrecked over a cup of joe. Disentangling my fingers from Gabriel's grasp, I opened the cupboard above the stove and took out a box of filters.

"Here," I said, putting them on the counter in front of Aleksei. "You're going to need one of these." With a low grunt that I interpreted as a thank-you, Aleksei resumed his work as a barista.

Noticing the faded blue jeans and T-shirt he wore, I was about to ask Aleksei who'd outfitted him when the answer came down the hall from the general direction of the utility room.

"I'm sorry, Aleksei, but I think your coat is destined for the bonfire." Tomas held the offending article in his hands. "I'm not sure even I can get all the bloodstains out, and did you know you've got brain matter on one shoulder?" He lifted one of the sleeves to his face. "I don't even care to speculate what that might be. I've never smelled anything like it before." The sentinel sighed. "It truly is beyond repair, laddie."

I imagined Tomas was the only person who could get away with calling Aleksei *laddie*. Probably having been with Aleksei from the start of his journey to becoming a vampire helped, but the sentinel's adopted Scottish accent, with its soft rolling burr, didn't hurt either.

"But I've had it a long time," Aleksei protested, sounding decidedly miserable.

"Yes, well, perhaps it's time for a new one. I'm sure you can go back to Moscow now. It's been what, seventy, eighty years since you were last there?" Aleksei nodded, looking dejected. "I doubt there's anyone still alive who would remember what happened. At least not in any detail," Tomas added.

"What did he do?" I blurted out.

Three heads swiveled in my direction, and I felt myself being pinned by three pairs of eyes. Gabriel's were filled with a quiet amusement, Aleksei's were slightly ashamed, while Tomas had the kind of look I'd last seen on my dad's face as he dealt with the unenviable task of helping me negotiate my way through puberty.

"I was drunk," the big guy stated miserably.

Oh ho, this is going to be good!

"I'm surprised you could still stand," Gabriel murmured with more than a touch of admiration.

I turned to Tomas, looking for an explanation. The sentinel shrugged as he began to stuff the army greatcoat into a heavy-duty black plastic bag.

"I'm sure it's not the first time Stalin woke up to find a heifer in his bedroom," he said, tying the corners of the bag together. "The difference being this one had four legs, not two."

"It was still disrespectful," Aleksei muttered.

"Did you say heifer? Like an actual, cud-chewing, milk-producing animal?" They gazed at me again, clearly wondering what other type of beast I might possibly be thinking of. "You put a cow in Stalin's bedroom? While he was asleep?"

"I think the effect would have been ruined if he'd been awake, lass," Tomas said.

I couldn't even begin to imagine the logistics involved in pulling off such a feat. "How did you get it into his bedroom?" I blurted.

"I carried it," Aleksei replied in a slightly bewildered tone. The rest of his explanation was in unintelligible Russian, and I just nodded in what I hoped were the appropriate places.

"As I said, no one will remember." Tomas patted the big guy on the shoulder before turning to me. "So, lassie, how are you feeling?"

"Good. A little tired."

"I would imagine so. May I offer some advice?" I nodded. If Tomas was going to give me one of his homemade remedies, I was all ears. "No more untruths between us."

"Untruths?"

"Aye, silly notes to tell me where you aren't going to be."

I felt the heat rush to my face. Obviously, the sentinel had seen through my ruse—telling him I was going to spend the night at a hotel when my true destination was my apartment. My intentions had been good. If Kartel was coming after me, and we still didn't know for sure he wasn't, he might think twice if I was in a place with a lot of people. And I'd thought that if Tomas was confronted by the blue-haired Original Vampire, he stood a better chance of getting away if he didn't also have to protect me. So I'd left him a note.

"Did you check with the hotel?" I had gone through all the motions of actually checking in, making sure the receptionist would be able to recall me if anyone asked.

Tomas gave me a disappointed look. Another reminder of my dad dealing with his teenage daughter. "I didn't need to, lass. Did you not recall I am a runecaster? Your words on the paper fairly jumped up and screamed they were a lie."

I ought to have known better. I've never been able to lie convincingly, and if I couldn't do it with Gabriel, why did I think I'd be able to fib to his sentinel? Even with a note. I didn't realize I was about to cry until I felt strong arms pivoting me toward a hard chest. A hand began to rub comforting circles on my back, and a voice above my head murmured soothing endearments. In Russian. I pulled back my head and was rewarded by puppy-dog brown eyes staring adoringly back at me.

Aw shit!

Awkwardly, I disentangled myself from Aleksei's embrace and looked over my shoulder at Gabriel, who was staring at both of us with a face that was calm, giving away nothing. Except I could feel the heat surging through him. I grabbed his hand and led him out of the kitchen toward the front door. He needed to get to his sarcophagus.

"Perhaps this isn't such a good idea," he murmured. "It might be better if I stayed."

I took hold of his chin and made him look at me. "Are you certain all he wants to do is hold my hand?"

Powerful shoulders moved slightly. "He may want to feed you dinner . . . while you sit on his lap."

I got an instant visual of the last time I'd sat on Gabriel's lap while he fed me. Strawberries and cream, as I recall, and we'd both been naked. I'd make certain Aleksei kept his clothes on. I sensed rather than saw both Tomas and Aleksei come into the living room. I don't think either of them actually believed Gabriel was going to leave, and they were waiting to see what I would do.

"Do you trust me?" I asked, looking up at my lover's face.

"Always."

I pulled his face toward me so I could kiss him. I made it fierce and hungry, my tongue lapping across his fangs when he dropped them. His erection was threatening to pop each and every button on his fly, so I slid my hand between us, covering it. "Save that for the next time you see me," I told him when I pulled my mouth away.

Gabriel grinned. Whatever uncertainty he may have been feeling, it wasn't about Aleksei. He never would have allowed the other vampire to stay with me if there were any doubt. Gabriel had simply needed reassurance from me. And I was pretty sure I'd just delivered in a way that was more than convincing.

He was almost at the door when he bent and picked something up from the floor. I remembered holding the pale blue jewelry box in my hand, thinking the knock on the door was the giver come to take it back from me. But it had been Aleksei standing on the other side, and I'd dropped the box to catch him. The necklace must have spilled out. To be honest, I'd forgotten all about it . . . until now. I don't know why I felt guilty, but I did. It was never my intention to hide the necklace from Gabriel, or to keep the visit from the demon who gave it to me a secret, but the way my heart was racing certainly made it seem that way. And from the look on Gabriel's face as he turned to me, he thought the same thing.

He held the strand of black opals in both hands. They gleamed in the light, the brilliant red and green striations glowing with their own kind of demonic brilliance. The necklace was much longer than I had realized. In the box it had appeared as a single strand, but then I hadn't spent a lot of time examining it. Now I could tell what Gabriel was holding in his hands was actually a lengthy rope of gemstones. I couldn't even begin to imagine their value. And then I saw Gabriel's body stiffen and felt a crackle in the air as he turned to me.

"When did you accept him?" he snarled. "Before or after you saved Aleksei?"

I was still trying to process his words, and the fury with which they were delivered, when I saw movement out the corner of my eye. The sheer curtains covering the wall of windows lifted as if a strong breeze had been welcomed inside to clear the air. I opened my mouth to speak, to ask Gabriel what he was talking about, but a second displacement of air knocked me off my feet back onto the couch.

"Don't even think about it!" Gabriel roared. "I will snap your neck like a twig if you try to insert yourself between me and my Promise!" His Promise. Not his fiancée, or lover, or even Rowan. Using my title reduced me to an object.

Pulling the hair out of my face, I saw Gabriel had Aleksei by the throat and was holding him up against the open brick wall at the far end of the room. This wasn't the first time the two of them had been involved in an altercation over me. Last time it had been Aleksei who was the aggressor. His knee-jerk reaction at hearing Petrov's name had been all the provocation necessary. Gabriel had been forced to intervene to make sure the big guy didn't hurt me. And now it seemed Gabriel was stopping Aleksei from getting to me again. Only I didn't think this time the Russian vampire wanted to hurt me. I think he was trying to protect me.

Gabriel tightened his fingers, and I heard Aleksei make a gurgling sound. The last time I saw Gabriel holding a vampire in this way it was psycho-bitch Katja. She'd fought him, fang and nail, to get free. It hadn't done her any good. Aleksei was doing nothing. His arms hung by his sides, and he made no attempt to either free himself or prevent Gabriel from slowly choking the life out of him. It occurred to me that perhaps he didn't have the strength.

"Gabriel, stop it—let him go!" I shrieked, seeing Aleksei's face begin to turn a pale shade of eggplant. I scrambled off the couch and threw myself at Gabriel, but he wrapped his free arm around my waist and held me off easily.

"Do you understand me?" He gave the vampire a hard shake and suddenly launched into a completely different language. I had no idea what he was saying, but I didn't need to know the words to understand the meaning. Aleksei was being issued a warning. It was, I suspected, the only one he would get. A gurgled response from the other vampire must have been the answer Gabriel was waiting for, because he opened his hand, and Aleksei crumpled to the floor.

Ignoring the sounds of wheezing gasps and coughing, Gabriel carried me across the room like a sack of potatoes, dumping me on the couch. "I asked you a question." He snapped his fingers in front of my face to make sure my focus was on him, and not Aleksei. "When did you accept him?"

"Accept him? Accept who? What the fuck are you talking about?"

My own temper was climbing up into the furious range. I was pissed Gabriel had threatened Aleksei for trying to help me, and scared to death his anger wouldn't let him hear me even if I had the chance to explain. I scrambled off the couch, banging my shin on the edge of the coffee table as I did so, and began to fall back. Gabriel automatically reached for me. I grasped his hand, pulling myself upright, before slapping it away in anger.

His eyes darkened at my rudeness, but I was beyond the point of caring about manners. I watched his nostrils flare and his chest expand as he took a deep breath and then let it out on a low whistle.

"Are you telling me you don't know where this came from?" He held out his hand to show the opal necklace roped around his fingers. He'd been holding it the entire time he had Aleksei pinned against the wall.

"No, of course not—"

"So you know what it is?"

"Yeah, it's a necklace."

No doubt a hugely expensive one, but still only a necklace. It had no meaning for me, and it never would. Given the fact that Gabriel's temper was walking an unstable line, I figured now was not the time to mention why I'd been given it, or when I was supposed to wear it. There are some things those you love are better off not knowing.

"No, it's more than a necklace." Gabriel's voice was eerily calm. "It's called a Bridal Night Chain, and is worn as proof."

"Proof of what?"

"Your complete submission to another, and acceptance of his dominance over you."

"Submission?"

"Guess your demon didn't tell you everything, did he?"

I could see I didn't need to worry about trying to protect Gabriel's feelings by not telling him the circumstances under which I'd been given the necklace. It seemed he already knew.

"He's not my fucking demon!" I yelled.

"No . . . not yet," Gabriel said coldly.

Running the string of gems through his long fingers, Gabriel held his arms out so I could appreciate the full length. The stones sparkled and fell like a river of black gold.

"I don't understand . . ."

"No, of course you don't," Gabriel muttered under his breath, his tone chastising me. "Let me explain." He fashioned the rope of opals into a loop, securing them in a way I couldn't see, and dropping the circlet over his fingers. "This goes around your neck, with the excess falling down your back. Oh, and did I mention you're completely naked?" He looked at me and I shook my head. "Surprised you hadn't worked that out for yourself, considering when it's supposed to be worn."

Gritting my teeth, I did my best to ignore his sarcasm. "Now, where was I? Ah yes, down the back. The necklace is then used to bind and secure your hands behind you until—" He held up the end of the strand where the largest opal was attached. The size of a damson plum, it seemed to change color, turning first red, then green, then black. "Until this little beauty can be inserted inside you." His eyes flicked to my crotch in case I didn't get his meaning. "It stays there until it is removed by your lover's tongue."

I know there are certain sex toys that can be inserted into a woman's body, and left there, for the sole purpose of creating pleasure as she goes about her daily routine. All I can say is it's not anything I've ever been even mildly curious enough to want to try. And seeing this massive, smooth opal wasn't making me change my mind.

"The opal is ensorcelled," Gabriel continued. "Once inserted, it can only be removed by the intended recipient as described. You remain bound until then."

I gasped, and this time when I fell backward on the couch Gabriel did not try to stop me. I closed my eyes, able to see in my mind the demon standing almost exactly where Gabriel now stood, hearing his voice in my head.

"When I take you, you will wear these . . . and only these."

"My Lord." Tomas's voice startled me. In truth I'd almost forgotten the sentinel was there. "I am certain your Promise had no idea of the gift's true purpose. She has made no declaration of agreement to the intent behind it. Perhaps if she were to explain the circumstances—"

"What is it that you think is beyond my comprehension, sentinel? Do you suppose a messenger was sent to act in his stead? If so, then I could allow for the possibility of confusion regarding intent." Gabriel's eyes were a dark, furious storm, and I could see the muscle in his jaw spasm with anger. "But we both know that didn't happen, don't we?" He fixed me with a stare. "We both know *he* was here, and you accepted his gift—"

"No, Gabriel, you're wrong. I didn't accept—"

"Don't lie to me!"

I'd never seen him so angry, and I knew it was a waste of time trying to explain what had happened. Even if Gabriel allowed me to speak, he was in no mood to listen. His hand clutched the string of opals in a grip so tight I saw his knuckles blanch. Would the precious stones caught in his palm be pulverized to dust from the pressure of his fist? He came toward me and reached for my hand with his free one, turning it palm up. Opening his fingers, he pooled the smooth stones in my palm, closing my fingers over them when he was done.

"I've told you before to never lie to me." His disappointment stung.

"Gabriel—please! I'm not lying! I didn't—"

"Shhh." He placed a finger against my mouth. "If you had refused . . . you could not hold the stones in your hand."

Chapter 6

The smell of fear, thick and heavy, forced Ryiel to rise from his sarcophagus before he was ready. The lone rune anchored over his heart scolded him with angry chittering sounds even as he plucked it free. Set to an appointed task, the runes did not take kindly to being forced to abandon their purpose before it was completed.

"What is it?" Stavros asked, meeting Ryiel at the chamber's doorway. The sentinel had felt the vampire surfacing moments before he'd appeared. Only a matter of the gravest importance would have caused him to waken before the sun was set.

"Something is wrong." Ryiel closed his eyes to better sense the world beyond the stone walls of the ancient monastery. "In the valley . . . there is chaos and fear." His fangs dropped and he gave an angry hiss. "Where is Katja?"

"Standing behind you."

Two heads turned to see the female vampire brace a hand against the stone wall and use the other to rub her temple in an effort to dispel the stabbing throb in her head. Like the sentinel, Katja's bond also made her sensitive to the Original Vampire. His need to rise had penetrated her own semi-comatose state, but she was less able to tolerate being awake with the sun. Seeing her wince, Ryiel turned his face to the west.

"The pain will disappear once the sun drops below the horizon," he told her.

She nodded and took her hand from the wall to massage the other side of her head. Seeing the iron manacle still attached to her wrist, Ryiel addressed his sentinel.

"She was with you?"

The bald head gleamed in the candlelight as Stavros nodded. "Until I put her in her chamber."

"She doesn't sleep with you?" Ryiel allowed his curiosity to momentarily distract him.

"He doesn't trust me that much." Katja made a rude noise. "I'm still being punished for bringing a knife to his bed."

"It's true," Stavros agreed.

Ryiel opened his mouth to comment, but whatever insight he was about to offer regarding the unusual arrangement between his sentinel and his progeny was lost as a high-pitched scream drowned out all other sound. Carried on the frigid air, it came from beyond the walls of the monastery.

"Tell me that was an animal," Katja murmured, her throbbing head forgotten as she closed the distance between herself and her maker. For the first time since her arrival, Ryiel heard the thread of fear in her voice.

The sound came again, shriller this time, and Ryiel saw Katja shudder.

"It is an animal," he answered, "but the kind that walks on two legs, not four."

Dark brows pulled together over amethyst eyes. "I don't understand."

"Don't you?" He arched a brow. "Do you not recognize your own kind, Katja?"

Her eyes widened as she stared at him. "Are you telling me that's a . . . *vampire?*"

"More than one, if I'm not mistaken."

"And you think they come from the valley?"

The question posed by his sentinel made Ryiel frown. He expected Katja to have doubts, but Stavros? Perhaps he was spending too much time fornicating with their guest.

"Forgive me, my Lord. I meant no disrespect," Stavros apologized hastily, seeing the look on the silver-eyed vampire's face. If Ryiel told him the sound was coming from the sirocco-swept sands of the Sahara, then it was. Stavros had never known him to be wrong.

"But how can it be vampires?" Katja asked, her frown deepening. "We cannot function in daylight, and the sun has yet to drop below the horizon."

"Indeed, that is puzzling," Ryiel noted, "but no other creature on earth makes such a noise." Ryiel put a hand on Stavros's wide shoulder. "We need to go, my friend, although I fear it is already too late."

"Too late? Too late for what?"

Katja's question echoed off the walls of an empty hallway. All she caught of Stavros was a glimpse of his broad back as it disappeared at the far end, and Ryiel had already vanished into his chamber. He reappeared a moment later, dressed in his customary leather pants and heavy-soled boots, and she grabbed onto his arm as he strode past her.

"Wait! Let me come with you."

"No." His refusal was firm as he peeled her fingers from his forearm. "You must remain here."

"Why? I could help you."

Ryiel looked at her. Though she pleaded prettily enough, he caught the glimmer of something sly in her eyes. "I don't think so, Katja. Not this time."

"When will you stop treating me like a child!" Amethyst eyes flashed purple fire. "If it is other vampires, I could be of help. He might be stronger than me"—she pointed a finger at the returning sentinel, now dressed in clothes more suited to brave the elements—"but he isn't faster."

"That I cannot dispute," Stavros grudgingly agreed.

"How strange it is that you choose the most inappropriate time to issue a compliment," Ryiel murmured. He nodded to his sentinel. "You will come with me, but you"—he caught hold of Katja's upper arm and squeezed it for emphasis—"are to remain here."

A string of invectives filled the hallway as Katja tried her best to break free of Ryiel's iron grip, but to no avail.

"Stop it!" he commanded, shaking her hard enough to make her head snap back.

Katja found the moment eerily reminiscent of the time she'd fought with Gabriel. Not wishing to be flung down the hallway, the female vampire stopped struggling. Instead she glared at her maker with malicious intent.

"I have no time for this foolishness," Ryiel snarled. "Must I break your legs to guarantee your obedience?"

"My bones will heal!" Katja snapped back with a snarl of her own.

"Not if I shatter them."

"You wouldn't!"

He dropped his fangs. "Try me."

Her shriek of frustration bounced off the stone walls. "Why must you treat me as if I were an imbecile lacking the ability to think and reason for myself? Do you truly believe fetching your stupid scrolls, sweeping floors, and fucking your sentinel are the limits of my capabilities?"

"If you don't want to fuck Stavros, then don't. He can always find another female."

The possibility of being so easily replaced, even in a place as remote as this, pricked Katja's vanity, and she muttered sulkily under her breath. Sensing Ryiel was running out of patience, she tried to soften her approach. "I don't think you realize all I could do for you," she cajoled, "how valuable I could be, if given the chance—"

"To do what?" Letting go of her arm, Ryiel caught hold of her face. His long fingers braced her jaw, squeezing and tilting her head until she looked up at him. "Don't play me for a fool, Katja. I know only too well the limit of your capabilities." His tone became cold and unforgiving. "And do not mistake my tolerance for affection. The only reason your head is still attached to your neck is because Gabriel asked I not take it."

"G-G-Gabriel?" she stuttered, shocked.

"Yes, I confess I too am perplexed by his request. You attempt to kill his Promise, and still he asks for mercy on your behalf." He pulled her face closer to his. "Gabriel always was the very best of us when we were celestial beings, so it comes as no surprise he remains that way still. There are limits to what even the Void can corrupt." Ryiel smiled, a rarity in itself, and Katja found herself trying to pull back from a mouthful of sharp white teeth, and fangs that put her own to shame. "Of course, what happens going forward is another matter entirely. Give me a reason and I will mete out whatever punishment I see fit."

"You're still not saying why I can't go with you." Her voice trembled, but she refused to back down.

Stavros let out a noisy sigh. "Tell her, Lord, it's the only way to stop her from following us."

Ryiel opened his mouth to speak, but as he did so another high scream broke the stillness. And this time Katja felt it lick her spine.

"That sound is the voice of a vampire caught in the thrall of bloodlust. Something I have not heard for many centuries, and never thought to hear again."

"If it's been that long, you could be mistaken," Katja pointed out. "Perhaps it is only the wind."

"It isn't." The surety in Ryiel's voice said he was speaking the truth.

"But how can it be vampires when the sun is still . . ." She paused and turned her head to the west. The terrible pain in her head suddenly vanished, confirming the sun had set. ". . . *was* still above the horizon," she finished.

"That's what I'm going to find out," Ryiel said. "How many and why."

"And you are positive it is vampires?"

He looked at her, his eyes turning almost completely silver with only tiny pinpricks of black in the center. "There are some things you never forget. That sound is one of them."

She shifted her stance, moving so her weight was now evenly balanced on the balls of her feet. Hands on her hips, she met her maker's eyes with a steady look of her own. "You still haven't explained why I can't go with you."

It wasn't Ryiel who answered her, but Stavros.

"Everyone in the valley has been slaughtered, and the smell will be—"

"I know what death smells like," Katja snapped irritably, interrupting him.

"Yes, you do," Ryiel agreed. "Have you ever been to a blood orgy? Participated in a feeding frenzy?"

She shook her head slowly.

"It isn't pretty," Ryiel continued, "but such gatherings will usually involve no more than twenty-five or thirty humans at the most. This will be more like a battlefield, with close to a thousand dead. It will carry a stench you will never forget."

"It isn't only the blood," Stavros continued, seeing her slightly bewildered expression, "or even the underlying smell of shit and piss and puke everywhere. It's the smell of panic, fear, and desperation tainting the air. It will pull the breath from your lungs and choke you." The sentinel paused, his bald head gleaming in the candlelight as he gave her a sad, knowing smile. "This is the stench of the battlefield. You may know death, Katja, but you know nothing of this kind of butchery . . . and I hope you never do."

It was the nicest thing he had ever said to her. Apart from the time he asked if the manacles were chafing her wrists.

"The scent of blood will overwhelm you. You will be consumed by bloodlust, wanting nothing more than to tear flesh and gorge yourself," Ryiel told her.

"But you said everyone was already dead."

Seeing the silver-eyed vampire nod his head, Katja hesitated, wondering what she was missing.

"Vampires cannot drink from the dead. It leads to madness."

Every vampire knew that. It was one of the first things they were ever taught. Never drink from a corpse, and stop at once if a human dies while you are feeding. Once the heart ceases to pump, the death process is initiated. Body temperature drops, organs shut down, changes in chemical composition occur. And to a being whose own existence is reliant on an infusion of healthy blood, such changes are catastrophic.

"This is why bloodlust is so dangerous," Ryiel told her. "Held in its thrall, a vampire cannot tell the difference between what is living and what is dead."

"What about you? Won't you also be affected?"

Ryiel shook his head.

"So what will happen if I do fall prey to this . . . bloodlust. What will you do to me?"

Reaching out, Ryiel took a strand of her blue-black hair, letting it spill over his fingers. "Then I will be forced to break my promise to Gabriel. I will take your head."

Chapter 7

"He doesn't believe me."

I stared at the apartment's open front door, still reeling from the impact of Gabriel's words. It was hard to say which hurt more—his anger or his disappointment at my assumed untruthfulness. But I wasn't lying. I hadn't made any agreement with the demon. Why didn't he believe me?

"If you had refused . . . you could not hold the stones in your hand."

I looked at the opals overflowing my palm and spilling onto my lap. What did Gabriel mean I couldn't hold them? Why not? They hadn't done anything to him when he held them, so what did he expect them to do to me?

Tomas came to stand before me, Aleksei by his side, and both wore looks of concern.

"Are you all right?" I asked the vampire, seeing the dark red blotches around his neck from Gabriel's fingers. He nodded and croaked something in Russian.

"Aleksei, if we're going to spend the next three days joined at the hip, then you're going to have to speak in English," I told him.

"He wants to know if he can sit next to you," Tomas translated. "He needs to be close to you physically."

"Oh, of course."

I patted the cushion next to me and managed to appear only mildly surprised when Aleksei's arm slid across the back of the couch, his hand wrapping around my shoulder while his thigh pressed against me. I was lucky he was in a weakened state or else he might have pushed me through the side of the couch and onto the floor. It crossed my mind that perhaps I'd be safer, and probably less bruised, sitting on his lap, but seeing the way his upper lip curled as he glanced at the black gemstones in my hand, I reconsidered the idea.

I stared up at Gabriel's sentinel. "Why doesn't he believe me, Tomas?"

"I don't know, lass."

"Yeah, you do." I narrowed my eyes and gave him a hard look. "It's why you don't believe me either."

"I never said that."

"Not in so many words, but I can see the doubt in your eyes." I paused before adding bitterly, "You think I'm a liar too."

"Aw, lass, don't make the mistake of assuming you know my thoughts." His voice remained calm, which only made me feel more pissed off.

"All right then, do you think I'm lying?" I became confrontational as feelings of hurt were now replaced by bitterness and anger.

Tomas narrowed his eyes and gave me a long, hard look of his own. Feeling the tension rise between us, Aleksei shifted uncomfortably next to me. I pressed my knee against his thigh as a way of letting him know my mood had nothing to do with him.

"I think you believe you are telling the truth," Tomas said slowly, "but it doesn't necessarily mean you are."

"I'm lying, but not on purpose, is that what you mean?"

"Aye, lass."

"Why doesn't Gabriel think that?" I pointed an angry finger at the front door, forgetting I still had multiple strands of opals in my grasp. They made a soft plinking sound as they jostled for space along my arm.

"Because he can't explain how you are able to touch the opals and suffer no ill effects."

I was already tired of hearing this. Tomas, apparently reading the frustration in my expression, held out his hand and made a *gimme* motion with his fingers.

"Give me the necklace, Rowan."

"Why? What are you going to do?" I asked suspiciously as I pulled my hand back.

"Hopefully prove a point."

"Don't you mean prove Gabriel right?" I muttered belligerently under my breath.

"I hope to prove you both right!" he snapped, executing the *gimme* with a little more authority.

A low snarl near my ear told me Aleksei wasn't too happy with the sentinel's attitude. For a moment I'd forgotten I was babysitting a vampire who was an emotional mess. I was confident the big guy would do nothing to hurt me, but I couldn't say he would be as considerate to anyone else. Thankfully Tomas not only heard the snarl but took note of it.

"Please, lass"—he gentled his voice—"let me hold the necklace."

I stared at Tomas's open hand. His palm and fingers were decorated with a number of calluses and scars. Casting runes was not so easy as it seemed; it involved more than repeating ancient incantations and making mysterious signs in the air. Strong fingers cupped my hand as Tomas carefully tipped the string of glittering black stones from my possession to his. He managed to hold onto the necklace for almost a minute before I saw wisps of smoke escape from between his fingers and the smell of charred skin reached my nose.

"Tomas! No—let go!"

I grabbed hold of his hand and pried his fingers loose, letting the necklace fall to the floor. It looked as if he was holding a handful of Red Hots, only instead of the cinnamon-flavored candies, he'd been cradling something a lot more sinister. His hand was an eruption of angry, red blisters that bubbled and hissed.

I was about to send Aleksei for the first-aid kit I kept in the bathroom, but Tomas stopped me.

"I've got something a wee bit better than any ointment," he hissed between clenched teeth.

He pulled a rune from his pocket. It looked like a small brass key, something used to safeguard secrets—a young girl's diary, perhaps, or a dancing ballerina jewelry box. Guilt washed over me in horrible waves. I watched him grimace in pain as he placed the rune in his palm and covered it with his injured fingers. He closed his eyes and his lips moved. The rhythmic cadence of the spell he uttered filled the room. A few months ago, I would have laughed derisively at the idea of curing a hurt with enchanted words, but a few months ago I had no idea I would be spending almost all my waking hours in the company of vampires. Now I knew better than to mock the unknown.

Tomas's voice continued to call on the magic of the spell, but now it had dropped to a low murmur. A deep ridge furrowed his brow, and

I forced myself to remain still, almost too afraid to breathe in case I disturbed his concentration. After a few moments, his lips stopped moving, his forehead smoothed out, and he looked at me and smiled. A shriveled, blackened piece of gunk that might have once been a key lay in his palm. Save for a few patches of pink, his hand was back to the callused, scarred appendage I'd seen before.

I put a hand to my throat. "Did you know that would happen?" I knew damn well I wouldn't have been able to hold onto the necklace for more than ten seconds at best. "Is that what Gabriel was expecting to happen to me?"

"Well, I canna say if you would have had the same reaction," he told me. "Each person is different, but there should have been something."

Whoa . . . no wonder your boyfriend is pissed.

I was angry, but it was hard to say who with. Gabriel for not giving me the benefit of the doubt, the asshole demon who created all this drama to begin with, Tomas for taking such drastic action to prove a point, or my inner bitch for her unwelcome observation. I went with the sentinel. Right now he was the easiest one to deal with.

"Don't ever do that to me again," I ordered. "You could have just told me what was going to happen."

"Sometimes a visual demonstration has a greater impact."

I glanced at the necklace on the floor. It seemed harmless, looking remarkably like a pile of rabbit droppings. "Did you know it would burn you?"

"No, but I'm not surprised," Tomas answered. "It is a product of the Dark Realm, where fire is the predominant element."

"Did it cross your mind that, should anything terrible happen to you, I'd have to tell Gabriel? What the fuck would I say?" I tried throwing my hands up in despair, but Tomas caught hold of them, putting my palms together and clasping them in his.

"Rowan, lass, calm yourself and listen to me." Who was I to disobey my personal version of Mr. Rogers, even if his accent was a result of watching *Braveheart* too many times? "I'm sorry if I scared you, it was nae my intention." He paused and had the decency to look a little shamefaced. "Well, it was and it wasn't, but I needed you to see what it is you have in your possession."

Without thinking about it, I bent and picked up the necklace. I knew it wouldn't hurt me. Retrieving the light blue box, I set the necklace inside it and closed the lid. "Is it safe in here?" I asked Tomas, reassured to see him nod. "Good, then it's going in a safe-deposit box."

"I understand why it did not burn Gabriel," Aleksei said, pulling me back down and tucking me against him. "He's an Original Vampire. Perhaps because Rowan is his Promise . . . ?"

"No." I gave him my hand to hold. "Being a Promise would not have made a difference, but I think I know what did."

The look on Tomas's face seemed even more worried than it had a few moments before. "What did you do, lass?"

"I asked Gabriel to give his protection to Laycee's baby and agreed to pay the cost without knowing what it would be." I didn't admit it was actually Laycee who had asked, or that it was the demon who'd planted the suggestion in her head.

"You dinna ask beforehand?"

I shook my head, feeling more miserable than ever. "It never crossed my mind it would mean Gabriel would have to . . ."

Shit. I couldn't even bring myself to tell him what I'd inadvertently sentenced Gabriel to do. It was a valuable lesson about the power of words spoken in haste when dealing with the realm of the supernatural. A lesson I had approximately twenty-five years to find a way to reverse. A task my demon was certain I would fail at.

Tomas came over to me and took hold of my hand. The one Aleksei wasn't holding. "Dinna feel so bad, lass," he said, giving me a kind smile. "Your impulsiveness may be the reason a demon is thinking he's taking a bride, but he's still got to get you before the altar. And that won't happen until you actually say the words."

"Perhaps I already have, and don't realize it."

"Which is why you're going to tell me everything that was said between the two of you. Not just words spoken, mind you. I want to know about each sigh that was breathed, the most insignificant gesture made, where you stood and walked and sat. And you"—he looked at Aleksei—"you can let go of her hand and go fix her something to eat. The lass is positively wasting away before my eyes, it's been so long since she last had a meal."

In between bites of scrambled eggs, buttered toast, and bacon cooked to the perfect crispness, I told him everything in as much detail as I could remember. Both of them seemed particularly fascinated by the demon's ability to change his appearance at will. "He wore the same ruby cufflinks and tie clasp from the first time you met him?" Tomas asked.

It was hard to tell if this was a detail of some significance, or if the sentinel was making an underhanded comment on a woman's eye for jewelry. "I'm pretty sure he was wearing the same suit," I added, not wanting him to think I was easily distracted by bright, shiny objects.

I have to admit it was easier not having Gabriel around when I described the cloven-hoofed, fork-tailed, corkscrew-horned appearance of the demon. Even so, judging from the burn on my cheeks, my face must have been beet-red as I recalled the enormity of its cock in this guise.

"How big was it?" Like any male, Aleksei's curiosity got the better of him.

I held my hands apart, well past the width of my shoulders. The look on both faces reflected my apparent inaccuracy estimating length. I might not have a problem with jewelry, but family jewels were another matter. Yeah right, whatever. Why do all guys have this curiosity about the size of each other's cocks? If there was a way they could openly admire one another's equipment without the fear of being thought gay, I swear it would be women who would complain about the amount of time *they* spent in the bathroom.

"And he was completely flaccid," I added with the tiniest hint of malicious glee.

Neither of them was impressed by my description of the demon's final manifestation, although I did notice Aleksei's hold on my hand tighten a little. "You liked the way he looked, yes?"

"It was the wings. I think I have a thing for feathers." I certainly wasn't going to admit I was also consumed by lust as I'd stared at the flip side of what Gabriel must have looked like as an angel. Since they had been created from the same sphere of light, was it any surprise the demon was able to elicit such a visceral response from me? I did, however, confess to falling to my knees before him and taking his hand as he helped me up. Did that constitute an acceptance?

"Nae, lass. Words must be spoken," Tomas assured me.

I felt better. At least I could see Tomas now believed me. "Will you tell him?"

We both knew who I meant, and he nodded.

"Do you think he'll listen?"

"Of course he will"—Tomas shrugged—"eventually."

I looked at the other vampire in the room, but Aleksei had no insight to share. Tomas gave me a brief hug as we said our good-byes. He gave me his assurance he would continue to search for an answer to my dilemma. I couldn't ask him to do anything else.

"When will you be back?" I opened the door for him.

"Three days"—he leaned forward and whispered in a low voice—"and I'll bring Anasztaizia with me."

Aleksei would no doubt need to feed by then, but not from me. Now all I had to do was deal with the equivalent of a two-hundred-and-seventy-five-pound lovesick puppy.

"C'mon, big guy," I said, taking him by the hand. "We need to set some ground rules about sleeping arrangements, and you not trying to break down the bathroom door when I have to go pee." The sudden flush on his face told me he'd actually considered it.

I had no idea what I was supposed to do with Aleksei for the next three days. I racked my brains trying to find something to make the time pass and came up with the only idea I could think of. "Wanna play beer pong?"

Chapter 8

The first thing that struck Ryiel was the silence. It hit him halfway through his descent to the valley floor. It wasn't the lack of human noise that bothered him, mainly because he already knew the reason for that. It was the stillness, indicating the absence of all life, that he found more disquieting. It was as if every creature within a twenty-five-mile radius had simply vanished.

"You hear it as well?" Ryiel asked Stavros, who stood with a puzzled look on his face.

"Hear what?"

"Exactly." The vampire put a hand on his shoulder. "I smell only minimal animal blood. Normal predatory spill, but nothing recent. I think the lesser beasts must have sensed what was coming and run before the vampires arrived."

"Smarter than their two-legged counterparts," Stavros said with a grunt.

"No. Just more attuned to any disturbance in their surroundings."

Stavros took in a deep breath, filling his lungs with cool air. "Is there no one left alive in the village?"

Ryiel shook his head, his long dark hair briefly revealing the tattoos on his chest with the movement. "None we care about or can help."

"What of those responsible?"

Ryiel didn't need to answer as the night was suddenly filled with the howl of a vampire caught in the throes of bloodlust. The pull too strong to ignore, the vampire could not resist it. Seeing another form of bloodlust shine in Stavros's eyes, Ryiel cautioned. "See if we can keep one alive. It would be helpful to know whose hand is responsible for such madness."

"You don't think it's one of them?" he asked, pointing in the general direction of the howling.

"The instigator will not stay if he knows I am coming, and I suspect he already does."

The sentinel put his hand on the vampire's forearm. "You think this might be a plot to bring you once more onto a battlefield?"

It had not been so long ago that both of them had witnessed first-hand the debacle humans called *double-you-double-you-eye-eye*. Seeing the sadistic brutality of the concentration camps had changed something in the silver-eyed vampire.

"They have the audacity to call us monsters." Ryiel's tone had been chilling enough to make the hairs on the back of his sentinel's neck rise, making him wonder if the vampire was thinking the same as he. Had Gabriel permitted the destruction of a generation, as Ryiel had once suggested, would it have prevented such madness, or merely postponed it? Since then Ryiel had ventured even less into the outside world, preferring to keep to the monastery and have contact only with those humans he wished to. Except now it seemed someone had decided the vampire had kept to himself for too long. If he wouldn't rejoin the modern world willingly, a way would be found to change his mind. Although why it was so important that he do so was the mystery.

The coppery smell of blood hit them a quarter mile out. Thick and heavy, it caused Stavros to bend over and eliminate whatever was in his stomach. After that, both of them breathed through their open mouths as much as possible.

In the spring, Ryiel would allow his sentinel to leave him and travel to Japan in order to see the *sakura*, or cherry blossoms. Stavros would spend a week in Osaka and Kyoto, admiring nature's perfection, before returning to the monastery. Now he wondered if someone was playing a cruel trick, because the trees on either side of the road were awash with pink and red blossoms. It took a few moments for his mind to comprehend what he was seeing were the trees' natural foliage stained with blood and tissue matter.

Bodies were strewn everywhere.

Young, old, male, female, it made no difference. The villagers lay where they'd fallen. Most of the dead showed evidence of having been mauled with varying degrees of savagery. On some the skin at the throat had been ripped open, so the network of veins and arteries were more easily found amongst the muscles and sinews. Others had been attacked so violently that spinal columns were completely severed.

"If this is the work of vampires," Stavros observed in disgust, "it's vampires who don't know how to feed."

"They don't," Ryiel agreed. "What you are seeing is evidence of newly made vampires. With no one to guide them, no code of conduct to follow, they rely on instinct alone."

"They've been turned and let loose?" Stavros found the idea incomprehensible. "You have seen such behavior before?"

Ryiel nodded his head. "Indeed I have."

"Where? When?" It wasn't only curiosity driving the sentinel's question. Never having dealt with a newly made vampire before, he was hoping for an edge to use against an unknown enemy.

"How do you think we started, Stavros? Myself and every Original made have, at one time, left bodies like these in our wake." His mouth fashioned itself into a grim line. "It is why the act of turning a human is never taken lightly."

"I think someone in your fraternity no longer shares the same philosophy."

"So it would appear," the vampire reluctantly agreed.

They moved systematically through the village, checking every building, every barn and stable, every chicken coop. An avenue of carnage lay before them, its broad width littered with dead bodies, both human and animal. Whoever was behind the slaughter had not discriminated. Cattle, horses, goats, and dogs had also had their throats ripped open. Blood was blood. It wasn't until they came to the large building that served as the village's meeting hall that they saw signs of a different vampire involvement.

Several young women lay side by side on the floor, all carefully positioned with hands folded neatly on their chests, feet crossed at the ankles, and eyes closed. They looked as if they were sleeping, drugged perhaps. Stavros gave a murmur of thanks, until Ryiel corrected him.

"They're not under some spell. They're all quite dead."

"But they look . . . peaceful."

Ryiel moved to the closest female and squatted by her head. With careful movements, he gently rolled the woman's head, exposing the wound in her neck. The slice was elegant, its precision boasting centuries of practice. As the wounds were deep enough to cut the carotid artery without having to waste any additional energy, Ryiel suspected each woman was dead before she realized her murderer was standing next to her.

"Are they all like that?" Seeing Ryiel nod, he queried, "A different vampire did this?"

"Most definitely," Ryiel told him. "You don't go from that"—he pointed to the doorway where a man who had been nearly decapitated lay—"to this in the blink of an eye."

"He took his time with them. Not the killing," the sentinel clarified, "but afterward. Laying them out in such a way."

"Yes, he did."

"So why do you think he didn't feed from them, or want any of the others to?"

Each woman had been positioned so her blood would drain through a slat in the floor and flow directly into the ground supporting the building.

"He's sending a message," Ryiel said, coming upright.

"A message? To whom?"

The vampire arched a brow. "As these are all women I have fed from, I can only assume it's meant for me."

Stavros opened his mouth to speak, but the sound of another howl ripped through the air. Part human, part animal, it was all vampire— and close by. The sentinel was nearly knocked over by the force of the enraged vampire moving past him, and the bloodlust howl was suddenly cut off in mid-shriek.

Still trying to regain his equilibrium, Stavros stumbled out of the building to find Ryiel standing no more than a few strides away with the body of an apparently dead vampire crumpled at his feet. The sentinel arched a brow. "What happened to keeping one alive?"

"I didn't kill him." Ryiel's eyes flashed a mercurial silver.

"He's dead, isn't he?" Stavros looked around, immediately on the alert.

"Yes, he's dead . . . he just fell down."

Stavros approached the body with caution. The vampire was male, in his early twenties, the sentinel guessed, although it was difficult to be sure because his face was locked in a spasm of excruciating pain: brows drawn tightly together, eyes squeezed shut, and nostrils flared wide open. His lips were pulled back from teeth clenched in a snarl, with fangs fully extended. "I don't understand," Stavros said. "How did he die?"

He wasn't doubting the word of the Original. If Ryiel said the vampire fell down, then he fell down, but what had caused the newly made vampire to collapse in agonizing pain?

Ryiel pointed at the body. "Look at his fangs. They haven't retracted."

Stavros reached out a finger to touch one of the incisors, hearing a warning hiss of caution from above his head as he did so. Whenever a vampire was incapacitated and unable to function or defend itself, its fangs automatically retracted. Although it had been many years, a few centuries actually, since Stavros had last come across the body of a dead vampire, Ryiel's statement suggested the mechanics had not changed. He pushed on the dead vampire's upper gum with the pad of his thumb. Even as long as an hour after death, applying pressure to the correct part of the gum would still make the fangs retract. These did not.

"I don't think they can," Stavros said. "Have you ever seen this happen before?"

Ryiel shook his head. Even Oscar, the vampire deliberately starved by Katja, was still able to retract his fangs. It was agony for him due to his debilitated condition, but not impossible. "No," he replied, "never." Ryiel paused and frowned as he looked at the dead vampire's face. "They're too big."

"What are?"

"His fangs. A newly made vampire shouldn't have fangs so big. Look—" He dropped his own to demonstrate. Fully extended, Ryiel's fangs fell past his chin, and like all vampires, he only exposed as much length as was needed. The dead vampire had fangs that were almost as long as the Original's: something impossible for a newly made vampire. And yet the evidence was impossible to ignore. Ryiel retracted his own fangs with a soft click. "See if he's carrying any identification."

Items such as driver's licenses and ID cards remained viable for some time after a human was turned, and even when they were no longer relevant, many vampires were loath to relinquish a reminder of the person they had once been. It seemed a safe bet that the vampire's wallet would contain a wealth of information. Unfortunately, it was a bet neither Ryiel nor his sentinel was going to collect on.

The moment Stavros's fingers grasped the edge of the vampire's coat, he felt a band of steel wrap around his upper body as he was slammed back into the hard wall of Ryiel's chest. The Original Vampire pulled his sentinel away from the figure on the ground, and they both watched the corpse before them disintegrate until it was nothing but a pile of ash.

"What the fuck . . . ?" Stavros muttered under his breath, hearing a grunt of agreement as Ryiel relinquished his hold. "I didn't know a vampire could do that," the sentinel said.

Dropping to his haunches, Ryiel sifted a handful of the fine, pale gray ash between his fingers. "They can't."

"Not even if they're fried by the sun?"

"Not even then. Sunlight will burn them, but it always leaves enough remains to be identified, besides . . ." Ryiel made a point of looking at the dark, star-filled sky.

"Oh . . ." Feeling slightly foolish, Stavros blushed.

"There's nothing here to make you think this was ever human," Ryiel continued. "It could just as easily be the remnants of a chair as of a vampire." He got to his feet, brushing the remaining ash from his hands. The hope of finding any survivors was no longer an option. If there had been a single heart still beating, no matter how faint, Ryiel would have heard it. But the valley was eerily silent, offering nothing audible from man, beast, or vampire. "Let's see how many more of these we can find." He kicked at the remnants, turning the toe of his boot gray.

"You think there will be more?"

"I'm certain of it."

In the end, they counted seventeen piles of cinders. All that remained of the attacking vampires.

"Seventeen vampires to slaughter a population of almost a thousand in less than, what? An hour at most?" The warrior side of the sentinel's nature couldn't help but be impressed by the efficiency.

"Eighteen," Ryiel corrected. "You forgot the one who let them loose."

Stavros shook his head. He was having difficulty processing the deaths of so many people for no apparent reason. Farmers he had planted springtime crops with, harvesting the same in the fall. Comely young women who had willingly invited him to share their beds. Smiling mothers who allowed him to cradle their infants in the safety of his huge hands. And none tore at his heart like the children. Girls who had sat on his lap sharing their secrets as they wove garlands of flowers for him to wear on his head and around his neck. Young boys also wanting to confide secrets of their own as they played rough-and-tumble games and climbed all over him. Now they were all gone.

"Why would someone do such a thing?" he asked, hearing the hitch in his voice as he covered his eyes with a weary hand.

Ryiel placed a hand on the back of Stavros's neck and pulled him into a fierce embrace. "I don't know, but they will pay for what they have done," the vampire promised. Releasing his hold, he looked into his sentinel's eyes. "In the meantime, we must take care of the dead."

"You think they will rise?"

"I don't know. They should not, but the vampires that slew them . . ." His voice trailed off, letting Stavros see he was not the only one sickened and left disheartened by the massacre of an entire people. And these murderers were no ordinary vampires. There were too many unknowns. "There is no way to be sure, but I will take no chances."

Stavros watched as Ryiel pulled free the claymore strapped to his back. It was a beautiful weapon measuring seventy-six inches overall, far longer than any other sword of its kind ever created, the sentinel wagered. Even now he could still recall the look of disbelief on the face of the swordsmith. The man had pointed out, as politely as he could without giving offense, the possible inaccuracy of the specifications he was being given. No one had ever made a sword of such size.

"Are you saying it is beyond your ability to fashion such a weapon? That you lack the skill?" The man had bristled at the insult.

"Perhaps I should ask another," Stavros had murmured slyly. *"I'm certain there is one here who could accommodate my request with fewer questions."*

The sound of clinking coins overcame the last of the craftsman's objections, but he was not, however, entirely finished with his protest.

"If I agree to make this sword to the size you require, you must promise not to hold me at fault, and you must guarantee me your protection when your master demonstrates his displeasure." There was only a hint of belligerence in the man's tone.

"Why do you suppose the sword is for another?" Curiosity made Stavros ask the question.

"Hold out your arm." The swordsmith was barely able to contain his glee when Stavros complied. With an expert eye he gauged the distance from outstretched limb to the ground, checking the instructions on the parchment he had been given. *"I'll wager the man who will wield this weapon is at least half a foot taller than you, wider at the shoulder with a broader stance."*

Stavros grinned. It was a small thing to allow the swordsmith his victory, especially when it guaranteed Ryiel would have the weapon he desired. He left, promising to return at the specified time and wondering if the man would be as insolent before Ryiel. He was not, but in all fairness it was probably difficult to talk with his mouth gaping open at the sight of the vampire brandishing the massive sword with only one hand.

In the years following, Ryiel had found a need to use the claymore no more than a half dozen times, and always for the same purpose: to separate a vampire from his head. He had not brought it with him when Gabriel requested his help in dealing with Katja, but that was because both of them had seriously underestimated her hatred of Rowan. Knowing she would never have Gabriel for herself, she was prepared to see his Promise dead, and had starved another vampire in order to achieve that end. Killing Oscar had been a kindness, and on reflection, Ryiel decided being without the claymore had probably been just as well. The shock on Rowan's face when he had used his hands to put the starving vampire out of his misery had been bad enough. Would seeing his blade slice through tissue, bone, and muscle have been better or worse?

Now the hilt of the claymore rested lightly in his hand, the weight of the blade perfectly balanced. Becoming a vampire was always a choice, and these bodies strewn before him had been given no choice. He had been truthful in telling Stavros he had no idea if they would rise as some form of vampire. They should not because they did not possess the required gene in their DNA, but he knew less than nothing about the vampires that had killed them. How had they been made?

Deciding it was not a risk he was willing to take, Ryiel nodded at his sentinel. Stavros would build the pyre while he decapitated each body he came across, and together they would burn them all.

Chapter 9

Katja scowled as she watched Ryiel and Stavros make their way down the side of the mountain. She could follow Ryiel with her senses until the vertical drop of over a thousand feet to the valley floor made it impossible for her to track him. She wasn't sure if it was the drop itself or the Original Vampire's will that interfered with her ability. No matter how hard she tried, she couldn't hold onto him, letting out a snarl of frustration every time he slipped away from her.

It had crossed her mind to defy Ryiel and test the seriousness of his threat if she were to follow him into the valley, but an inexplicable feeling of terror had filled her when he spoke of shattering her legs. She told herself it was nothing but coincidence, her mind momentarily succumbing to the power of suggestion, but why take the chance? Though the silver-eyed vampire had made her, she knew little about him. For centuries the only recollection she had of her maker was a vague memory of liquid platinum eyes and glossy black hair. And no matter how hard she tried to get a feel for him, she was not strong enough to take advantage of the connection they shared. She could sense his presence within her but could not follow the thread back to him; thus he remained elusive.

The only vampire she had no difficulty sensing at any place or time was Vladimir, the Carpathian goat herder who had begged Ryiel to turn her for him, but the desire was one-sided. Once in his presence, Katja could hardly wait to be away from him. No matter how much time passed or how urbane his lifestyle, Vladimir always smelled like goat piss to her. She didn't remember it bothering her when she was human, but then her senses were not as heightened. He was the first male ever to fall so completely under her spell, and she reveled in her power over him. When he told her the truth about what he was, and how she could become a vampire too, Katja had jumped at the chance. She'd embraced her new life as if she had been born with fangs.

But even with her heightened senses and newfound awareness, Katja never saw Vladimir as anything more than a coarse, uncultured peasant. She barely made it through her first year before deciding there was nothing left he could teach her. It wasn't until a few centuries later that she learned the sad-eyed goat herder was a particular favorite of Ryiel.

Then, older and shrewder, Katja wondered if she had foolishly overlooked an opportunity. Few vampires enjoyed any type of regular contact with an Original, but if Vladimir was able to boast of such a connection, it was an opening worth pursuing. She sought to rekindle their relationship, but her former lover had changed during her prolonged absence. No longer a lovesick puppy, Vladimir had grown up. He did not welcome her back with open arms. Instead, he was suspicious and openly questioned her motive for seeking him out. What was more, he showed his disdain by refusing her his bed. Unused to rejection in any form, Katja's pride was hurt by his cold manner. For someone who had once been so enraptured by her beauty, who had begged his reluctant maker to turn her, Vladimir's change in attitude was wounding. But Katja was, if nothing else, tenacious. If Vladimir no longer wanted her as a lover, she would become what he did want—a surrogate daughter, obedient to her father's bidding for as long as it suited her purpose.

She was secretly thrilled when he told her she might be going to St. Petersburg.

"The choice is yours," Vladimir told her. "You cannot be compelled to do this, and no one will think the less of you if you refuse."

Curiosity already had her saying yes. "What is it I'm being asked to do?"

A voice spoke from the shadows. A low rumble that ignited an unexpected flame deep inside her. Turning, Katja stared at the white-haired vampire who stepped out from the shadows toward her.

"I have a recently turned vampire in my care," he said, "who is in need of assistance I cannot provide."

Katja felt her pulse quicken and her heart pound in her chest as her fangs dropped. The newcomer's only response was to give a self-deprecating smile, as if her reaction was an all too familiar one. And perhaps it was, but it didn't change the fact that he needed something from her.

Vladimir's voice next to her ear was a rude reminder she wasn't alone with the vampire demigod. "Katja . . . this is Gabriel."

She nodded and, although her insides had been rearranged by some unknown hand, managed to gather her heavy skirts in both hands to execute a flawless curtsey.

"The vampire in your care"—she favored Gabriel with her most brilliant smile—"who turned him?"

Finding her question both brazen and disrespectful, Vladimir dropped his fangs with a hiss. Katja had no idea why he would be so upset, especially when Gabriel seemed more amused than offended by her boldness.

"It's all right, Vladimir," he chuckled richly, "she has the right to ask." Neon-blue eyes, dazzling in their intensity, looked at her from behind thick lashes. "He was turned by me."

So this was another Original Vampire. My God, he was magnificent!

"What do you need me to do?"

Taking her by the hand, Gabriel led her to a seat across the room. "As I said, the vampire under my care is recently turned. He is still trying to master control over what it means to be a vampire."

"And what aspect is he having difficulty with?"

"Lust." The look Gabriel gave her said he appreciated her candor in getting to the heart of the matter. "He accidentally took a life and is filled with remorse. Reconciling himself to the incident is difficult for him, although I am confident he will find a way to put it in its proper perspective. Killing is, after all, part of being a vampire, and though regrettable, it is a mistake we have all made at some time or another."

Katja glanced at Vladimir to see him nod in agreement with Gabriel's words. She quickly looked away. For all the humans she had killed, and there had been many, she hadn't felt the slightest remorse. Of course, none of those deaths had been accidental, so perhaps that was the difference. Fixing her gaze on the Original Vampire, she noticed his brows pulled together in concern.

"He shows great potential as a vampire," he continued, "but without control . . ." There was no need for him to finish his sentence. A vampire who could not exercise control over his needs, both physical and emotional, was a danger to both himself and the entire vampire community. There would be no choice but to put him down, and make sure he could not rise again.

Resting her chin on her hand, Katja looked thoughtful. "Surely St. Petersburg can provide the necessary experience to benefit your protégé. Could he not avail himself of the city's whores?" Arching a brow, she smiled with womanly confidence. "Might I suggest perhaps more than one at the same time?"

"Your suggestion has merit, but those women are all human, and he is fearful that when he feeds again he will take another life."

"But how can that be?" She ignored Vladimir's hiss from across the room. Apparently one did not question an Original Vampire. "Copulation beforehand will always lessen the ferocity of a feeding."

"Unless you're a virgin."

Katja's mouth fell open in stunned surprise. She had never known a vampire who was a virgin. Of course she'd heard the rumors; they'd all heard the rumors. The loss of a vampire's virginity was so intense no human could survive the experience. If the feeding didn't kill them, the fucking would. She had always thought such tales to be nothing more than the fanciful musings of bored vampires, but in light of Gabriel's statement, she might reconsider her opinion. Only, if such stories were true, who cared about a few dead whores if it helped to deflower a newly made vampire? A glance from beneath her lashes suggested at least two other vampires who did.

"Are you sure he's a virgin?"

"*Katja!*" Vladimir's outrage was unmistakable.

"Yes," Gabriel assured her, calming her father with a wave of his hand. "He has never been with a woman."

"And you want me to be his first?"

"I would do it myself, but I'm the wrong gender."

"I didn't think such a notion was possible."

Across the room Vladimir had an apoplectic fit.

Gender had never been a primary requirement for most vampires when it came to sex. The ability to achieve orgasm was the primary goal. By what manner, and with whom, was usually no more than a secondary concern.

"My protégé shows no inclination toward his own sex." Gabriel shrugged at the querying look on Katja's face. "It happens sometimes, and I take no offense at his preference. His initiation into the pleasures of the bedchamber would be preferable without the possibility of his killing his teacher in the process. For that I need an experienced vampire. A female vampire."

"Of course," she murmured, lowering her eyes.

"The choice is still yours," Vladimir reminded her. "You can always refuse." But he knew she would not. He could already see the seed of her infatuation with Gabriel taking root. Had she shown a similar passion for her own maker, Vladimir would not have been concerned. It was to be expected, but to be so deeply obsessed with an Original she had no bond with was . . . troubling.

"What will you do if your vampire becomes attached to me? It can happen."

"I would welcome your presence in my household, for as long as it lasts," Gabriel told her with a dazzling display of fangs.

It was the answer she wanted to hear. In order to stay close to Gabriel, she fully intended to convince this new vampire his cock would fall off if he so much as allowed anyone else to even look at it. Three days later, she left for St. Petersburg. She did not say good-bye to Vladimir.

All the servants in Gabriel's house treated Katja like a great lady, with the exception of Tomas. His attitude toward her was one of polite indifference, but as he was never overtly rude or deliberately hostile, she had nothing to complain of. On the third night after her arrival, she was shown into a sumptuous bedroom where a newly made vampire named Aleksei waited for her. He was nervous, but also handsome and well-muscled, and Katja decided she much preferred the smell of hay and horses to goat piss. Four nights later she emerged, leaving in her wake one exhausted, but extremely satisfied vampire.

When Gabriel came to her later, to offer his gratitude as she rested, curiosity got the better of her. "What made you choose me?"

"I didn't," he admitted candidly. "It was Ryiel's suggestion. He thought you would be amenable."

It was stupid, but for some reason Katja had convinced herself Gabriel had sought her out of his own accord. Learning he knew nothing of her existence until her maker told him stung more than her pride. She turned her head away from him so he would not see the telltale brightness in her eyes. But she wasn't quick enough. Realizing his error, Gabriel took her in his arms, holding her to him as she wept silent tears.

"I'm sorry," he told her. "I assumed you already knew what was expected before we met. I thought your questions were for Vladimir's sake. I didn't realize they were for yours." He tilted her head up and gently wiped her wet cheeks with the pad of his thumb. "It was wrong of Ryiel not to have told you. I will speak to him—"

"No, you must not!" she protested. "He is my maker. It is not my place to question how he uses me." She gave him a feeble poke in the chest. "Or yours either."

Gabriel clearly did not comprehend the relationship between Katja and her maker, but he decided to abide by her wishes and stay silent on the matter.

"As you wish." He placed a chaste kiss on her forehead "But it would not hurt to remind him what century it is. Common courtesies are not only observed, but expected." Staring up at him, Katja fell even more in love with him.

Now, after all this time, she could still feel the softness of his lips against her skin. It reminded her how cruel and unfair the hand of fate could be. How different her life would have been if only Gabriel had been the one to turn her. With their shared connection, he might never have felt the need to seek out his Promise. After all, in five hundred years Ryiel had never expressed a desire to find his. She sighed. The game of *what if* was an old one, ending always in stalemate.

"A beautiful woman should never look so sad."

Katja whipped her head around at the unfamiliar voice. A vampire was leaning in the open doorway, looking at her. Narrowing her eyes, she stared at him. He was bathed in silver from the rising moon behind him, and the arrogant smile on his face told her to take as long as she needed to examine him. He stared back, showing Katja the palest green eyes she had ever seen.

Chapter 10

"Perhaps I have good reason to be sad," Katja said, wondering who the vampire was, and if his timing was more than a little fortuitous. She doubted he was here to see Stavros, so whatever business he had must be with Ryiel. And that made her cautious, because Ryiel never conducted business from his home.

"Aren't you going to invite me in?" the vampire asked, making the smile a little less arrogant and a little warmer.

His voice was smooth and melodic, with a hint of an accent. *Somewhere from the Southern Hemisphere,* Katja told herself, and while the voice did not have the same effect as Gabriel's, it nevertheless stirred something inside her.

"This is the home of a vampire, you need no invitation"—she paused, showing the tips of her fangs—"but I suspect you already know that."

She was not some naïve, newly made vampire. Did he imagine she couldn't tell what he was?

With a slight shake of his head, the vampire stepped over the threshold. "I was trying to be polite and not make assumptions."

Really, about what?

As he came farther into the kitchen, Katja was surprised to see there was nothing silver about him at all. It had merely been a trick of the light reflecting off the pale gray clothing he wore. She watched as he slipped out of the long duster he was wearing, letting it fall to the floor behind him. Apparently he liked gray. Everything he wore was a varying hue of the same color. Katja pursed her lips. Although she wouldn't be caught dead in such an insipid shade, she had to admit it was a perfect complement for his pale eyes and shocking blue hair.

The sleeves of his silk shirt were rolled back to above the elbow, and her eyes opened wide as she saw the markings tattooed on the inside of his forearms. The resemblance to the glyphs on Ryiel's chest was uncanny. Although all vampires had a visceral connection to the Original who sired them, many had no memory of any physical traits. A hazy recollection of eyes and fangs was, at best, all that was remembered. Katja had a superior advantage in being on a first-name basis with two Original Vampires. Now it would appear she was going to meet a third. Perhaps fate was trying to make up for giving her Ryiel as her maker.

"Versace?" She gestured to the pants and silk shirt the vampire wore.

"You know your designers. Can't say I'm familiar with yours, although I do find the camouflage print intriguing."

She gave a hollow laugh. "Not my choice, and you don't strike me as the type of guy who's ever heard of Pro Bass Outfitters."

"And what is your choice?"

Her look turned wistful. "I've always had a weakness for Valentino."

"He does know how to dress a woman, especially a beautiful one. I'm sure you would look stunning in anything from his latest collection."

Katja couldn't decide if he was being polite or if his flirtatious behavior was deliberate. She decided she didn't care. It had been too long since someone had last paid her a compliment. "Well, I don't think I'm going to have the chance to follow up on that anytime soon."

"What if I told you it was possible?"

The denial she was about to make was cut off by a piercing howl that filled the night air. It reminded Katja where Ryiel was, and suddenly she wasn't sure if being alone with this unknown Original Vampire was such a good idea.

"If I wanted to kill you, it would have already happened," he said, correctly interpreting the change of expression on her face.

He was bigger, stronger, and faster than she was, and she did not doubt him for a moment. Tilting her head toward the still-open door, and as the dying howl carried on the wind, she asked, "Is that your doing?"

"What if it is?"

"I'm curious. Do you mean to kill them all?"

"Of course."

"But . . . why?"

"I'm conducting an experiment."

Katja stared at him, nonplussed. "What kind of experiment?"

"A secret one." He leaned insolently against the wall. "Do you know how amazing it is, in this era of instant communication, to come across humans the rest of the world knows nothing about?"

"And that is important why?" Katja asked. "In case your experiment fails?"

He laughed. "I have every confidence that won't happen."

It was obvious he wasn't going to tell her anything more, and she still couldn't decide if he was being truthful or simply playing with her. But why would he? What did he hope to gain from it? Another howl crested the mountainside, only this time it was abruptly cut off in mid-shriek.

"Ah . . . it would seem your maker has come across one of my test subjects."

"Doesn't sound like it went well," Katja observed. "I don't think he'll be reporting back to you."

"But I don't expect any of them to report back to me." Mainly because he assumed Ryiel would kill all of them. "It isn't part of this particular test."

"So how many vampires did you let loose in the valley?"

"No more than a score." Seeing the slight furrow in Katja's forehead, he asked, "What are you trying to figure out?"

"How long it would take less than twenty vampires to decimate a population of a thousand humans."

"My, my, beauty and brains. I knew I was going to like you. So tell me, is Ryiel still burying his nose in those ancient scrolls he rescued from the library?" He held up a hand. "You don't have to answer; I can still smell the smoke." He came toward her and took a lock of her hair, corkscrewing it around his finger. "But what brought you to this godforsaken place? You don't strike me as the scholarly type."

Being all-powerful did not equate to being all-knowing.

"I'm being punished," Katja told him, deciding it was pointless to lie.

Pale green eyes darkened with curious excitement. The finger twisting her hair halted in mid-curl. "You must have done something pretty awful to earn a front-row seat for this particular brand of purgatory."

He dropped the lock of hair from his fingers and cupped her cheek with his hand. To Katja it seemed as if centuries had passed since she had last been offered comfort in any form. Impulsively, she leaned into him, thinking how wonderful it was to be caressed by someone who didn't smell of boiled beets or cabbage.

"I tried to kill a Promise," she murmured.

His chuckle was a deep rumble that seemed to reach the rafters of the ceiling high above them. "So the rumors about Ryiel's Promise are true? She is so beautiful she fills the heart of every other female with jealousy?"

Katja tilted her head back and looked up at him, her amethyst eyes sparkling with puzzlement. "I know nothing about Ryiel's Promise. As far as I know, she remains hidden, and he has not sought her out. The Promise I tried to kill belonged to another."

He placed a finger beneath her chin so she could not look away. "Who?"

"Gabriel."

"What a shame you didn't succeed. You would have done us all a favor."

A ribbon of excitement unfurled inside Katja. "You know who she is?"

"We've met—quite recently, in fact—although I must admit I wasn't impressed." He gave her a chilling smile before continuing. "A word of advice? The next time you get the chance, make sure you finish her off."

Katja's amethyst eyes looked startled. Did he have any idea what he was saying? "You're giving me permission to take the life of a Promise," she murmured.

His fingers resumed playing with the lock of her hair. "What do I care? Take her life or not, it's all the same to me. Personally I think Promises are overrated. I know mine was, and I've yet to see how no longer having one has put me at a disadvantage."

Katja frowned. "I thought each Original Vampire was given a Promise."

"They are, or rather they were. But no one said we had to keep them." Katja wasn't sure what to say, or if she was expected to say anything at all. "So," he tugged on the lock of hair around his finger, "do you want to stay here, isolated from the rest of the world, or would you like to come with me?"

Now it was Katja's turn to release her hair from around the vampire's finger, after which she took a few steps back. Perhaps he had never kept a vampire prisoner and thus did not comprehend the limitations involved.

"My maker has enforced a restriction prohibiting me from moving beyond the boundaries of the mountain under any circumstances," she explained.

"Are you sure? What if I told you I could change those circumstances?"

Fate, she decided, had a wickedly twisted sense of humor. She was conversing with an Original Vampire, but one who had taken one too many blows to the head at some point during his life span. Pretty to look at, but dumb as a box of rocks and unable to grasp fully the ramifications of her confinement.

"I cannot leave. I am physically bound to this place until my maker sets me free."

He looked thoughtful. "What happens if you try to go past this impossible barrier?"

I'll immediately gain sixty pounds, have a unibrow, and my skin will be covered with warts and liver spots.

"I'll die," she told him. It was pretty much the same thing.

"And if I knew of a way to stop that from happening?"

Now it was Katja's turn to think she was the one with swelling on the brain. "It's not possible. What you are suggesting would mean destroying the bond between vampire and maker. Something that can only happen with my death." She arched a brow and gave him a withering look. "Hardly an acceptable alternative from where I stand."

She couldn't decide if he was deranged or dangerous. Or maybe both. Did he not comprehend the one irrefutable truth about being a vampire? Without a connection to his maker, a vampire would simply cease to exist. And if an Original Vampire was somehow killed, all the vampires he had ever made also died. Of course, it was a truth that had never been put to the test, but all vampires who had been turned had the knowledge implanted inside their heads. Like knowing there wasn't an SPF number high enough to let them walk in the sunlight.

"Katja, there is a way you could survive breaking your bond with

Ryiel." The green of his eyes darkened to a deep emerald. "But only if you're brave enough to try it."

The sound of her name on his lips was as startling as his words. "You know who I am?"

He nodded and gave her a sly smile. "Do I look like I go traipsing around the Himalayas for fun?" No, she'd figured he was here for a reason, but she'd assumed it was connected to Ryiel. One Original Vampire to another. It had never crossed her mind that he had come for her. "I won't ask again, Katja. If you could leave this place, and be free of your maker's influence, would you go?"

She stared into his eyes, which had resumed their pale hue. "Of course I would."

Going to his duster, the vampire removed a flat case from an inside pocket and opened the lid. Inside was a syringe filled with a brilliant blue liquid. It sparkled like a sapphire in the candlelight.

"It matches your hair," she told him.

The vampire narrowed his eyes and gave a sly grin. "A small vanity permitted by the alchemist."

She pondered his use of the old-fashioned word. "But what will happen to me? If I'm not bonded to Ryiel, will I not perish?"

His expression made her consider refusing him because it said he didn't know. Not with any certainty. But Katja wasn't going to refuse because she already knew it was too late. His secret experiment hadn't been confined to the vampires in the valley. She was also a part of it. "How can I not be bonded?"

He frowned as if he were seriously mulling through every possible consideration her question posed. The arrogant smile returned. "Perhaps I misspoke. The bond between you and Ryiel would break, but it would be replaced."

She pursed her lips as understanding swept through her. "I'll be bonded to you instead."

"As I said, beautiful and smart."

Katja had been a vampire for so long, she couldn't imagine not being connected to someone more powerful than herself. Ever since she was a small child, when her father realized others would pay to use the body attached to such an exotic face, she had been used by those who were stronger and more powerful. The key to surviving her harrowing childhood had been the uncanny ability to always recognize who was the strongest of those around her and use it to her advantage. This situation was no different. She suspected Ryiel was actually stronger than the one who stood before her, but Ryiel was not here. She looked at the syringe in the vampire's fingers, the bright color twinkling in the candlelight. If she refused, he would only overpower her and take what he wanted.

So what choice did she have? When Ryiel discovered another vampire had been here, he would either kill her or keep her in this god-awful place until she lost her mind. Did she want to suffer a century or more in this place under such dismal conditions? The only thing Ryiel had ever done for her was introduce her to Gabriel, and that hadn't gone the way she had hoped. And now she was reduced to indentured servitude, a life of drudgery, with her only relief the faint hope she might fuck Stavros to death. It made no difference that she knew nothing about the vampire standing in front of her. For reasons of his own, he had sought her out, and that had to count for something. That he had also orchestrated the death of a thousand humans meant nothing to her.

And now he was offering her a chance to do something no other vampire had ever done before. She'd be lying if she said she wasn't intrigued by the proposal, supposing it could actually work. He tapped the barrel of the syringe with a well-manicured nail.

"So . . . yes or no, Katja?"

She held out her arm, the pale skin accentuating the vein in the crook of her arm. "Yes."

Raising his head, Stavros noticed an apricot blush painting the peaks of the far-off mountains. It was close to dawn. He watched as Ryiel gently placed the last corpse on the funeral pyre, the small body of a child soon consumed by a blanket of flame. Knowing their task had been necessary did not make it any the less tragic for either of them.

"What now?" Stavros asked, his face and hands streaked black from tending the fire.

"Sleep. We both need to rest, and I have a journey to make."

"Where are you going?"

"I must let Gabriel know what has happened here."

The sentinel frowned. This was not the first scene of mass slaughter they had come across, as either participants or witnesses. It was, however, the first time Ryiel had ever expressed the need to discuss it with any other Original Vampire. It was proof enough of his concern.

"Is it because of the vampires?"

Ryiel nodded, his own chest glistening with sweat. "These are a different kind of vampire, and I suspect the manner of their creation is unnatural."

"You could just call him, or send an e-mail," Stavros suggested.

Ryiel's disdain for modern technology did not mean he was foolish enough to ignore it. He simply believed in being circumspect in its use. Still, it always baffled the sentinel that Ryiel was able to achieve a connection, especially from their current location.

"I could," Ryiel agreed, "but I have other news that needs to be delivered in person, and as soon as possible."

For the first time, Stavros permitted himself a smile. "You have found the answer his Promise seeks?"

"Indeed I ha—*AAAAAARGH!*"

The claymore fell from the Original Vampire's fingers as he clutched his head with his hands and fell to his knees in obvious agony. Rushing to his side, Stavros stared helplessly as his master writhed on the ground, his lips curled back, fangs fully exposed. Seeing the vampire fist his hands in his hair, the sentinel threw himself onto the powerful chest and gripped Ryiel's wrists in order to prevent him from pulling out his hair.

For what seemed like an eternity, the sentinel did his best to ride out the violent storm that had taken hold of his master. Knees locked on either side of Ryiel's torso, Stavros prayed to his long-forgotten gods to be forgiven for any ribs he cracked. And then, with an unprecedented surge of strength, the sentinel felt himself being caressed by a rush of air as the vampire heaved himself up. Landing on the opposite side of the pyre, Stavros felt his head strike the hard, unforgiving ground. Blood filled his mouth as his teeth sliced through the tip of his tongue, but before he had time to consider what the scent of fresh blood might mean to his master, the vampire was on him.

"My service is my life, and both I give to you," Stavros said as he looked into the face of the vampire he had chosen to follow out of the Void too long ago for either of them to recall with any clarity of detail. Something flickered in Ryiel's eyes, changing them to a form more bestial than human. And then the vampire threw back his head, letting loose a snarling, shrieking howl that came from an animal who had ceased to prowl the night eons ago. Stavros trembled, causing Ryiel to look down at him. His eyes glowed as bright as the moon before rolling up into his head as he fell off his faithful servant in an unconscious heap.

Chapter 11

"**D**ahlink!"

Anasztaizia threw herself at me as I opened the front door. The slight shudder of her body as she held onto me was the only sign she gave of how traumatic these past few days had been for her. My lack of apparent enthusiasm made her pull back and look at me with concern. I held up wet hands, suds dripping on the floor. She made a dismissive gesture and yanked me forward for another tight embrace. Now the tremble of her body was accompanied by some wet snuffling in the side of my neck as she cried and gently fell to pieces. I hugged her back. If she didn't care about wet handprints on her silk blouse, why should I?

A polite harrumph from the hallway made us break apart. Tomas moved past us carrying a sack of groceries in each arm. He came to a stop a few feet inside the door.

"What the hell have you been doing?"

I could feel the color flush my face. I'd been hoping to have my living room look more like a living room and less like the morning after at some high-end college frat house party. I say high-end because most movies depicting college parties usually involved a kegger. I had no beer, save for a six-pack of something imported in the fridge, but every other conceivable surface displayed a bottle of alcohol. Some were actually unopened, but most were not.

I cleared a space on the kitchen counter for Tomas to put the grocery bags. This too was crowded with bottles, but these were all mixers. And garnishes. Tomas seemed momentarily mesmerized by the jar of olives he now held in his hand. I had only ever thought olives came in one kind. Apparently not. There were also pearl onions, red and green maraschino cherries, salt, sugar, and powdered chocolate for rim dipping, as well as a crate of fresh fruit. Lemons, limes, oranges, three pineapples, two coconuts, and a bunch of bananas.

Anasztaizia followed us in, wiping at her eyes with a tissue. "There now," I smiled. "My favorite raccoon." I've always been of the opinion that waterproof mascara is a lie. Water-resistant to some degree maybe, but waterproof? Not when it comes to crying.

The lovely Magyar kissed me on both cheeks, paying no attention to her ruined makeup. "Well, now I know why you smell like you've been on a three-day drunk, dahlink," she told me. "I can see that you have been."

"Yeah, well, it was my idea to play beer pong, but your boyfriend decided on a different game. One that required a copy of the *Bartenders Ultimate Guide*."

"That was in his coat pocket," Tomas said. "I left it on the washer when I took his coat."

"Gee, thanks." At least now I knew where it had come from.

Anasztaizia gave a little shrug. "Whenever we go out, Aleksei always likes to try a new cocktail."

Imagining the big guy ordering a drink with either fruit or an umbrella as decoration was mildly disturbing. Especially in a public place. "Yeah, well, I think he's gonna need a new book. That one's toast."

"You've spent three days drinking cocktails?"

It was difficult to tell if Tomas was delighted or disappointed by the fact that I was still standing and reasonably functional. "Aleksei suggested we binge watch *Downton Abbey* and play the Tea Game. He told me it would be fun."

"I'm almost afraid to ask," Tomas said, "but what the hell is the Tea Game?"

"Any time the word *tea* is mentioned by any character, or they are shown drinking the disgusting stuff, or if you spot a teapot, or someone holding a tea cup, you hit the pause button and try a new cocktail," I paused and looked at both of them. "It was *Downton Abbey*, for Christ's sake! Do you have any idea how much tea those people drink?"

"Oh dear," Anasztaizia mumbled under her breath and tried to smother a laugh.

"It's not funny," I admonished. She gave me a suitably contrite look.

Tomas just seemed curious. "Where did all the liquor come from?"

"I'm pretty sure Aleksei has just paid a year's college tuition for the eldest Bradleigh boy. Don't be surprised when you receive an invitation to his graduation party," I added, smiling at Anasztaizia.

"Who's Bradleigh?"

"Mr. Bradleigh, the elder, owns the liquor store on Main Avenue. By the time Aleksei came to the end of his list they were on first-name terms. Al and Al, which is really quite funny, if you think about it."

"This all came from one store?" Tomas seemed flabbergasted.

"A year's tuition in the bag. I get the feeling they can't wait for Christmas and New Year's. It might be easier—and cheaper—to become an honorary aunt and uncle."

"I can't believe you drank this much." Tomas gave a sad shake of his head.

"It wasn't only me. Aleksei did his fair share." He was making it sound as if I was the only lush in the building. Well, I might be, but it was rude to say so. "Besides, I think it helped him."

Picking up a bottle, Tomas sniffed the open neck. He jerked his head back, wearing the same expression I'd worn when he asked if I'd like to try blood pudding. Not only no, but hell no. "How could this help a vampire?" He scowled.

"Didn't you know a steady consumption of alcohol can enable a vampire to go without sleep for a few days?" I relished the opportunity to display my knowledge even if I was being rather smug about it. "The problem, as I see it, is having someone around to stop said vampire from doing something stupid if he gets too drunk. Luckily for Aleksei, my boyfriend is also a vampire." I pointed at the wall of windows that normally gave a spectacular view of the river and the Greenley Heights financial district. The glass behind the floor-to-ceiling sheers was covered by steel shutters—something Gabriel had installed under the guise of security. "No chance of a drunk vampire accidentally exposing himself to sunlight."

"But why didn't Aleksei want to sleep?" his girlfriend asked.

My finger now waved in her direction. "My darling girl, your boyfriend was consumed with guilt about wanting to sleep with me." I paused and frowned. "Well, not *sleep* with me, but sleep with me."

She nodded. It was a good thing one of us understood what I was saying. "So where is he now?"

"Oh, he finally crashed this morning," I told her. "I think it was the first time he was able to think about sleeping without me. That's a good thing, right?" This last I addressed to Tomas, who nodded.

"Yes, it is." He gave me the same kind of look my dad had used when I came home drunk from my senior prom. "And you haven't slept either?"

"I didn't say that," I corrected. "I did pass out a couple of times." Two sets of raised brows needed details. "One time I know was after Mr. Bates was arrested and charged with the murder of his ex-wife. I was drinking a Wisconsin Lunchbox at the time. Then I'm pretty sure I passed out again after Sex with an Alligator when poor lady Edith found out she was pregnant."

"Lady Edith had sex with an alligator?" Anasztaizia queried.

"No, silly, I had the libation, but maybe if Lady Edith had had one, she might have had better luck with men."

"How long since you last drank anything?" Tomas inquired.

"Well . . . does the chocolate martini I had for breakfast count?" I watched a vertical line form between his eyebrows. "And nothing but water since. I wanted to clean up before you guys got here."

Anasztaizia opened the fridge and began making space for the perishables she unloaded from the grocery sacks. "Don't worry about it. You've done more than enough. Aleksei can finish when he wakes up."

"Uh-huh." Somehow I didn't think washing dirty glassware was going to be high on the big guy's to-do list.

"So, dahlink . . . where is he?" Anasztaizia paused, a carton of eggs in her hand.

"In my bed," I answered without thinking.

Now it was Anasztaizia's turn to blush.

"Oh, don't worry, I think he was expecting you."

"Did you tell him Tomas was bringing me?" She put the eggs in the fridge and closed the door.

I shook my head. I wasn't going to say anything to the big guy unless I knew for sure. Even though Tomas told me he would bring the lovely Magyar with him, I had no idea if Anasztaizia would agree to come, or what her reaction would be to what had happened. I took her hand in mine. "You do know why he broke his bond with you, right?"

"To protect me." Her voice took on a raspy quality. "But until I hear him tell me in his own words . . ." She shrugged, not finishing her sentence.

"And you know why he came to me instead of you?"

If I didn't know what to look for, putting myself in her place, I would have missed the flash of hurt in her eyes. "Gabriel told me he was the one who sent Aleksei to you."

"Gabriel? You spoke to Gabriel about this?"

She nodded. "Yes, he came to see me."

Was that before or after he decided you were a liar?

"He said it would be better," Anasztaizia added.

Yeah? For who?

I could hear something in her undertone. Not so much bitterness, more frustration because she had been unable to help the love of her life at one of his darkest hours.

"Anasztaizia"—I squeezed her fingers gently—"the only reason Gabriel sent Aleksei to me was because he couldn't get to him in time. I have Gabriel's blood in me, and it was the next best thing."

And he also couldn't kill us if he took too much. Might turn us into drooling vegetables, but death was off the table.

"By the time Gabriel arrived," I continued, "he was able to supplement what Aleksei had already taken from me and help accelerate the healing process." I paused to make sure she understood me. I also decided it was best if I didn't tell her about the whole feeling my boob part. Hopefully the big guy would have enough sense to also omit that particular detail. "I guess it also explains why he didn't even get woozy drinking all these cocktails."

She laughed. It was a small chuckle, but more than enough. "So if you didn't tell him I was coming"—she wiped her eyes, smudging what was left of her makeup—"why do you think he's expecting me?"

I wasn't going to tell her about how I'd awoken on the couch to the sound of Aleksei vacuuming. Or the fact that he'd put clean sheets on the bed or spent all night airing out the room in an effort to dispel my scent. He wasn't going to be able to get rid of it completely— it was my apartment, after all—but thankfully Anasztaizia didn't possess a vampire's heightened sense of smell. As long as the bed linens were fresh, or smelled only of Aleksei, there wouldn't be a problem.

And the fresh-cut bouquets of roses, sweet peas, and stephanotis would help.

"Just a feeling," I replied. "There's another bathroom down the hall. Why don't you go freshen up?" She patted my hand and grabbed the large tote she'd brought with her and disappeared. Behind me, Tomas continued to put away groceries. I watched him for a few minutes before asking, "How long are you expecting Aleksei and Anasztaizia to be here?" I knew the big guy could eat, but even so it looked like Tomas was planning to feed an army battalion.

"I'm not sure, but this is probably the safest place for Aleksei right now, and once he's reestablished his bond with Anasztaizia—"

"She'll be safe here too."

I wished I felt as confident about it as Gabriel's sentinel did. I explained to Tomas how Gabriel had been able to cross my threshold without an invitation, something that I was still mildly resentful about. The idea that my lover had bought the entire apartment building was amusing enough to make Tomas grin.

"Ah, but Gabriel is an Original," he explained. "The first time Aleksei came to the penthouse he needed to be invited in."

As if I didn't have enough on my plate trying to keep up with regular vampire rules, now there existed a different playbook for the Originals.

"So that means Petrov couldn't get in, but Kartel could?"

The humor disappeared from Tomas's face. "That would be correct."

"And you're hoping what? Kartel doesn't know about this place?"

"I'm hoping Petrov doesn't know. Where Aleksei is concerned, Kartel isn't the one who's been carrying a grudge for three hundred years."

"Yeah, I would've thought he'd have gotten over it by now."

With my fridge containing more than a six-pack of imported beer, and cupboards now stocked to bursting, Tomas picked up one of the liquor bottles from the counter, sniffed the neck warily, and made a disgusted snorting sound. I didn't need to know what language he was muttering to understand the sentiment.

Taking the bottle of advocaat from his hand, I poured a measured amount into a clean glass. "How brave are you, Tomas?"

He rose to the challenge with an expression that begged me to do my worst, watching as I added chocolate liqueur and Bailey's Irish

Cream to the same glass. I have to say the shudder as he downed the contents of the glass was one of the most dramatic and spectacular body spasms I'd ever seen.

"I'm almost too afraid to ask, lass, but what in the name of God and all that's holy was that?"

I grinned. "Now you can tell all your friends I made you Lick Out a Sheep."

Obviously, staying at the apartment was out of the question for me. By my reckoning, it was going to take Aleksei a grand total of thirty seconds before reestablishing his bond with Anasztaizia—a process that would involve sex and feeding on what could possibly be a scale of biblical proportions. I certainly had no intention of being a fifth wheel, even though there was a good chance that I was so tired, I'd sleep through the event. Besides, Aleksei and I needed a breather from each other. Our relationship had changed, but in what way was still up for grabs. Whatever. We'd deal with it.

I yawned. Passing out while cocktail sampling did not equate to beneficial, restful sleep, and raising my arm over my head told me I could also benefit from a shower.

"I don't think I should be driving," I told Tomas, imagining the scenario in my head if I was pulled over by a state trooper.

Have you had anything to drink this evening, miss?

No officer, not this particular evening, but that's only because I'm still pretty wasted from the past two days.

Uh-huh, and just what have you had to drink?

Oh, lemme see . . . there was a Paralyzer, a Four Horsemen, a Red-headed Slut, a Leg Spreader, a Naughty Angel, an Adios Mother-fucker, a Jamaican Ten Speed, and a Melon Ball.

I see . . . anything else?

Give me a moment. I'm sure I'll remember the rest.

I'm not quite sure what would have happened next in my little scenario, but I figured both the cop and I would have been pretty much in agreement that there was a good chance I'd melt his breath-alyzer if I blew into it. Handing Tomas my car keys was a no-brainer.

I don't know why, but for some weird reason I assumed he would take me back to the hotel I'd lied about staying in. I hadn't checked out, so presumably the room was still being charged to my credit card. I managed to stumble only once on our way to the car, and I was asleep before Tomas had backed out of the parking space. I didn't open my eyes again until we were in a different garage, one that housed Gabriel's car collection.

"Why did you bring me here?" I asked, fumbling with the door latch.

Tomas gave me an odd look. "Where else should I have taken you, lass?"

"Back to the hotel. I haven't checked out yet."

"Actually, you have," he informed me, "and do you really believe he'd let me take another breath if I put you back amongst strangers?"

"Not your decision to make."

"Not yours either."

Awww shit!

"What makes you think I'm going to be better off upstairs?" I muttered sourly. "Have you managed to convince him I'm not lying?"

Part of me was hoping Tomas would say no because the idea that Gabriel would accept the word of his sentinel over mine was . . . was . . . I didn't know what it was, except not what I wanted to hear.

"I don't know," Tomas said, getting out of the car and closing the door. I quickly did the same. Having Gabriel open my door for me was one thing; having Tomas do it felt weird. "I haven't spoken to him."

The admission surprised me. I was certain Gabriel would have vented his frustration to his sentinel. Placing his hand on my elbow, Tomas steered me across the parking substructure to the elevator. The sound of our shoes striking the concrete was a hollow ring.

"He's all right, isn't he?" I had no idea how much giving blood to both Aleksei and me had taken out of him, but the need for his sarcophagus's restorative powers had been evident. Of course, that was before he blew up at me.

Tomas pushed the button on the wall. It went from orange to green, indicating the elevator was on its way. "As far as I know, yes, he's all right."

As far as he knew? What did that mean? It wasn't like Tomas to be so ambiguous.

A soft ping heralded the elevator's arrival, and a moment later a familiar mechanical swoosh accompanied the opening of the doors. Tomas's hand moved from my elbow to the small of my back as he gently pushed me inside the steel box.

"Wait!" I started, seeing he was still standing on the garage side. "Aren't you coming up with me?"

He shook his head. "Some conversations, lass, need to be kept private. This is one of them."

A lump filled my throat as I watched the elevator doors whisper closed.

Chapter 12

The door to the penthouse was open, as if someone knew I wouldn't have my key on me. I stepped through, closing it behind me, and stared at the open space of the living room. Something was different. None of the furniture was missing or had been replaced, as best as I could tell, but something wasn't quite right. It wasn't until I took my second sweep around the room that I noticed it. How I didn't see it right away I can only blame on the hangover effect of too many cocktails.

Gabriel's sword was buried in the wall.

I couldn't even begin to imagine the rage that had given his arm the strength to do such a thing. Surely this was about more than me and a stupid necklace? I walked over to the wall, seeing the spiderweb of cracks running top and bottom from the point of impact. I ran my forefinger across the inch or so of visible blade before working my way along the hilt and handle, and yes, there it was. I curled my fingers around the grip, almost laughing out loud when they failed to meet. I'd need two hands to hold this wicked baby.

I sighed and turned away. I had no idea what had propelled Gabriel to this particular act of mayhem. I was too tired, my brain too fuddled, to even try and come up with a remotely plausible explanation. For now, I would accept that I had a massive celestial weapon embedded in the wall. Eat your heart out, *Architectural Digest*. I held my breath and listened. Nothing but silence. A glance at the sky through the sliding-glass patio doors said it was almost night. I had no doubt that if Gabriel was still in his sarcophagus, he would be surfacing soon. The image of the large bed we shared suddenly filled my head, only I wasn't thinking about sex. All I wanted right now was to sleep. I made my way to the master bedroom. Still no sign of my vampire lover. I peeked into the walk-in closet just to see if the door to the hidden chamber at the far end was open or closed. It remained closed. He was still submerged. Perhaps setting Aleksei back on the path to a full recovery and the subsequent uproar with me had taken more out of him than I'd realized.

I turned my head and caught a whiff of myself. Ugh! No way was I getting into bed smelling like this. Twenty minutes and one vigorous scrubbing with a washcloth later, I was glowing pink and smelling of honeysuckle and ginger. I crawled beneath the big poufy duvet. The last thought on my mind as I headed for la-la land was how much I was beginning to dislike sleeping alone.

At some point in the night, I rolled over and felt Gabriel's arms wrap around me. His scent was intoxicating, and the feel of his hair whispering across my skin was like silk. His mouth and hands teased me, suckling and stroking my body to the point that I was nothing more than a pool of wanton desire, drenched in my own need for him.

I was supposed to be angry with him, and I should have turned away. Refused to allow his tongue to slide seductively into my mouth. Ignored the urge to glide my own between his fangs. I should have silenced my lustful moans as he palmed my breasts and brought my nipples to hard points by blowing lightly across them. I should have suppressed the involuntary gasp from between my lips as his fangs scraped along the side of my neck and over my collarbone.

I should have . . . but I didn't.

Even when I felt his hand slip between my thighs, his fingers dipping inside me, I responded to him with a measure of lust beyond my control. Unable to deny him, I opened myself up and begged him to fill me. He entered me with strong, steady thrusts, and it took little encouragement for my body to match his rhythm. And right at the point when I was standing at the edge of the abyss, when the promise of untold pleasure was within my grasp and the soft click of descending fangs told me Gabriel was a heartbeat away from puncturing my vein, I gripped his hips with my knees and went completely still.

Confusion filled his eyes as he snapped back his head and stared down at me. Carefully I untangled my fingers from the hair at the nape of his neck and took his face in my hands, forcing him to look at me. His mouth was open, his breathing ragged, and his fangs were longer than I had ever seen them.

"I didn't . . . lie . . . to you," I told him.

Gabriel continued to stare at me, his locked elbows keeping him suspended above me. A sheen of perspiration covered his chest and abdomen with an almost unearthly glow. For a moment, I thought he was going to contradict me, and then I saw his eyes change. Confusion was replaced by awareness and perception. I slid my hands down his neck and across his shoulders, moving to his waist as he dropped his head to my neck. His lips brushed against the outer edge of my ear, and he hesitated for only a moment before murmuring, "I know."

And I felt the sweet sting as he punctured my neck, bringing me to a climax that threatened to break me in two.

Several hours later, I stumbled into the kitchen, looking for coffee, and found Gabriel taking inventory at the bar. He had his phone to his ear, deep in conversation with someone. If I had to guess, I would say it was probably Tomas.

". . . no, what? . . . yeah, I checked there, too . . . no, I don't see any . . . I don't think it's something we've ever had . . . yeah, I can ask, but don't hold your breath . . . why? She can be stubborn, that's why." He chuckled as he ended his call, coming into the kitchen and taking the mug I had poured for him from my hand.

"Anything I can do?" I said, pointing to his phone and indicating I'd overheard part of his conversation.

"I think you've already done it." Gabriel smirked. "Tomas wants to make sure it isn't repeated."

"What?"

"Whatever you made for him with advocaat. He was asking me to check to make sure we didn't have a bottle stashed away in the bar." His arched brow asked the question his mouth did not, so I told him how the cocktail was made. He also shuddered in a dramatic fashion.

"Lick Out a Sheep? Honestly?"

"Hey, I didn't come up with the name, and if you want to blame anyone, blame Aleksei."

"I see—he asked you to play the Tea Game, didn't he?"

"You know about that?"

Gabriel flushed. "I taught it to him."

"You guys watched *Downton Abbey?*"

"*Upstairs, Downstairs,*" he said with a shake of his head. "So, how far did he get?"

"With what?" The question had any number of possible meanings. All of them somewhat unnerving.

"The bartender book."

"He needs an updated version," I muttered.

"Well, if it meant he wasn't going to sleep with you, it was worth it."

"Was that really a concern for you?"

Gabriel shook his head. "Not with Aleksei."

A less secure girl might have wondered if there was some hidden meaning in his reply. Perhaps a question of her own fidelity being raised. But the dull ache between my legs served as a reminder that my faithfulness was not the issue. We both knew whose actions were of concern. I stirred a spoonful of sugar into my mug. As we were alone, with no distractions, it seemed like as good a time as any to talk about . . . things.

"I'm so sorry, Gabriel, this is all my fault. If I hadn't badgered you into giving your protection to Laycee's baby, then none of this—"

My insistence that he ease my best friend's fears had brought us to this point. If I hadn't been so quick to agree, if I'd taken the time to understand just what I was asking Gabriel to do, then neither of us would be standing at the edge of the abyss facing the very real possibility of being separated from one another. He came and took me in his arms, the soft pressure of his lips preventing me from saying anything else. I felt slightly dizzy when his mouth released me.

"First of all, you have never badgered me into doing anything I didn't want to do," he said. "Had I known how afraid Laycee was, how deep the scar within her runs because of what she witnessed, I would have made the offer myself."

"Would you?" I didn't try to hide my disappointment. "Even knowing how the debt is to be repaid, you would have still offered?"

"So you know about that, do you?"

I nodded and carefully extricated myself from his arms. "It's why the demon gave me the opals. He said I had already consented to your infidelity, which meant our relationship is pretty much over." I could feel the tears pricking my eyelids, and I made an effort to steady my voice. "It doesn't matter how much time I originally bargained for. Twenty-five years from now, you'll have to sleep with

Laycee's daughter. He told me Jenna's virginity was the price for your protection. Blood for blood."

"Well, he's not wrong."

In that moment I realized that was exactly what I'd been hoping. That somehow the demon had made a mistake and Gabriel would laugh and tell me to stop being silly. There was no way he was going to be unfaithful to me, no matter what the circumstances.

"But you still would have offered?" I repeated stubbornly.

"Yes, because usually there is some leeway in exactly how this type of debt is paid."

"But not this time, huh?" I murmured.

"The terms, including responsibility of payment, must be specified before the agreement is made," he confirmed.

"And I didn't allow for any such terms."

It was true. I went ahead and agreed to pay whatever was owed so that my lover would give his protection to my best friend's child, and now my recklessness meant I was going to lose the best thing that had ever happened to me. This time I didn't try to stop the tears. Enveloping me in his arms again, Gabriel began to rock me as he stroked my hair and made soft *shushing* noises.

"It's all my fault," I sobbed against his chest. "If I had just used my head and thought things through—"

"Stop!" With his finger beneath my chin, Gabriel made me look up at him. "Do you think your impulsive behavior is something I'm not aware of? It's part of what makes you who you are, Rowan. It's why I didn't hesitate to send Aleksei to you. I knew you wouldn't waste time questioning the implications of what had to be done. Aleksei was dying, and you were the only one who could help him. You didn't question whether you should, you simply did."

"It's not quite the same thing."

"Perhaps not, but you acted out of the same generosity of spirit. Laycee was afraid for her child, and you wanted to ease her fears."

"At least now we know who planted the idea in her head to ask for your protection." I pulled back and looked up at him. "Is it true Jenna will die if you don't sleep with her?"

He nodded, and I mentally cursed myself for the position I'd put him in. Saving Jenna would mean losing me, something Gabriel could never accept. And saving me meant losing Jenna, something I could never accept. And we were supposed to find a way out of this lose-lose situation?

"Because he showed his hand, we have twenty-five years to find a way around the problem," Gabriel pointed out.

His words might not make me feel better, but they did carry some weight. If my demon had kept to himself in the Dark Realm, I would never have known what was going to happen a quarter of a century from now. What was that saying about clouds and silver linings? Overly optimistic maybe, but it sure beat a poke in the eye with a sharp stick.

Why the fuck do vampires have to be so goddamned dramatic?

I had absolutely no idea, but speaking of ongoing drama . . . "So why do you think I can handle the necklace without it hurting me?"

Gabriel frowned and shook his head as he let me go. "I have no idea. I know what's supposed to happen—"

"Yeah, Tomas showed me."

"He did?"

"I'm sorry, wasn't he supposed to?" A shiver went through me at the memory of Tomas's blistered fingers. "At least I know why you freaked out when nothing weird happened to me."

Gabriel pulled a seat out from the breakfast bar and pulled me onto his lap. "Tomas must like you very much to do such a thing for you." He tucked a stray curl behind my ear.

I sighed and silently promised never to make the sentinel drink advocaat again. "If it makes you feel any better, Tomas doesn't understand it either. He made me tell him every moment of what happened between me and *him*."

My lover gave a soft grunt and leaned back in his chair, his brows coming together as he pondered the conundrum. "I guess we'll have to find you another apartment."

"Not until we know Aleksei and Anasztaizia are safe."

I hated to be the one to point out the other problem lurking on our horizon, but ignoring it would be an act of gross stupidity. We hadn't heard the last of either Kartel or Aleksei's possible half brother. "Has there been any sight of Petrov?"

Gabriel shook his head. He seemed to be doing a lot of that recently, and I could tell it didn't sit well with him. "No, he seems to have gone to ground, but I've let it be known I want to speak with him. He will surface. With Kartel as his maker, I doubt he has many who will hide him."

"And what about Vampire Smurf?" With hair that blue it was hard for me to call Kartel anything else. "Do you think he actually went to Death Valley to see if you would show up?"

"Not when I'm sure he was the one behind Aleksei's abduction. Oh, if I had continued on to California, I'm certain I would have found two dead vampires staked out for me to find." His mouth became a grim line. "And one would have been decapitated."

And if all had gone according to plan, Aleksei would have been dead thanks to a drug-crazed member of the Ursidae family, breaking the bond between maker and progeny. It might have been enough to make Gabriel think the blackened body of a dead vampire was Aleksei.

"Do you have any idea what he's up to?"

"Who . . . Kartel?" I nodded. "I don't know, but whatever it is, he has already decided it will not meet with my approval."

"You don't trust him, do you?"

"I never did."

"I'm surprised he's part of your"—your what? gang? posse? crew?— "group," I finished lamely. "He's so different from you and Ryiel. Are the other Original Vampires like you and Ryiel, or like him?"

There were, I knew, nine Original Vampires.

Gabriel closed his eyes as if needing a moment to gather his thoughts. "In the beginning we believed"—he paused before amending his statement—"*I* believed Kartel shared the same vision as the rest of us, but it wasn't long before we saw it was not true. Though his tongue was persuasive, his heart was false. In the end he became so entangled in his own web of deceit, he was unable to escape the punishment that befell us all. It came as no surprise to learn he had accepted the Wraith's offer when it was presented. Kartel is, if nothing else, a survivor."

"Surely there was a way to stop him from becoming a vampire?"

"How? None of us knew who had been approached, and even if we did, we knew nothing of what awaited us in this new existence we had agreed to. Looking back, I don't think any of us expected Kartel to survive his first year as a vampire." He gave me a wry grin. "I know I didn't. No one was more surprised to discover he'd not only survived five hundred years, but thrived as well. There was nothing to be done except watch and limit the scope of any destruction unleashed by his hand."

"What kind of destruction?"

"Kartel specializes in conflict. He has the uncanny knack of knowing when a simple dispute, words taken out of context, can be escalated into something much bigger."

"You're talking about starting a war," I said, appalled. Gabriel did not correct me. "And you haven't tried to stop him?"

Arching a brow, my lover gave me a puzzled look. "Why would we? He's doing what he was created to do. Curbing the growth of a species that has lost all respect for the planet it inhabits. A species that refuses to practice reason when it comes to utilizing resources and does little to protect its own kind, much less those it considers weaker." He caught my chin in his hand, his long fingers holding me gently yet firmly. "Kartel is doing exactly what the lesser beasts required of him. Do not forget that we are predators, Rowan, and the human race is our hunting ground."

"When you next talk to Ryiel, will you tell him about the necklace?" I asked.

Despite Ryiel's professed dislike for modern technology, I knew he wasn't so foolish as to avoid it when the need arose.

Letting go of my chin, Gabriel said, "You want me to ask if he has any insight on your non-aversion to demonic gifts?"

It suddenly occurred to me that our priorities had now shifted. The mysteries surrounding my relationship with the demon suddenly didn't seem quite as pressing as they had a few moments ago. We had twenty-five years to play mind games with him. Whatever Kartel was up to, I didn't think he was going to give us nearly that long.

I frowned as he took the mug from my hand. "If you wanted more coffee," I started irritably, "why didn't you ask me to fix you some?"

"Sorry, sweetheart."

It took me a minute to realize the second half of my comment, along with Gabriel's subsequent apology, were both voiced in a different room. I was now sitting on the living room couch with my mug on the coffee table, watching as Gabriel pulled open the sliding-glass door in time to catch the barely conscious vampire falling into his arms.

Chapter 13

"**R**owan, quickly—the panic room!"

I jumped up from my seat and ran down the hall, through our bedroom to the control panel in the wall at the far end of the walk-in closet. The only reason I was able to beat Gabriel there was because he was slowed by the inert body he carried in his arms. I punched in the code, grateful to hear the soft displacement of air as the section of wall slid open.

"Oh my God!" I gasped, recognizing the raven-black hair pooling over Gabriel's arm. "Ryiel."

"Rowan—his boots," Gabriel ordered, laying the vampire on the cool marble surface of his sarcophagus. It immediately began to change color as the neon-blue gave way to a trio of black, white, and silver. "Rowan, hurry. We don't have much time."

I moved to the end of the sarcophagus. The silver-eyed vampire was old-school, as was his choice of footwear. Military-style combat boots, steel-toed judging from the weight, were laced up the front to mid-calf. No fancy buckles or zippers, just thick, heavy-duty nylon laces . . . and some major knots. Shit! I pulled and tugged at the bindings, but the tie might as well have been steel cable. "Gabriel, I can't undo them!" I yelled in frustration.

Long fingers wrapped around my arm, moving me to one side, and I stared in confusion as Gabriel bent his head toward Ryiel's feet. How was sniffing going to undo the intricate knots that had been tied? The white head moved from toe to shin, repeating the motion on the other leg. "Try now," Gabriel instructed.

Gabriel had bypassed the knots by slicing through the nylon bindings with his fangs, loosening both halves of the boot. With one hand cupping the heel and the other the toe, I was able to work the boot off, dropping it to the floor with a loud thud. I stifled the unseemly urge to laugh on seeing Ryiel's socks. The dark wool had *Toes in first* stitched in bright red across the instep. It was nice to know the serious vampire had a sense of humor.

"Everything," Gabriel instructed, the upturn at the corner of his mouth indicating he'd also seen Ryiel's footwear.

I'd finished stuffing the socks inside the boots when Gabriel's voice said, "Grab his pants."

"What?"

"He can't wear any clothing in the sarcophagus."

Of course he couldn't. I knew that. Hadn't I seen Gabriel lying on the deep-blue marble slab enough times? Completely naked and usually with an erection. Only this wasn't Gabriel, and I wasn't sure how I felt about seeing another man naked—or, more to the point, how Gabriel was going to feel about it. But this wasn't another man or even another vampire. This was another Original, and whatever connection existed between the two, it was strong enough to bring Ryiel to Gabriel for help.

I shot a quick look at Ryiel's hips. Gabriel had already unbuckled the belt and was now working the buttons on the fly. From the amount of skin already exposed, it was obvious Ryiel wasn't a Fruit of the Loom guy, or anything else for that matter. He might go commando, but at least he didn't appear to have an erection. Gabriel grunted and rolled the vampire onto his side as he worked the leather pants down over Ryiel's buttocks. I turned my head, not sure which of us I was trying to save from embarrassment.

"Okay, Rowan, you should be able to pull them off now."

Gabriel positioned himself in such a way that my only view of the recumbent vampire was from toes to mid-thigh. The offending pants were now bunched around Ryiel's knees, but I was still able to see how muscular his mid-thigh was. I seized the waistband and pulled, sliding the clothing off with ease. I picked up the boots and socks, and with the pants over my arm, made my way to the open door as the sarcophagus began to pulse.

I was so accustomed to seeing the entire spectrum of the color blue decorate the walls of the panic room, it took my breath away to see a palette predominately made up of black, white, and silver. I know colors are designated as being either warm or cold, and what I was seeing now would be considered cold, but never had a descriptor been more wrong. Then again, what do I know? I think blue is one of the hottest colors in the continuum.

Gabriel was leaning down, his lips next to Ryiel's ear, whispering something. I hoped they were words of encouragement, telling the vampire to come back to us. I couldn't imagine him saying anything else, and the sudden rise and fall of Ryiel's chest seemed to confirm that the comatose vampire knew he was safe.

Slowly I made my way toward the door, still slightly mesmerized by the night-sky effect in the room. I think I had stars in my eyes when I turned and walked back out into the closet and into the arms of the bald-headed man standing just past the doorway.

"Ooomph!" I ricocheted off the unexpected obstruction, clumsily getting myself tangled in the winter coats hanging from the overhead rail. A hand reached out to steady me. "Who the hell are you?" I yelped, immediately slapping a hand over my mouth to apologize for the profanity.

His weary smile, coupled with the anxious look in his eyes, forgave me. He introduced himself with a slight nod of his head as he looked past me into the room I'd just left. "I am Stavros."

He looks like that guy who was in The Ten Commandments, my inner bitch murmured quietly inside my head. An unexpected visitor to the closet was worthy of her interest.

He doesn't look anything like Charlton Heston, I snorted back. I'm beginning to wonder if, when we watch a movie, we're all actually seeing the same thing on the screen. I've had my doubts of late.

Not him! The guy who played his brother. Ramses whatever. You know, the guy who squished slaves under massive blocks of stone while building a temple to honor his dad. Although why he couldn't have gotten him a tie like any other son is beyond me.

His dad was the pharaoh. I don't think they had ties back then.

Okay, new eyeliner pencil then.

Yeah right . . . definitely not seeing the same thing during movie night.

Yul Brynner.

You'll do what?

The actor's name was Yul Brynner. Baldy here reminds me of him.

She was right, he did. A little. His gaze turned back to me, and from his concerned expression, I had to wonder if he could hear the conversation in my head. I held out my hand. "I'm Rowan."

"Yes, I know."

"You came with Ryiel?" I vaguely recalled seeing someone else beyond the glass door as I made my mad dash from couch to closet. The man nodded. From his general bulldog build and thick neck, I could take an educated guess as to his relationship to the vampire, but being around Tomas had taught me not to make assumptions about anyone. For all I knew the Yul Brynner look-alike could be Ryiel's sock guy. It was always best to ask. "Are you his sentinel?"

Bingo! Sentinel it was. The smile he wore positively transformed him, making him less evil son of a pharaoh and more friendly garden gnome.

"May I?" he held out a hand for the pants draped over my arm. He'd already picked up the dropped boots and socks combo.

"Yeah, sure." I nodded at the boots. "Sorry about the laces. It was the only way we could get them off. Oh, and there's something weird on the pants. Not sure what it is."

"It's all right, I know."

I couldn't be a hundred percent sure, but it sounded like he muttered the words *spinal fluid* under his breath. I was about to ask, but Gabriel's appearance behind me flooded the other man's face with more than relief. Gratitude, appreciation, and hope were some of the emotions I caught. The items in his hands fell to the floor as he clasped Gabriel by the forearms and started speaking in something I wasn't entirely convinced was a real language. The odd clicks and grunts made me wonder if Stavros was a sci-fi fan, but Gabriel seemed to give an affirmative answer to every question fired at him, and I didn't think he was simply placating the sentinel.

I glanced at the floor and felt my cheeks flush with heat. There was a scrap of satin and lace on the floor next to the sentinel's foot. A pair of my panties. It was time to bring the conversation out of the closet, and I pounced when Stavros paused to take a breath.

"Will Ryiel be okay?" I put my hand on Gabriel's arm.

"We won't know for a while."

"But he's safe now, and you've done everything you can, right?" Gabriel nodded and pressed his lips to my temple. "Then I'm sure you and Mr. Stavros can continue your conversation in the living room while I fix us all something to eat."

The alarmed look in Gabriel's eye was not reassuring. Tomas, who spent a great deal of time preparing meals for Gabriel, had delightedly assumed I would want him to cook for me also. I thought it would be rude to disappoint him, so my culinary skills, which were questionable at best, were in danger of deteriorating from lack of use—a fact Gabriel had managed to convey with his expression because the sentinel took my hand.

"Please, it is only Stavros," he corrected kindly, "and you must allow me to cook for you. I talk better when my hands are occupied."

"You know Tomas is jealous about his kitchen," I murmured to Gabriel.

"Tomas—hah! We are old friends." Stavros grinned. "He will not mind me being in his kitchen. Who do you think helped him perfect his baba ghanoush?" My expression obviously conveyed my ignorance because the sentinel took my hand and patted the back of it. "Don't worry, I will make for you yak stew, and you will be of great help to me."

My help was limited to chopping vegetables, although I didn't fail to notice the sidelong glance from the sentinel when I first picked up the knife. "Am I holding it wrong?" He shook his head. "Then why are you looking at me like that? I promise you I'm perfectly capable of chopping a few vegetables."

"Your skill is not in question. I was recently given reason to be wary around females with knives." I shrugged and let the comment pass, focusing on the mound of vegetables placed before me. How many people was the sentinel planning on feeding? "It freezes well," he said, picking up on my consternation.

Sadly, we were all out of yak meat, but Stavros refused to allow such a minor detail to deter him from creating a gastronomic masterpiece. Buffalo was an acceptable substitute. I chopped vegetables. Potatoes, carrots, onions, leeks. Leeks? Seriously? I had no idea that was a vegetable.

"Wait till I introduce you to parsnips," Stavros promised.

"Can't wait."

Despite having to settle for inferior buffalo, the stew was good, even the leeks, but the dinner conversation was not so pleasant. The sentinel described in detail the complete annihilation of the village situated below the monastery. A village of people with no connection to the outside world, but who had nevertheless welcomed both Stavros and Ryiel into their midst.

"Did they know what Ryiel was?" I asked curiously.

"Oh yes," Stavros confirmed. "Their culture's history included accounts of vampires, and the village elders were extremely pleased to see one for themselves. Ryiel was greatly admired by all." Knowing the vampire's disdain for the modern world, as well as his preference for self-imposed isolation, I wondered if he'd found the sudden rock-star attention difficult to handle. "Not at all," the sentinel assured me, "although if they had tried to put him on YouTube, it might have been different."

We all laughed at the notion.

"They were proud he had chosen them," Stavros continued, "and were pleased to offer themselves to him when needed. In return, they accepted his offer of protection. We had no idea something like this would happen." His face crumpled as big, glossy tears slid down either side of his nose to fall from his quivering chin. "I have never seen Ryiel so devastated," he added hoarsely.

"But Ryiel was certain it was the work of vampires?" Gabriel asked.

Stavros nodded and used the linen napkin on his lap to wipe his eyes. "He told me they were newly made and had been let loose with no guidance. He said their savagery was like when he was first made."

"Newly made vampires don't behave in such a way," Gabriel frowned. "Our DNA prevents such barbarity."

Stavros slapped his hand on the table, making me jump. "Ryiel thought their creation was unnatural. I am such an idiot for not telling you this first." Possible, but I wasn't going to be the one to say it. "And they disintegrated," he continued. "Did I tell you that?"

A shiver went down my spine. How did you create a vampire in a way unnatural enough to make it disintegrate?

Gabriel was filled with curiosity. "How did they disintegrate? After Ryiel took their heads?"

Stavros described the piles of ash as well as the one vampire who had simply fallen at Ryiel's feet and become a pile of ash in a matter of moments.

"There must have been something left behind," Gabriel said. "Bone fragments or fangs?"

Stavros shook his head, which shone in the soft overhead light. His head wasn't smooth like a bowling ball or anything else. The surface was bumpy and scarred and, for some strange reason, made me think of pictures I'd seen of the moon's surface. It was kind of ap-

propriate when I thought about how well he matched Ryiel's silvery
gaze.

"No," he replied, answering Gabriel's question, "they became
nothing but dust. Fine gray dust. If I hadn't seen it with my own eyes,
I never would have known I was looking at the remains of what had
once been sentient creatures."

"Are you sure?" I asked. "About the sentient part, I mean."

"I don't know how they were changed or why, but I am certain
they were all someone's son or daughter at one time."

I dropped my eyes, suitably humbled by the gentle rebuke. Gabriel's
hand covered mine in understanding.

"And what happened to Ryiel?"

Stavros seemed as perplexed as Gabriel by the other Original
Vampire's condition. He recalled the details as best as he could. The
swiftness of the assault, the agony it produced, and his very real belief that Ryiel would take his life. Getting up from the table, Gabriel
went to the bar, returning with a bottle of cognac. He poured a hefty
amount into the sentinel's after-dinner coffee.

"Did his eyes look different?" he queried in a low voice.

The sentinel paled and described the sudden change in the vampire he served. "Do you know what has happened to him?"

"I'm not sure," Gabriel replied, "but I think Ryiel has been broken back to his first transition. It would explain the unfettered rage I
could feel pulsing through him."

From the way Stavros fussed with his utensils, it was obvious to
me he wanted to ask for an explanation, but I guess he thought it
would be impolite for him to do so. Luckily I had no such problem.
"What's the first transition?"

Gabriel's hand returned to mine and squeezed my fingers. "It's
when two species join to become one. You witnessed mine," he
added solemnly.

I would never forget. The clearing in the forest, the icy cold of the
night. Gabriel falling to the ground and the large cat-like creature
that brushed past me to give the best of himself to a disgraced celestial being in the hope of creating a superior predator in return. The
sacrifice and the reward. Both had been magnificent.

"What's happening to Ryiel now?" I asked, seeing Stavros take a
big gulp of his doctored coffee.

Gabriel closed his fingers around my hand and placed it on his chest over his heart. "The beast within us never dies, Rowan. It is present in every single breath we take, and sometimes, when necessary, it will remind us it is there." I thought about the times I had heard Gabriel growl. Not the playful noise he sometimes made to excite me in bed. This was a more feral sound that made the hair at the back of my neck stand up. "I believe Ryiel has lost the link to his beast. He has gone to the only place where he can reclaim the beast as his own."

"The Void . . ."

Gabriel nodded. "The only true power in the Dark Realm."

"Will Ryiel find himself again?"

"If he doesn't, I'm going to be really pissed with him," Gabriel declared, leaning forward to kiss me quickly on the mouth.

"Is there anything we can do?" This, too, I asked more for Stavros than myself.

"We can wait. For as long as it takes," he added anticipating my next question.

A sudden realization struck me. "But that means you can't use your sarcophagus."

"No, I can't, but it is not an issue. I would do the same again, Rowan, as I know he would for me." Proof of the respect and affection Gabriel had for the vampire.

From across the table, Stavros drained his mug and looked at both of us with an expression that was almost fearful. "There's something else I need to tell both of you." He cleared his throat. "It's about Katja."

Shit. I'd forgotten all about her. Of course, she was Ryiel's progeny, and like any good, caring parent, he had put her under house arrest for trying to kill me. Personally I thought it was kind of lenient as punishments go. I would have preferred something slow and horribly agonizing, but there were some areas where my opinion didn't actually carry much weight. This was one of them.

"What about her?" Gabriel was cautious.

Stavros poured another measure of cognac into his mug, and then pushed the bottle across the table to Gabriel. "She's gone."

Chapter 14

Ryiel felt as if someone had taken a molten-hot metal spike and was determined to drive it through his forehead and out the back of his skull. The agony was unbearable.

The Void welcomed him like a prodigal son returning home. It pulled him into the dark heart of its embrace with no promise of release. But freedom from the Void held no appeal for Ryiel. He had made his choice long ago, which explained why he kept his Promise secluded from the world. Taking back his soul to receive redemption and reclaim his rank in the Celestial Hierarchy was not a future he coveted. And it would take an extraordinary set of circumstances to make him change his mind.

He gave himself to the Void completely. The absence of stimuli was as familiar to Ryiel as the tattoos across his chest. Those he had committed to memory, seeing in his mind's eye every sweep and curve that tarnished his smooth skin. The hand that had sought to shame him with the markings had failed in its endeavor. The vampire wore his disfiguration with pride. It was why he had selected his torso for the application, and why he never covered them up. He felt no shame, no dishonor, for having stood at Gabriel's side so long ago.

Drawn deeper inside the Void's sphere, Ryiel emptied himself of all emotion. He knew that, when the moment presented itself, the Void would reveal his purpose and set him on his path. It was a journey he had taken before, but then it had always been his choice. This time was different.

This journey was not of his choosing. It had been forced on him by another, and events had unfolded contrary to his wishes. Whatever had happened in the valley, the breaking of his bond with a vampire he had not voluntarily released had nearly broken him as well. Ryiel had barely survived, and he was grateful Gabriel had not tried to reach him through the bond they shared. Had he done so, he would have found only echoes of a long-forgotten past, with nothing to identify him as the vampire he knew.

But Gabriel had been astute enough to recognize that Ryiel needed to return to the source that had been instrumental in their creation. The Void had taken the best of each of them, melding it with the choice of the lesser beasts. Each animal, sacrificing itself freely for the greater good, had blended seamlessly with its chosen fallen angel, until no Original Vampire could tell where he ended and the beast began. And now this unprecedented catastrophe had ripped Ryiel's beast from him. He felt lost and, for the first time in too many millennia to measure, terrifyingly alone.

Unable to register the concept of time, he did not sleep, he did not wake, he just was. Hunger and thirst were unknown to him. He existed in a place where, it was rumored, the light came to die. At first, he had been able to distinguish the sound of his own heartbeat, the whisper of his own breath, but he had ceased to hear either long ago. Was his heart still pumping? Did it need to? If it did, did it make a difference? He was in a sea of nothing, surrounded by nothing.

Ryiel continued to drift, unaware he was surrounded by insidious forces wanting to steal what was left of his senses. He might have continued in this non-existence for eternity, and perhaps in some part of the time continuum he did, but the Void was obligated by an agreement made long ago. A private covenant made with the Creator, which continued no matter who ruled the Dark Realm. Any Original Vampire that returned to the Void, no matter the reason, was to be sent back to the world of men, whole and intact.

With fang and claw and hot, boiling blood, the beast was slammed back into Ryiel with the same violence that had been used to separate it from him. Feeling the rush of blood once more filling his heart and pumping through his body, the vampire returned from the brink. Muscles expanded and tendons flexed, and slowly his mind woke up, and he was aware of two things. The first did not surprise him, but the second did.

He knew exactly how Katja had broken her bond with him. And he had summoned Sinisia to him. Though why he would need the keeper of his soul, he could not say.

Chapter 15

For the first time ever, Gabriel went to bed angry with me. Actually, angry might be a little dramatic. Irritated? Definitely. Exasperated? Oh yeah, and then some. And all because of my choice in sleeping attire.

"You're kidding, right?" he said as I pulled on a pair of shorts and a faded tank top.

"Surely you don't expect me to sleep naked?"

"Why not? You usually do."

"Yes, but this is different."

"Different how?"

"Well, Ryiel is here. What if he needs to pee like a racehorse in the middle of the night?"

"Highly unlikely." Gabriel arched a brow. "But what if he did?"

"Um, he has to walk right past our bed to get there." I pointed from the closet to the open doorway on the other side of the room that led to the bathroom.

"So?"

"So you have no problem with him possibly seeing me in my birthday suit?"

"You'd be asleep."

"What if I woke up?"

He sighed and got out of bed, his naked backside giving me an incredible show as he disappeared into the closet. Gabriel had absolutely no qualms about Ryiel or anyone else seeing him naked, so he had a hard time understanding my own insecurities about how I looked without clothes. No matter how many times he told me he worshipped every curve of my body, every freckle, every dimple, unless I could wake up with a body to rival Gisele Bündchen's I wasn't about to dance on the dining room table in my birthday suit. Even if it was one of his most ardent fantasies.

"If you insist on wearing something to bed"—he held a padded hanger out toward me—"at least wear something sexy."

I stared at the black garment, which seemed to stare reproachfully back, as if it knew it wasn't coming off the hanger tonight. Purchased during Gabriel's Fifty Shades of Undies moment, it was one of the items I'd yet to model for him. Yes, he had impeccable taste. Yes, it was practically indecent how sinfully gorgeous every piece of lingerie felt next to my skin. Yes, I had forgiven him for his arrogance . . . well, almost. The black material shimmered as Gabriel waved the hanger back and forth.

"That's not something you wear to sleep in," I pointed out.

"I know." He gave me a sexy smile. "How about if I make sure you're too exhausted to wake up unexpectedly?" The glazed look in his eyes left no doubt about how he intended to make sure I reached such a state. Unfortunately, his fantasies were also going to be taken off the menu.

"Um, yeah, about that . . ." I shook my head and took a step back.

His brows pulled together as he realized what I was saying. The sharp vertical line looked positively painful. "Are you serious?" he growled. I tried explaining how it was when family came to stay for the holidays. At least how it was in Laycee's house. She was always having to give up her room for some elderly relative, and with the multitude of cousins, there was absolutely no privacy. "Are you saying we would never have had sex in your father's house if he were still alive?"

"Something like that," I mumbled, pulling the end of my braid through nervous fingers.

"But this isn't—"

"I know, but it feels the same." If I had to choose, I'd prefer the dark-haired vampire got an eyeful of me starkers than with Gabriel's cock in my mouth. Of course, it would be even better if I didn't have to make a choice.

"You're being ridiculous," he snapped, stalking back into the closet to return the lingerie to its place on the rail.

Feeling both miserable and angry, I got into bed. My unhappiness was compounded when I felt Gabriel get into bed but roll away from me. For the first time ever, he did not take me in his arms, or stroke my skin, or kiss me goodnight. And by the time I got up the nerve to approach him, he had already succumbed to the daylight and was in a state of inertia.

I didn't recall falling asleep, but I must have because the sound of the shower woke me. Automatically I stretched out my hand, but the other side of the bed was empty. I threw back the covers and walked quickly over to the closet. The far wall remained solid, telling me our guest was still on the other side. I knew there was no way I could overcome all my anxieties and confidence issues overnight, but there was one way to get back in my lover's good graces. Gabriel was inordinately fond of sex in the shower.

I stripped and unbraided my hair and, feeling the burn of anticipation running through me, headed for the bathroom. Clouds of steam billowed out from above the top of the shower door, creating a scene to rival anything Victorian London had to offer. Condensation glistened on the tiled wall and fogged the mirrors. Gabriel, it would seem, had been in the shower for some time. Sliding open the glass door, I stepped in behind him.

With his hands braced on the wall in front of him, he was bent far enough over to allow the spray to pound the back of his neck and shoulders. I reached past him for the bottle of body wash, but the hand on the wall unexpectedly dropped and long fingers gripped my wrist.

"You don't want to do that."

Three things hit me all at the same time. His voice had changed, his grip felt different, and—oh shit, shit, shit!—there were no tattoos on his spine. And, in case I needed confirmation, that wasn't the light playing tricks with a cloud of steam, but a ribbon of dark hair falling over his wide shoulder. Not dark as in water-wet, but dark as in natural color dark. The noise that escaped my mouth sounded a lot like a cat being strangled.

"I'm going to let you go, and not turn around," Ryiel said, "and no one will ever have to know."

I'm pretty sure I had the sliding door to the shower already open before he let go of me. Grabbing a towel from the rack, I backpedaled as fast as I could, closing the bathroom door once I was back on the bedroom side. I turned around, fully expecting to see Gabriel standing behind me, but as luck would have it, I was still alone. Perhaps he was still mad at me. If so, I'd never been so grateful.

Dressing quickly, I forced myself to take a couple of deep breaths. My fingers were shaking so much I could barely do up my shirt. I was lucky my hair was only damp, not wet, and I was able to pull it up into a loose ponytail. The sound of the shower cutting off pushed me out of the room. In the kitchen, I fixed myself a cup of coffee. If either Tomas or Stavros noticed the way I blew past Gabriel, they kept their comments to themselves. I was spooning sugar into my cup when I felt strong arms around my waist.

"I'm sorry about last night," he murmured, nuzzling the back of my neck. "It was childish and immature of me, and I promise it will never happen again."

Suddenly overwhelmed at being saved from making the world's worst mistake, I turned in Gabriel's arms and pulled his head down so I could kiss him. Surprised by my unexpected demonstration of forgiveness, he quickly matched my passion. Guilt may have been the initial reason behind my action, but it was quickly swept away by lust as I slid my tongue between dropped fangs.

"Oh for the love of—not on my kitchen counter!"

Tomas's censure was as effective as a bucket of cold water. Burning with embarrassment, I buried my head in Gabriel's neck as he picked me up and carried me into the living room.

"So I'm forgiven?" Gabriel asked, lowering himself onto the couch and pulling me onto his lap.

"Ryiel's awake," I blurted out.

"Oh, so you've seen him then?"

More than I expected. "He was in the shower."

"That explains it."

"Explains what?"

"Why you look so guilty."

Shit! Shit! Shit!

"You were worried he might catch you getting dressed," Gabriel concluded with a grin.

I didn't say anything. I didn't have to. The flush on my cheeks spoke for me, and it seemed the wisest thing to let him think that. One day, many, many years from now, I would tell him about what nearly happened. One day when I was certain he would be able to see the funny side. One day . . . yeah, right, when pigs fly.

The sound of raised voices made us turn our heads in the direction of the kitchen. Tomas and Stavros appeared to be in the midst of a heated discussion. At least Ryiel's sentinel hadn't been mistaken when he'd told me Tomas wouldn't mind him using his kitchen. When the two of them met, it was almost magical. They hugged, made loud smacking noises as they kissed each other on the cheek, and hugged again. The affection had made me wonder if they were related, even though they looked nothing alike.

"They are in a way," Gabriel said, "as all sentinels come from the Void."

"So did you."

"Yes, but I was something else to begin with. In the Void I was reborn."

I considered what he was telling me. "So you're saying all your sentinels were actually created in the Void?" Gabriel nodded. "Will they return there?"

"They do, periodically."

I suddenly recalled him mentioning something about Tomas being five hundred years old. "Is Tomas returning anytime soon?" I couldn't imagine him not being here.

Gabriel shrugged. "The Void will call him back when it chooses to. Sometimes it will wait a thousand years, sometimes it will be sooner."

"And what then? Does he get to come back to you?"

"Only if the Void permits it."

"That's not right!" I protested.

"Actually it is," Gabriel corrected with a smile. "Just as the Void agreed to provide each Original Vampire with a Promise, it also agreed to provide a sentinel. But unlike a Promise, a sentinel belongs entirely to the Void, is a part of it, and has no choice but to obey its command."

"So the Void will give you a sentinel, just not necessarily the same one it took from you?"

"Precisely."

"Well, that sucks." I pouted for a moment. "Will a new sentinel know who you are, and how to take care of you?"

"Of course, but I'll let you in on a secret. Though he has looked different in the past, I've never had anyone but Tomas."

"And he was always a runecaster?"

"Yes. That has never changed."

I jumped at the sound of a fist being slammed on the kitchen counter. A little more force and the tiles would break. Both Tomas and Stavros seemed equally short-tempered over whatever it was they were discussing. "I hope they're not talking about me."

"They're not," Gabriel smiled. "It's a lively disagreement about haggis."

"Haggis? Sounds horrible."

"It's a dish made from a sheep's stomach filled with the animal's heart, liver, and lungs, plus oatmeal, onions, stock, and spices."

I felt my nose wrinkle and my lip curl in disgust as I looked at him. "You're joking, right?"

Gabriel shook his head, doing his best to hide his smile with his hand.

"And they're arguing about it?"

He nodded. What the hell could there be to argue about, unless of course it was the merits of making the awful meal to begin with. Watching my face, Gabriel's smile broadened, becoming a grin he could not hide.

"I don't really want to know, do I?" I sighed.

"Probably not."

From somewhere Tomas had pulled out a book that looked more like a grimoire than anything Betty Crocker dreamed up. It might have been something Macbeth's three witches would have used if they were making haggis. I watched as Mr. Rogers and our Yul Brynner look-alike pored over the book's contents. I didn't need to understand what they were saying; their body language spoke volumes. Tomas let out a yell and threw up his hands in a gesture of I-told-you-so triumph. Whatever the basis for the haggis argument, it seemed the ancient manual had proved his point. Stavros conceded with more grace than I would have done.

"Do you believe him?"

"Who?"

"Stavros. Do you think Katja is really gone?" Gabriel shook his head, confirming what I already suspected. If he truly thought Katja was loose in the world, he would have shown more concern. "So is he lying?"

"No, Stavros is telling the truth, at least his version of it. I think Katja was hiding—probably still is—somewhere in the monastery. It's not possible for her to leave the physical confines Ryiel set for her." He raised my hand to his mouth and kissed my fingers, one by one.

"That, my friend, is where you are wrong."

"Ryiel!"

Gabriel didn't exactly toss me off his lap, but it was close. I watched the two vampires embrace. Not some fake hand-to-hand-chest-bump thing I see a lot of guys do these days. The kind of contact that's supposed to be a declaration of how comfortable they are with their own masculinity. Gabriel and Ryiel had no such concerns. They embraced with true affection. The dark-haired vampire broke away and looked directly at me. Whatever he had been through had left its mark. Purple shadows colored the skin beneath his eyes, and the hollowness of his cheeks gave him a gaunt appearance. He seemed smaller somehow, but it might have been an illusion because he was standing next to Gabriel. The sight of his ribs, and the low ride of his pants on his hips, however, was not an illusion.

"Hello, Rowan, it's a pleasure to see you again."

The last vampire who'd expressed a similar sentiment at meeting me had been lying through his fangs. And we'd both known it. The timbre of Ryiel's voice was deeper, his accent different, but I knew he meant every word he said.

"It's nice to see you again," I told him, "only I think this time I'm not the one who's at a disadvantage."

He smiled and came toward me, taking his time as if each step was a carefully considered act he had to put into motion. He was barefoot, and I watched him flex his toes and roll his foot, feeling the smooth surface of the hardwood floor with each step he took. I hoped his humorous socks hadn't been misplaced. Standing before me, he slid his fingers into the open neck of my shirt and pulled the material back, exposing my shoulder. Never mind the fact I'd been buck-naked with him in the shower. He'd been enough of a gentleman to keep his eyes averted, and now the idea of Ryiel seeing my lacey bra strap seemed highly improper. Long fingers danced lightly down my neck and skimmed across the top of my shoulder, making the breath catch in my throat.

"I'm glad to see Katja did not scar you." He smiled enough to show his fangs and ignored the low growl we both heard. "Down, puppy. I already know I have nothing to tempt your Promise to my bed."

After a statement like that, you might want to reconsider telling lover boy you took a shower with Ryiel.

I didn't take a shower—I was barely in there long enough to get wet!

You think that's gonna make a difference to him?

Ryiel straightened my collar and smoothed the material with his hand. His eyes were liquid silver, framed by thick black lashes, and though somewhat eerie to look at, they suited him perfectly. He smiled at me, and I knew my indiscretion was safe with him. He would never tell Gabriel. Whatever the bond existing between the two of them, it ran far deeper than ordinary friendship.

"I have news for you," the dark-haired vampire continued, "but I fear it may not be what you hope to hear."

My mind began to race. There was only one type of news Ryiel would need to give me. My heart was pounding in my chest, and beads of perspiration broke out on my forehead, my temples, and the nape of my neck. Suddenly I couldn't pull any air into my lungs. An invisible hand was wrapped around my throat, squeezing slowly as it inexorably choked the life from me. Dark spots floated in front of my eyes, and I felt as if I'd just stepped into a sauna. I was hot and sweaty and starting to shake.

I didn't want to hear what Ryiel had to say, because I already knew what he was going to tell me. It wasn't that he hadn't been able to find a way to break the agreement I had made with a demon. He hadn't had anywhere near enough time to exhaust all the resources at his disposal. Instead, he must have found irrefutable proof the agreement *could never* be broken. It was the only thing important enough to justify telling me in person.

Gabriel's arms wrapped around me, and I felt myself pulled back against his hard chest. The slow, steady beat of his heart pounded rhythmically against my back, trying to persuade my own pathetic organ to match it, beat for beat. Picking up on my free fall into a full-fledged anxiety attack, Gabriel took me in his arms and held me to him, enveloping me in the scent of pine trees and snow. It was his way of telling me I was safe. Except I wasn't sure I was safe. Not anymore.

But instead of addressing the issue of my demon, Ryiel said, "Stavros was not lying. Katja *has* broken her bond with me."

Chapter 16

"How?" Gabriel's voice was a rough whisper next to my ear, and I felt his arms tighten around me.

Ryiel curled his lip in disgust. "Through the use of drugs."

"And she's not dead?"

Ryiel shook his head. His hair reached almost to his waist, and it swirled across his chest with his movement, alternately covering and revealing the tattoos on his torso. The glyphs, though different in detail, bore enough similarity to the ones on Gabriel's spine to tell me they had been designed by the same hand. Whether the hand had been angelic or demonic in nature was another matter.

"Are you certain the bond is broken?" Gabriel asked.

"She no longer stands within my influence." Ryiel frowned and leaned forward. Elbows on his thighs, he let his hands fall into the open space between his knees. "I know she still lives, I can feel that much, but she could be in the next room suffering the most horrible torture and I would not know it."

"We should be so lucky," I murmured under my breath. I had momentarily forgotten I was surrounded by beings with exceptional hearing, until I felt their eyes fixed on me. "Don't ask me to apologize," I said stiffly. "I won't forget what she did to Oscar."

Deliberately starving another vampire to the point that Ryiel had no choice but to put him out of his misery was not something I was ever going to forget. And I refused to pretend I wasn't waiting for the day the psycho vampire bitch got a taste of her own cruelty. What goes around, comes around.

Gabriel rubbed my arm before asking, "If Katja is no longer bonded to you, and she's not dead, then . . . ?"

"She's bonded to Kartel," Ryiel told him.

"Son of a bitch!" My arm suddenly felt like it was caught in a vise.

"So my home is not the only one to be contaminated by his presence recently," the other Original noted, startled by Gabriel's vehement response.

Gabriel sighed and loosened his grip on my arm. It took some effort, but he managed to put his anger aside. "Do you have any idea how it happened?"

"It would seem Kartel took advantage of the massacre in the village to pay a visit to the monastery. As Katja was alone, she had to be the reason for his stopover. I have to assume he was the one who subsequently injected her with the chemical severing the bond between us." The silver color of his eyes turned a hard iron-gray. "And allowing her to ally herself to him."

"She may not have had a choice," Gabriel murmured, "if the alternative was death."

"Kartel would have killed her?" I asked.

"He wouldn't have had to. In all probability, breaking the bond with her maker would have done that, unless she had another Original to bond with right away."

"Vampires can switch who they're bonded to?"

Gabriel shook his head. "No, that's the point—they can't. It's always been known that breaking the bond is a death sentence for a regular vampire."

"Not anymore apparently."

"It was almost a death sentence for me." Ryiel's voice was low. "If Stavros hadn't brought me to you in time . . ." The vampire shook his head. "It's not the first time you've both saved my life."

"How do you know Katja was actually injected with something?" I wanted to know what evidence there had been to make him suppose this.

"I could taste the compound in my head, but my knowledge of such matters is not comprehensive enough to identify the individual components."

And there was I, thinking he was going to tell me he'd found a syringe or some other paraphernalia left behind.

"So Kartel has found a way to chemically transfer a vampire's bond to himself," Gabriel said glumly.

"But why?" Ryiel seemed perplexed. "What would he gain from it?"

The answer seemed obvious to me, but I bit my tongue so as not to blurt it out. Better to get a few more ducks in a row first. I was dickering over how to get Ryiel to tell me what I wanted to know when Gabriel spoke. It was probably coincidence, but I told myself we were riding the same thought wave.

"Stavros has already given an account of the massacre at the village, but I would be interested to hear your perspective." He wasn't asking because he thought the tale was lacking in some way, but Ryiel would notice things his sentinel would not. "And I will tell you about our encounter with Kartel. Perhaps together we will see what links the two events."

"So you do not think it is chance?"

Gabriel snorted. "Have you ever known Kartel to do anything by chance?"

It didn't take long for the dark-haired vampire to relate what had occurred, and his details varied little from what we had already heard. Except for a few personal observations, it was the same story. A harrowing tale of the cold-blooded murder of close to a thousand people.

"And you're certain it was vampires?"

Ryiel nodded. "Newly made, but unlike any vampires I ever turned." He drummed his fingers on the arms of the chair. "And Kartel was definitely involved."

"There can be no doubt?" Gabriel asked in a quiet voice.

"The one that died at my feet carried enough of his signature for me to be sure."

In my head I could picture a stamp on the back of every vampire's neck, much like a kid's toy doll. Only instead of saying Made in China or Made by Mattel, this would say Made by Kartel, or Made by Ryiel, or Made by Gabriel. The sudden urge to giggle horrified me, and I smothered it as quickly as I could. In light of the deaths of over a thousand people, it was both inappropriate and horribly inexcusable.

Well, you do realize you have Gabriel's name tattooed on your ass . . . my inner bitch reminded me. I decided to ignore her and focus on the discussion at hand.

"So you believe the annihilation of a village was a way to get Katja alone in order to conduct an experiment?" Gabriel was asking.

"I don't think so." Ryiel leaned back in the chair. "I feel as if the two events were of equal importance, and undertaken for the same reason."

"Can you tell me what it felt like?" I asked. "When the bond broke?"

The vampire put his elbows on the arms of the chair and rested his chin on his folded hands. "It felt as if someone had taken a hot branding iron and dragged it across my chest, and then there was a sharp burning sensation that came from a cold so deep I was certain it would paralyze me. And then . . . nothing."

"How does it feel to you if you try to sense her now?"

"Like trying to grasp a leaf in a hurricane."

"Or hold quicksilver in your fingers?"

He gave me a puzzled look and nodded. "Yes, that would be a good description." I couldn't see the expression on Gabriel's face, but if it was anything like mine, it was probably shocked surprise with a hint of I-didn't-actually-believe-he-could-do-it thrown in. However, it was enough to make Ryiel ask, "What is it that you know?"

I turned my head and looked up at Gabriel. "Are you thinking what I'm thinking?"

He nodded. "Petrov has been playing with his chemistry set."

Ryiel looked confused at this new addition. "Who is Petrov?"

It took less than ten minutes to bring him up to speed. He bared his fangs at hearing the abuse I'd suffered at the hand of Kartel's vampire. "You are thinking he has improved this drug that did not work on Rowan?"

I felt Gabriel nod behind me, and then nothing was said. Both vampires appeared to be deep in thought, searching for the common denominator. Unable to stand the silence any longer, I asked, "If Kartel needed a guinea pig to test his formula on, why choose Katja?"

"To avoid retribution from any of us, he would need a vampire who wanted more than anything else to break the bond. Katja was the perfect choice."

Choice or not, I was genuinely curious to know why the universe would bring together two vampires I detested so completely. "Why? What made her so?"

"Her current circumstances," Gabriel said.

"I don't understand."

Gabriel took my hand. "The bond between a vampire and a human can be broken in one of two ways. Either the vampire can release the human as an act of free will, which is what Aleksei did with Anasztaizia, or death will sever the link." He paused for a moment, and I felt his thumb glide across the inside of my wrist. "Breaking the bond between a vampire and its maker is a little more complicated. It has never been attempted before as it usually means death for the vampire."

"But you don't know for sure. You said it was all speculation."

He shrugged.

"Well, now you know," I muttered under my breath.

"Yes," Gabriel agreed, pressing his lips to my temple. "Now we know."

"I find it hard to believe Katja was actually willing to risk her life."

She might be a psycho vampire bitch, but the exotic beauty had never struck me as someone who would become so despondent about her circumstances that she would willingly accept the chance of death as an alternative. Then again, Katja was a vampire who appeared to have embraced the modern age with gusto. Being incarcerated had probably felt like being hurled back to the Stone Age. It was difficult to know how anyone, human or vampire, would react to a punishment so draconian.

Hearing me, Ryiel waved a hand in the direction of the kitchen, beckoning his sentinel to join us. "Stavros has a more intimate knowledge of her mind-set." He instructed the man to speak freely.

With a hand clapped to the back of his thick neck, the muscular guardian began. "Katja believed her punishment was too harsh, that she had been judged unfairly." He gave a half smile. "She protested her innocence every chance she got. It was one of the reasons I was forced to gag her during sex—and to stop her from biting me, of course." The last he added as if I had no idea she was a vampire or the damage that could be inflicted by her fangs.

"You were sleeping with her?" I muttered, aghast.

Stavros looked perplexed by my dismay. "Sleeping? No, I did not trust her enough to sleep with her, especially not after she brought a knife to bed that one time."

"As I recall, it was a sizable blade." Ryiel chuckled.

I stared from vampire to sentinel, watching as they shared the private joke. I don't know why I should be disheartened at the idea of Stavros having sex with Katja. She had learned from a very young *human* age that her physical appearance could get her the things she wanted. Why would I expect her attitude to be any different as a vampire?

"Okay, so we're saying Katja was depressed enough to agree to let Kartel give her his drug and switch her loyalty from you"—I pointed at Ryiel—"to him. Is that it?" Ryiel nodded. "But what does Katja have that Kartel wants?"

"What if this isn't Katja so much, but all made vampires? And what if Kartel doesn't give a damn about retribution?"

The voice coming from behind us had Gabriel and I swiveling our heads. Tomas had been quiet for so long, I'd forgotten he was standing there.

"Tomas?" Gabriel's query was an invite for clarification.

The other sentinel pushed up the sleeves of his Mr. Rogers cardigan and folded his arms across his chest as he spoke. "As you say, Katja was the obvious choice for Kartel to try his experimental formula on. He needed a willing vampire, but only, as has been already pointed out, to protect himself against any possible retribution if his drug *failed*." Tomas stroked his chin thoughtfully. "In my experience, cooperation has never been a requirement for any drug to work, but now that Kartel is aware of the drug's success, what's to stop him from giving it to other vampires?"

"Fuck," Ryiel spluttered. "If Kartel can do that, then he can turn all made vampires to his will—"

"—and add in the assassination squad he seems to have created—"

"—and didn't you say he had a talent for turning a mild disagreement into something much more deadly?"

The last comment was mine, and with it Gabriel turned ashen. He gazed into my eyes, though what he saw I couldn't say, before glancing over my head at Ryiel. There were a few moments of tense silence as the two Original Vampires participated in some sort of silent, and very intense, form of communication.

I saw Ryiel nod. "He wants to start a war," the dark-haired vampire said grimly.

"Well, it will have to be a damn quick one," I said, pulling us all back from the edge of a pit labeled Doom and Gloom.

"Why do you say that?"

I looked at Ryiel. "Didn't you say those other vampires, the newly made ones, just poofed out of existence?"

He nodded, and I saw his brow furrow as he tried to see where I was going with my train of thought. I think behind me Gabriel shook his head, warning the other vampire not to try. Cheek!

"Do you think Kartel knows how they died, or do you suppose he'll assume you killed them all?" I saw the light switch on inside Ryiel's brain. "You said these vampires were created differently. Is it so far-fetched to think it possible Petrov has found a way to manipulate human DNA so more vampires can be made?"

"With human cloning anything is possible," Gabriel murmured in my ear.

I whipped my head around. "We're cloning people?"

"Oh yeah, it's being done."

Shit!

"But Kartel doesn't know there's a time limit to his vampire killers," Ryiel said, picking up my train of thought and running with it.

"Well, neither do we," I pointed out. "If—and this is a big if—those vampires were created unnaturally with the help of a drug, you need to find the expiration date." I began to count on my fingers. "How long after being given the drug could they be turned? How long after being turned could they be let loose? How long does it take them to go poof?"

"How can we find this out?" Stavros asked, sounding excited by the prospect.

"Finding Petrov would be a good place to start," Gabriel said.

"Yeah, but we don't know where he is," I told him dejectedly.

"Says who?" We all turned this time, and I was delighted to see a grinning Aleksei leaning in the open archway to the hall. "I know exactly where the bastard is."

Chapter 17

I scrambled out of Gabriel's arms and met the big Russian vampire halfway across the room. Apparently there were some lingering effects from our encounter that hadn't quite been eradicated. My need for a bear hug more than anything else in the world, it seemed. And Aleksei's enthusiastic willingness to indulge me.

"I thought you told me she was Gabriel's Promise?" Stavros gave Tomas a pointed look.

"She is," he protested. "The situation recently became . . . complicated."

"Ah, so that's what they're calling it these days, *complicated*." An unexpected grunt told me the sentinel had just met the business end of Tomas's sharp elbow.

I couldn't say if I would be happy, sad, or relieved when this pull toward the big guy finally came to an end, and I had no idea what still drew me to him. I would have thought any of my blood left in his veins would have been replaced by now, but maybe not. Perhaps it only took a single drop still swooshing around his body, or maybe it was the fact we had become as intimate as two individuals can be without crossing the line. I looked around him, hoping our affectionate behavior wasn't embarrassing his lovely blond companion, but he appeared to be alone.

"Where's Anasztaizia?"

"I left her sleeping. She needs her rest, but don't worry, I taped note to bathroom mirror."

Depending on how it was worded, it could be a comfort, or not. I let it go. At least he'd been thoughtful enough to tell her he was gone.

"Are you two okay now?"

The Christmas-tree effect on his face kind of destroyed the whole

nonchalant routine. "We have been"—he grinned—"getting reac-
quainted with each other."

If I was any judge of vampire behavior, this would involve the
kind of physical activity where clothing was strictly optional. No
wonder the lovely Magyar needed some rest.

The sound of throat clearing behind us made me turn around.
Gabriel stood only a few paces away, wearing a not-all-that-amused
look as his gaze focused on the large hand I could feel splayed
against the small of my back. Guilt consumed me as I disentangled
myself from Aleksei's embrace. And I wasn't the only one. The big
guy, realizing who was staring at him, flushed fire-engine red.

"Sorry," I apologized, wrapping an arm around Gabriel's waist.
"Guess there are still some residual effects."

He looked at me, and I saw his eyes highlighted with a ring of
brilliant gold. A sure sign another appetite was rising. Taking hold
of the arm I had around him, Gabriel moved me so I stood in front
of him with my back pressed against his muscular chest. He did this
for two reasons. One was a purposeful, showy display of possessive-
ness. His hands on either side of my neck, long fingers circling my
throat and shoulders like a collar, told everyone present I belonged to
him. The other reason was even less subtle. Gabriel wanted to make
sure I could feel his erection pressed against my backside.

Tomas and Stavros were watching Aleksei's embarrassment with
some curiosity, while I noticed the sparkle of amusement in Ryiel's
silvery eyes as he looked from Aleksei to me to Gabriel, and back to
Aleksei. Everyone seemed to be waiting for someone else to speak,
so I decided to go first.

"Was it safe for Aleksei to come here?" I turned my head and
looked up at my lover. My concern had nothing to do with safety inside the penthouse. We were probably safer than the doomsday seed
vault, but considering Aleksei had been abducted from his own
home, I worried about him traveling across town.

"I don't think anyone is going to make him waltz with a bear
again," Gabriel said grimly, answering me. His hand dropped, and I
felt his fingers slip inside the opening of my shirt. "I sent a reminder
of the consequences of hurting what belongs to me."

I didn't want to think of the details involved in such a reminder,
but I had to wonder how many vampires had been encouraged to

visit the place where Aleksei had been thrown into a bear pit. And how long before permission was given for the bodies to be removed.

"So," Gabriel's fingers began to stroke the swell of my breast, "let's talk about Petrov and his whereabouts."

A sudden rush of air across my face and I was suddenly in the kitchen. I gasped and stared, nonplussed, across the breakfast bar as my lover herded everyone else back into the living room, where a plan of action could be formed. I wasn't pissed—well, I was, kind of—but I knew removing me wasn't anywhere near as sexist as the hands-around-the-neck display had been. It might look as if Gabriel was relegating me to the position of little woman in the kitchen, whose job was to rustle up some vittles so the menfolk could have a hearty meal before going off to battle, but I knew better. Gabriel needed all of Aleksei's attention to be focused on the task at hand. Removing me from the setting said more about Aleksei's control than mine. I sighed and wondered how long it would be before I would no longer want to cuddle the big guy whenever I saw him.

As both Tomas and Stavros were being included in the testosterone talk, I figured I could make myself useful instead of merely decorative. I couldn't do much in the kitchen, mainly because Tomas had palpitations whenever he saw me at the stove, but I had finally worked out how the coffeemaker operated. With Aleksei here, it was an excuse to break out the good Russian coffee. Too bad vampires don't need much time to formulate a plan. They were done before the pot finished brewing.

Gabriel took me back to our bedroom for some privacy. I thought he was going to share whatever they had planned, but unless Petrov was holed up in a Turkish bath and they all had to get naked, I was in the wrong discussion. Making short work of the buttons on my shirt, he had my jeans unzipped and pulled off, ripping the side seam of my panties just as I managed to get his fly open. Using his hands as support, he lifted me up. I wrapped my legs around his hips, hearing a throaty growl as he buried himself inside me. I've never climaxed so fast or so hard, but feeling his body quiver as he peaked made me realize how much he needed this. And it was more than still feeling unsettled because of Aleksei.

"When you get back," I whispered huskily, tangling my fingers in his hair and pulling on his ear lobe with my teeth, "I promise I'll wear the black lace."

He stared at me with glazed eyes, before licking me in a single swipe from between my breasts to the sweet spot behind my ear. "I'll hold you to that," he promised. I assumed the tug on my own ear lobe was simply him returning the favor, until a sharp prick told me he'd pierced it with his fang. I laughed as he carried me across the room and deposited me on the bed.

Gabriel didn't mention Ryiel was staying behind until they all got into the elevator and it became obvious one of the merry group was missing. The omission was highly suspicious, almost as if Gabriel suspected I might raise some objection to having a babysitter.

"You can ask him about the necklace," he murmured as his lips drifted across my mouth.

"Necklace?"

"Hmmm . . . see if he knows why you can handle it."

Ah . . . that. In truth I'd foolishly hoped Gabriel might have forgotten all about the damn thing, which was ridiculous. He didn't forget anything. He might no longer be angry with me, but it didn't mean the incident wasn't tucked away somewhere inside his brain, ready to be paraded out at the appropriate moment. But that moment was not now.

"Be careful," I told him. It was a ridiculous thing to say to an Original Vampire, but we both knew it was for my benefit more than his. "No unnecessary risks."

"I promise."

"Come back to me."

"Always."

And then he was gone. I stood in the open doorway listening to the mechanical whirr of the elevator descending, and I closed the penthouse door when it faded completely.

Ryiel was in the kitchen, and he poured me a cup of coffee from the pot I'd made. That was one of the other things I loved about Aleksei's Russian blend—no bitter aftertaste, even when it had been sitting for a while. "Rowan, we need to talk."

I had been dreading this, ever since he'd first mentioned he had news I wasn't going to like. Part of me had been hoping Katja's escape was the news, but now it seemed that had nothing to do with whatever the silver-eyed vampire needed to say. I took the mug from his outstretched hand and bought myself a thirty-second delay as I added sugar and creamer.

"I don't suppose this could wait until Gabriel got back?" I asked. "Honestly, I'd feel better if he could hear it as well."

Ryiel actually seemed to be considering my request, but then he shook his head. "No," he told me, "if you decide to tell Gabriel, it will be your choice, but I would advise you to do it with no one else present."

"That bad, huh?"

"I am not sure you will want to share any of this with him."

Oh shit, it was going to be so much more than bad. "We don't keep secrets from each other," I stated with a hint of defiance.

Ryiel sighed and gave me an understanding, if forlorn, look. "This one, I suspect you will. If you love him enough."

"I don't—"

The rest of my sentence was cut off as the strains of classical music filled the air. I was getting quite fond of Beethoven's "Ode to Joy," and hearing Ludwig's entire Ninth Symphony was on my to-do list. I picked up the phone, relieved and not too terribly surprised to see Laycee's name on the caller ID. Baby Jenna had a while to go yet before she slept through the night, so her momma being awake at four in the morning wasn't unusual. Recently, we'd had some of our best conversations as Laycee rocked her baby back to sleep after a post-midnight feeding.

I automatically apologized to Ryiel for the interruption as I picked up the phone, except Laycee didn't speak. She was sobbing too hard to verbalize anything coherently. From the little I could make out, she needed me to come right away and bring Gabriel with me. A strange request from someone who had declared, more than once, that she wanted nothing to do with vampires.

Ryiel took the phone from my hand. "We are coming," he told Laycee, before disconnecting the call and handing the phone back to me. I stared at him, dumbfounded. Why would he include himself? "Shoes," he said, putting a hand on my shoulder and turning me around.

"I, uh, what?"

"You're barefoot, Rowan. Find some shoes."

I stuffed my feet into an old pair of Crocs and hurried to join Ryiel, who was already waiting for me in the elevator. As we descended to the garage, I chewed my lip and worried. Whatever was going on with Laycee, it was more than new-baby hormones still running amok. I followed Ryiel out into the garage before realizing my car keys were in my purse, which was still upstairs.

"We'll take your boyfriend's car," Ryiel said when I alerted him to my dilemma. "No keys needed."

"Do you even know how to drive?"

He took only mild offense at my question. "Of course."

"Tell me the last thing you drove."

"Chariot at the Circus Maximus in Rome."

I came to a skidding halt. "You're kidding me, right?"

He grinned and opened the passenger door of a big black vehicle, motioning for me to get in. "Let's find out, shall we?"

"Yeah well, this has a lot more horsepower," I cautioned.

"But easier to handle." Seeing the questioning look on my face, he added, "It's not going to catch the scent of sweet grass on the air and want to take off to go grazing."

There was no response to such a statement. I stopped and put my hand on the car door. "This belongs to Aleksei."

"I know."

"You said we were taking one of Gabriel's cars."

"I believe I said your boyfriend."

"He's not my boyfriend," I snapped irritably.

He smiled and pushed me down into the luxurious leather seat. "You can enlighten me on the way."

As it turned out, Ryiel handled the V-12 Mercedes-Maybach like a pro. Managing to squeeze every available gallop from the 523-horsepower engine, he cut the normal forty-five minutes to a little under half the time. Still, it was long enough for me to tell him about Aleksei showing up at death's door as well as mine.

"But Gabriel did send him to you?" he asked, seeking confirmation.

"Yes, but I don't think that makes what happened any easier for him to deal with. You saw how he was when Aleksei showed up."

"Well, it didn't help having you throw yourself into his arms," Ryiel chided.

"No I s'pose not," I agreed with a miserable mumble.

"And yet it could also have been a lot worse, which is why it's a good thing the Russian came to you at Gabriel's instruction."

"I don't see how."

"Well, you're both still breathing, aren't you?"

Yeah . . . there was that.

Pulling into the driveway of the house that used to be mine, Ryiel brought the two-and-a-half-ton vehicle to a smooth stop and was opening my door before I'd even unbuckled the seat belt. "You've made some changes," he said, looking around him.

"Laycee and Jake have," I corrected, informing him that I had given the house to them as a gift when I moved in with Gabriel. Still, I was impressed he'd even noticed, considering the circumstances of his only visit.

Aside from replacing my paving-stone driveway with a proper concrete one, Jake had also re-landscaped the entire front yard. I know that had been Laycee's idea. She wanted as few reminders as possible of seeing Katja trying to rip my throat open. The psycho vampire bitch had almost succeeded, too. I shuddered to think she was now on the loose, but that particular tidbit I was going to keep to myself for as long as possible.

I had climbed the three steps and was standing on the porch when the front door was yanked open. Someone who looked like my best friend, albeit a disheveled version, glared at me. And then past me. I didn't need to be told where Ryiel was now standing. Laycee's expression said it all. She shoved me hard enough to make me stumble backward and let rip a blood-curdling scream before launching herself at Ryiel.

Chapter 18

Ryiel caught the small blonde woman as she hurled herself at him. One arm wrapped about her waist, he held her against his hip like a wrestler about to throw an opponent to the mat. Strong fingers secured her flailing hands at both wrists as she struggled against him. She was like an eel, he thought—no, more like a mountain lion intent on protecting her den and offspring. He was content to let her exhaust herself railing against him, but when she sank her teeth into his arm, he decided he'd had enough. Not that her bite would hurt him, but there was no way to know, if she broke the skin, how his blood might affect her, angry as she was. Tightening his hold, he squeezed until she let go and began gasping for breath.

"Enough," he ordered.

The sight of his silver eyes and dark brows pulled to a sharp V between them was more than she could take. Ceasing her struggles, Laycee brought another, more formidable weapon to bear against him. Tears.

"I thought . . . I thought . . . you were him . . ." she sobbed. "I thought he'd come back."

Ryiel set her on her feet, and she immediately stepped away and began swiping at her face with her hands. He held out a hand to Rowan, who got to her feet, green eyes shimmering with concern as she looked at her friend.

"It's the hair," Laycee continued with a sniff, pointing at him. "It's black like the other vampire's, and you all seem to have the same build . . ." The rest of her sentence trailed off as she pulled her lower lip between her teeth. Ryiel had the distinct impression she was taking a mental picture of him from head to toe. "I'm sorry. I should have realized you weren't him. He was wearing more clothes."

He failed to see what difference his attire, or lack of it, made, but he accepted her apology with a soft grunt. "You were watching, from there." He raised a hand to a window on the upper floor of the house. "I remember Aleksei bringing you out of the house. Your wrists were broken, as I recall." He reached for her hand and turned it over, the tips of his fingers skimming lightly across her skin. "I'm sorry if I hurt you."

"You didn't."

Rowan brushed imaginary dirt off the seat of her pants as she stared at both of them. "You wanna tell me what the hell's going on, Lace?"

As she moved past him, Ryiel caught her scent. She was infused with the perfume of motherhood. A blend of regurgitated formula mixed with the innocence of her infant child, but then he caught the scent of something else. Another fragrance that was not so wholesome or, he imagined, so welcome.

"What is it?" Rowan asked, seeing his lip curl in distaste.

"Your friend has the smell of the Dark Realm about her."

"The smell of what?" Though Laycee acted surprised, Ryiel could tell she was not. She knew better than she should what he was referring to.

Rowan came forward and took hold of her friend's hands, asking, "Laycee . . . where's Jenna?"

Realizing Rowan was asking about the infant, Ryiel watched as Laycee turned petulant. He thought it an odd response. Her chin jutted out, and she speared a look of defiance at the Promise. The two women were friends, he knew, but something between them had changed. One held the life of a vampire in her hands, the other that of a child. Each female was prepared to do whatever was required to safeguard the life of the one she loved. Perhaps it was a reluctance to accept the change in the status quo that was causing the measure of distrust he could feel. Or perhaps it was something else. Rowan repeated her question, giving Laycee's arms a little shake for emphasis.

"She's in her crib sleeping," Laycee snapped irritably, shaking herself free of Rowan's hold. "You lied to me, Rowan. Both you and Eye Candy. You shouldn't have done that."

"Eye Candy?" Ryiel muttered.

"She means Gabriel," Rowan told him.

He frowned. He might not know Rowan as well as he knew Gabriel, but he did not picture her as a liar. He looked at her friend with renewed interest. Was her statement a result of the taint she carried from the Dark Realm, or was motherhood confusing her? He knew little about new mothers, but it seemed to him the dark circles beneath Laycee's eyes and her overall agitation were caused by more than natural fatigue. She had not slept well for some time, and while some deprivation was to be expected, this had the markings of something more.

"Where's your man?" he asked.

China doll blue eyes narrowed slightly. "My . . . oh, you mean Jake. He's away for work."

"And when will he return?"

"Wednesday."

"Then you must come with us." Ryiel was stern. "It is not safe for you or your child to be here alone."

"And being with a bunch of lying vampires is so much better?" Her laugh was scornful. "I don't think so. Besides, I'm not safe anywhere, it seems."

Rowan made a spluttering noise of frustration. "What are you talking about? Why do you think we lied to you?"

The petite blonde went from angry to fearful in a heartbeat. Her face crumpled, and she began to cry again. "You t-t-t-told me no v-v-vampires would get to her," she sobbed, unable to stop the flow of moisture from her eyes. "Gabriel said his b-b-blood would p-p-protect her."

Ryiel started in surprise. "Gabriel agreed to give his protection to the child? Who is standing as surety for the payment?"

"I think I am," Rowan admitted, refusing to meet his gaze.

His surprise was replaced by a stunned awareness. "Why would you do such a thing? Given the terms of your agreement with—"

Rowan snapped her head up, freezing him with a look. "Yeah well, about that—let's say I kinda agreed to it without knowing all the facts, okay?" She stepped forward and placed a hand on his arm. Her eyes darkened as she looked up at him earnestly.

"So it's true then?" They both turned to look at Laycee. "Gabriel is supposed to sleep with my daughter as payment for his so-called protection?" She stared at Rowan with contempt. "And you agreed to this? You would let him do this—*to my daughter?*"

"No, Laycee, you've got it wrong. That's not going to happen—"

"Damn straight—not if I have anything to say about it!"

"What were you thinking?" Ryiel said, his words making Rowan round on him.

"If you can't be helpful, then shut the fuck up." She paused, and pulled in a breath, ignoring the ferocious glare he gave her. He couldn't recall the last time he'd been spoken to with such insolence. Even Katja knew better. "Look, I'm sorry," Rowan apologized. "I need to talk to you about this, but is there a chance we might be able to talk about it later, in private?"

"I don't know why you're so worried," Laycee interjected sourly. "The whole thing was a lie. There's no protection for my baby."

"Of course there is," Ryiel snorted.

"Oh yeah? Then you wanna tell me how a vampire was able to come inside my house, *uninvited?*"

The answer was obvious to Ryiel, but he took his cue from Rowan. This was her friend, and he had no idea the extent of her knowledge.

"Is it possible you invited him in without knowing he was a vampire?" Rowan asked, offering a possible explanation.

Laycee frowned and bit her lip. "No, I'd never seen him before, but he knew what Gabriel had done. He asked if I wanted to see how worthless his word was."

"What did he do?"

"What do you think he did? He walked right in as if he owned the place."

Rowan turned to look at Ryiel. *How was it possible for a vampire to do that?*

It wasn't . . . unless he wasn't a vampire to begin with.

Rowan turned her attention back to her friend. "Did he tell you who he was?" Laycee shook her head and sniffed. The combative attitude was waning, and weariness was taking its place. "Describe him to me, Laycee," Rowan said in a low voice.

Ryiel listened as the other woman spoke, but his concentration was on Rowan, watching her body language. The telltale signs told him all he needed to know. He cared little about Armani suits or ruby cufflinks; it was enough that Rowan recognized her demon. How unfair was it that vampires were the only supernatural beings requiring an invitation to cross a threshold?

"You know who he is, don't you?" Laycee fixed Rowan with a horrified stare.

"He isn't a vampire—"

"Bullshit!"

"No, Laycee! You must listen to me—"

A peal of hysterical laughter trilled on the night air. "Believe you? But I did believe you, Rowan, and it was a lie. The protection you said I had was a lie. If it wasn't, he wouldn't have been able to come in, and he wouldn't have been able to . . ." She clutched her throat, wide-eyed with terror. "*He picked Jenna up from her crib and held her in his arms!*"

Desperation fueled Rowan to repeat herself. "Laycee, believe me when I tell you he wasn't a—"

"*I saw his fucking fangs!*"

The stunned look on Rowan's face, her uncertainty when faced with the onslaught of her friend's conviction, propelled Ryiel to act. He called the petite blonde by name three times before she heard him.

"*What?!*" she finally snapped, whirling about to face him.

"Do you believe I am a vampire?"

Same response, but this time delivered with a puzzled hesitancy. He folded his arms across his chest. For the first time the smaller woman looked at him, *really* looked at him, seeing more than the physique that she was doing her best to ignore. Now she recognized the strength of his build and the strange tattoos across his chest. He brushed back his long hair and slowly dropped his fangs, but the sharp intake of breath he heard came from Rowan.

"Yes, I believe you're a vampire," Laycee muttered. "Why do you ask?"

"Because I'm going to show you something," he paused, "and believe me when I say this is going to hurt."

Rowan stared at him and caught his glance at the open doorway. To be fair, she tried to stop him. He saw her mouth form the word *no,* and a millisecond later he saw her fall to her knees. She reached for Laycee, pulling the other woman down with her as they both protected their ears from the small sonic boom that resonated through the house as he tried to breach the threshold uninvited. Even though Ryiel relaxed his muscles, knowing it was the best way to absorb the force that pushed back against him, he hadn't been prepared for how much it hurt. He was lifted bodily, sent flying over the porch railing, and landed in a flowerbed of thorny roses a good twenty feet or so from the house. He let loose a string of colorful curses in a half-dozen different languages, ending with an easily understood "*Son of a bitch—that hurts!*"

Rowan cleared the porch steps and ran to his side. "You fucking moron! You have the nerve to ask *me* what I was thinking?"

Disentangling himself from a particularly prickly rose cane, Ryiel glanced toward the house, where Laycee watched them. Her face was even paler than before as she shook her head from side to side. No doubt she was experiencing some ringing in her ears, but he could sense that her anxiety level was approaching critical mass. "Do you think you can get the baby out of the house?" he asked, lowering his voice.

"Sure, I think so." Surprised by his whispering, she added, "I don't think she can hear us."

"She's not the one I'm worried about."

"Oh . . . okay." Coming to his side, Rowan placed her mouth next to his ear. "Why do you need me to get Jenna?"

"Your friend is a good mother, and she will follow her child."

Rowan pulled her head back and looked at him, her expression betraying her emotions. He reminded himself to tell Stavros not to play cards with her. "And you really think she's in danger if she stays here?"

"You know him better than I. What do you think?"

"We need to get her out of here. If nothing else, she needs some sleep." She hesitated before asking, "Will she be able to return once Jake is back? It might make it easier to get her to leave now."

He nodded. "The demon prefers one-on-one interaction."

"Guess that explains his visit to me."

"He came to see you? When? What happened?"

Her face became a mix of embarrassment and worry, the flush on her cheeks becoming. "I told you there was something else I wanted to talk to you about."

It was easy to see why Gabriel had become so enamored with her. She had captured his heart the first time he saw her standing in the back of the Warlord's tent. Did she remember that moment, Ryiel wondered?

"Are you going to be okay?" Her voice pulled him out of the past. He nodded and rolled his neck, making his cervical vertebrae crack. "I understand why you did it," she continued. "I just had no idea it would be so painful for you."

"Only because I didn't stick the landing."

"Oh, well, if you're gonna joke about it, then I gotta say as my first flying vampire, you impressed me."

He dismissed her with a wave of his hand. "Go see to your friend."

As she jogged back to the house, Ryiel dropped to one knee, putting his palm flat on the ground as he took a deep breath. Katja's loss was still affecting him. He thought about the other times he had crossed a threshold uninvited. He could count the number of times on the fingers of one hand. Each had been accidental. This was his first deliberate attempt, but he had to admit the Promise's admiration for his foolish gesture almost made the pain worthwhile.

"Well, that was spectacularly stupid of you."

Ryiel turned to see the blue-haired vampire step from the shadow of the trees and walk toward him. He had sensed someone was watching, but thought it might be a minion sent by Rowan's demon. To see the vampire was an unpleasant surprise.

"What brings you here, Kartel?"

"Truthfully? It was my intention to do Gabriel a favor and get rid of that millstone around his neck. Surely even you can see his life would be so much better without her."

"I doubt he would agree with you."

"Well, it hardly matters now, does it? After overhearing your conversation, I realize my aid is not required." He gave a short laugh. "Persuading Gabriel to give his protection to a squalling brat, without knowing the consequences? Tell me, Ryiel, is she truly *that* incompetent?" He shook his head and made a tutting noise. "I'll admit I was impressed that she managed to make a deal with a demon—especially that particular one—but now I'm of the mind that it was nothing but sheer luck. After all, why bother going to the trouble of saving Gabriel when she unravels everything with a few foolish words? Her deal with the demon will be nullified the moment Gabriel takes the virginity of her friend's child." He paused and made a theatrical show of shock. "You don't suppose she's grown tired of Gabriel already?"

Getting to his feet, Ryiel looked at the other Original Vampire with distaste. "How did you know where to find us?"

"How do you think?" he snickered. "I do hope you're not going to hold a grudge about my taking Katja from you. It's not like you were using her for anything." A furrow wrinkled his smooth brow. "Of course, I had no idea taking her would nearly kill you as well."

He might not have known then, but he did now, and Ryiel could tell he regarded it as an unexpected bonus. "Were those things in the village your creation also?" he snarled.

"Ah, my human DNA project. I should thank you for disposing of them for me. I really hadn't thought much beyond proving their worth."

"You know Gabriel has your vampire, Petrov."

Kartel made a show of looking puzzled. "Who? Oh him, no matter. He stopped being useful some time ago."

"You're not worried he'll betray you?"

The vampire sneered. "You spend far too much time with your dusty old tomes, Ryiel. It would do you good to get out in the real world more often. See how the rest of humanity and other vampires live. Petrov can tell Gabriel anything he wants. His words are useless without proof."

"You don't think he could recreate your drug from memory?"

"Ah, but would it be the *same* drug, I wonder? That's always been a problem with re-creating it exactly."

Kartel's smugness confirmed Ryiel's guess. "He doesn't know all the components, does he? You left something out, or added something he doesn't know about."

"I'm not stupid, Ryiel. You might want to remind Gabriel of that, although"—he glanced toward the house—"I think he's got his hands full trying to save his Promise from her own stupidity."

"What are you up to, Kartel?"

He shrugged. "Oh, you know me. I love to dabble in things."

"Yes, I do know you, Kartel. Only too well."

The sound of raised female voices turned the heads of the two vampires, prompting Kartel to say, "Well, as I doubt my reception with the Promise will be a warm one, you must allow me to be on my way." He gave the dark-haired vampire a thoughtful look. "You can't always be there to save Gabriel, Ryiel." He tipped his head in the direction of the house. "She betrayed him once before, and she'll do it again, mark my words. I'll never understand why he made her his Promise."

"Don't you? Then you're the only one of us who doesn't. Perhaps it's because you don't know Gabriel as well as you think you do." He watched as the blue-haired vampire turned on his heel and disappeared into the trees that acted as a natural property line.

You're wrong, Kartel, Rowan didn't betray Gabriel. She was as much a victim of the Warlord's schemes as the rest of us. Did you suppose being his daughter gave her some insight? Did you think he would take her into his confidence? If you knew as much about humans as you profess, you would have known the man trusted no one, least of all those he sired.

He used her, and when she failed him, he made her witness the consequences of her failure. You would have known that, Kartel, if you had been with us. You should have known that.

But you are right about my not being able to save Gabriel. That task is no longer my responsibility. It will be up to his Promise to prove that his love and faith in her are justified. I cannot stop what is coming, but I can remove one of the obstacles deliberately set to confuse and confound them. An impediment sowing the seeds of distrust and suspicion, malevolence and spite. In the grand scheme of things, my small gesture may prove to be meaningless, or it might be just enough to give Rowan the courage she needs to do what she must.

Chapter 19

I followed Laycee down the hall, my senses still reeling from the foolishness of Ryiel's action. He could have been killed! Well, maybe not. He was an Original Vampire, after all, but who knew how much he'd been compromised by what Katja had done. Of course, I had no idea trying to cross an uninvited threshold would result in such a spectacular display of aerodynamics, but even I'd suspected it would involve more than just a simple refusal.

Didn't I already say vampires were overly dramatic?

"You could invite him in now," I said to Laycee's retreating back. I was actually kind of pissed by her total lack of concern for Ryiel.

She whirled around and gave a bewildered look. "You're kidding, right? That"—she pointed in the direction of the front door—"doesn't mean squat. I don't feel in the least bit sorry for him."

I was shocked by the utter lack of sympathy in her voice. What had happened to the woman who had been my BFF since grade school? The Laycee I knew would never have been so unconcerned. Surely this wasn't all part of being a mother? Of course, I expected her priorities to change, and I knew I would slip down on her list, but having her refuse to accept proof of being manipulated into believing something that wasn't true? It hurt that she thought I would lie to her.

But you have lied to her. You never told her everything that happened to you in the Dark Realm . . . perhaps if she had known, she might have recognized him—

If she knew about the demon, he'd only change the way he looked.

Yeah, well, if he can conjure up being a bad-ass horny self with a forked tail, I doubt he'd have much of a problem with fangs.

I didn't have time to argue with my inner bitch—and told her so.

I also hate it when she's right, and this was not the time to have my own shortcomings pointed out to me.

"Laycee, I don't know who was here—"

Liar . . .

"—but won't you at least admit the possibility it might not have been a vampire?"

"I know what I saw."

"Oh, for God's sake!" Stubborn wasn't the word for it.

I sighed and put a hand to my forehead. This kind of arguing was going to get us nowhere. Sometimes I have to be reminded that 99.9 percent of the human race has no idea supernatural beings are a part of the everyday world. Laycee is ahead of the curve knowing about the existence of vampires, but I wasn't sure she could handle knowing what else was out there. The situation before me was starting to unravel and would continue to do so unless I could convince my best friend she had to leave—and now.

"Laycee, I don't think it's a good idea for you and the baby to be here alone. Come stay with me until Jake returns." It seemed as if she was actually considering the idea, but she shook her head. I held out my hand in a palm-up, non-threatening gesture and softened my voice. "Laycee, sweetheart, I've known you all my life. You have to trust me when I tell you the man you saw wasn't a vampire."

"*Bitch!*"

I couldn't say which shocked me more. The name-calling or the fact that she slapped me across the face. Hard. With a hand on my cheek, I saw her make a move toward me. I'll never know if she was intending to apologize or if she wanted to slap me again because I reacted instinctively. I shoved her away from me, hard enough that the back of her head hit the wall, and she went down like a sack of potatoes.

"Oh fuck!" I became paralyzed with indecision as she slid down the wall, her butt making a *whumping* sound as it hit the floor and she keeled over to one side.

From the open doorway I heard Ryiel hiss. "Rowan—drag her over here."

"What?"

"Laycee—get her here to the door. I can get her in the car, and we can get the hell out of here."

I stared at the figure crumpled by my feet. She wasn't moving. "Oh God, Ryiel . . . I think I've killed her."

"You haven't," he reassured me. "I can still hear her heart beating." Oh yeah . . . right. Good thing about having a vampire around, they can always tell you if you've committed murder. "You have to hurry, Rowan. The sun's going to be coming up soon, and I need to get you back. With or without your friend."

A sudden moan from the area at my feet galvanized me into action. Dragging an inert body across a hardwood polished floor isn't the piece of cake you might expect it to be. Getting Laycee to the front door was a bit more cumbersome than I'd imagined. I grabbed her beneath the armpits and began to pull but had to stop every few feet or so because I was also pulling her loose-fitting yoga pants down. Handing her over to Ryiel with a bare ass wasn't something I wanted to deal with. Not now, not ever. I almost had her to the door when the sudden crackle of electricity told me Ryiel was reaching forward to help, and in danger of going airborne again.

"Get back," I snapped. "Let me get her outside."

Once her head and shoulders had cleared the open doorway, it was easy. I watched as Ryiel picked her up and carried her to the big black Mercedes.

"Rowan—get the baby!"

Yeah, right.

I ran up the stairs to the nursery, where the world's most adorable baby girl was fast asleep, completely unaware of the hell trying to break loose downstairs. I scooped her up, pink blanket and all. She began to fuss as I slipped her into the carrying car seat and fastened her in. A diaper bag was on the changing table. It seemed to be full of the kind of stuff you'd expect to find in a diaper bag, so I picked it up and slung it over my shoulder. I may not know much about babies, but I do know they need changing—often. Seeing a large unopened plastic bag of newborn Huggies, I grabbed those too, doing my best not to let the cumbersome bag trip me on my way down the stairs.

Ryiel stood framed in the doorway waiting for me. "Here, get her strapped in." I handed him the car seat and set the other items on the porch.

"Where are you going?" he hissed.

"Kitchen."

"What for?"

"Formula." The other thing I know about babies is they need feeding. Like almost all the time.

"Isn't she breast-feeding?"

He sounded annoyed, but this was hardly the moment to be defending the merits of bottle over breast, or for me to wonder why such a thing was of concern to a vampire. Ignoring him, I hustled down the hall to the kitchen. Cans of powdered baby formula sat on the counter, along with clean bottles. I snagged a plastic bag from the stash behind the pantry door and filled it with everything I figured I'd need. On a hunch, I opened the fridge, almost crying with happiness to see some already made-up bottles nestled in the shelf in the door. Putting those in a separate bag, I was about to head out when something caught my eye. Something I'd seen the moment I walked in but my mind had dismissed as unimportant. Only it wasn't unimportant. It was a message. A message for me.

Why else would there be a black feather as long as my arm on the kitchen table?

Laycee slept for fifteen hours straight, and I made a vow never to underestimate the restorative power of sleep. Especially when it was aided by a small rune pressed into the back of her hand. Laycee had not regained consciousness during the drive back to the city, and I was concerned about the rune's effect. Tomas assured me all would be well.

"Poor lass is exhausted," he noted before fixing me with the same look I'd seen on many a teacher faced with no other option but to give me after-school detention. "It's a nasty bump. How did she hit her head?"

"Um, I shoved her." It seemed pointless to fib.

"A wee bit too hard, I'm thinking." I waited for him to ask why I had found it necessary to render my friend insensible, but he surprised me by asking for no explanation. "She'll not even wake with a headache" was the last reference he made to the matter. Grateful, I covered Laycee with a light blanket and followed the sentinel from the room.

Gabriel was holding Jenna in his arms. Tiny fingers clutched a handful of his hair, and from the look on his face, he was captivated by her. It was enough to wake the green-eyed monster inside me. Though the rational part of my brain acknowledged she was a baby,

I could not deny my feelings. Perhaps it was the idea that in a quarter of a century he might be holding her in a very different way that made me jealous.

I was saved by Stavros, who appeared at my elbow with a burp cloth in one hand and a bottle in the other. "Time to get your vampire back," he murmured to me in a low voice. If I didn't know better, I would have sworn he had just read my mind.

I looked at the bottle in his hand. "Are you sure you know how to do that?"

"You think I've never tended to a babe before?" My inclination was to say yes, that was exactly what I'd been thinking, but he seemed so hurt by the suggestion, I decided to say nothing. "There's not much to it at this age. All she'll want to do is eat and sleep and poop."

"And cuddle up to vampires," I murmured.

"Ah yes, there is that." He paused and gave a sly grin. "Now, were she a few months older, I might ask Tomas to see if she shows an affinity for the runes."

"You wouldn't!"

"Talent will not be denied, and she already has the look of a caster about her."

He winked and went to relieve Gabriel of his charge, muttering something I didn't quite catch about promises and bed. I took the hint, knowing Jenna was far better off in the sentinel's capable hands than mine. Besides, I wanted to ask Gabriel what had happened with Petrov.

"Later," he told me, once we were alone. "We'll talk about it after we've all had some rest."

It wasn't like him to be so reticent. "You didn't find him, did you?"

He shook his head. "No. He was already gone, and the building was empty."

"Gabriel, I'm sorry."

"So am I, but I think this situation with Laycee is the one we need to be more concerned about right now."

"Did Ryiel tell you what happened?"

"Some, and you were right to bring them both here."

"But—" A finger against my lips prevented me from saying anything more.

"No, Rowan. Sleep. You and Laycee both crossed a line tonight.

If you have any desire to heal the wound between you, you need your rest as much as she does. Words can be tricky—"

Tell me about it.

"—and it would be a shame to lose a friendship due to a weary slip of the tongue."

He was right, and so I let him take me in his arms and hold me until I fell asleep, but knowing there was a baby in the penthouse had everyone behaving differently. I woke earlier than usual, only to find that both Gabriel and Ryiel had risen before me. Seated at the large dining room table, Ryiel had Jenna fast asleep in his arms. I wondered what Laycee would make of her daughter's apparent ability to charm every vampire she met. Perhaps they needed to be protected from her, instead of the other way around.

I took my customary seat next to Gabriel, and as he poured coffee for me, I watched the intricate dance between Tomas and Stavros as they covered every available inch of the dining table with plates of food. The number of dishes was alarming. Enough to feed an army or possibly two—no, surely it was three—hungry vampires.

"Is Aleksei here?"

Both Ryiel and Gabriel answered in the negative. The combination of the previous night's activities plus the effort of still working through his emotional need for me had left him exhausted.

"He went back to your apartment to be with Anasztaizia," Gabriel said as he passed me the sugar and a small jug of half-and-half.

"How did he get there? We took his car."

"I let him take Lola," Gabriel confessed.

The night must have been more of a bust than Gabriel had let on if he was willing to part with his precious Lamborghini. "What happened with Petrov?"

His expression became a study in exasperation. "Aleksei's information was good. The building had been used to both manufacture and distribute the drug, but they knew we were coming. Everything was gone. Including Petrov."

"What about the informant?" In most cop shows I watched, they were nearly always untrustworthy.

"I'm sure everything was exactly as he said it was when he supplied the information."

Ryiel looked up; a small hand was wrapped around his finger, and he paused as Jenna blew bubbles in her sleep.

"Yeah, you wait until she's doing that from the other end," I cautioned.

He gave me one of his rare smiles before turning to Gabriel. "It wouldn't have made any difference," he said. "Petrov could not have told you how the drug was made."

"But I thought it was his creation," I said. Had Kartel messed with his brain cells or something? I wouldn't put anything past Vampire Smurf.

"It was, but he didn't know all the ingredients."

"How do you know that?"

"Kartel told me."

I almost sprayed a mouthful of coffee across the table. "When did you see Kartel?"

"Last night, when we were at your house."

Gabriel's quick reflexes caught the mug as it slipped from my grasp. "He was there . . . ? What did he say?"

"Just that. The alchemist didn't know all the ingredients . . . and his usefulness was at an end." He stared across the table. "I suspect if he isn't dead already, he soon will be."

"Something to work to our advantage." Gabriel looked thoughtful.

Intrigued, I asked how.

"Petrov is, if nothing else, a survivor. If he knows his life is forfeit, he may try to find another source of protection."

Ryiel gently wiggled the finger Jenna was holding. "How fortunate there are two Original Vampires close by."

"*Fortunate?*" I was outraged. "You can't be serious—are you forgetting Petrov murdered Aleksei's family? In front of him?"

"Of course not," Gabriel replied, "but if he believes an offer of safety could be exchanged for information, it would be foolish not to hear him out."

"Assuming he takes the bait," Ryiel cautioned.

Takes the bait . . . then this was a ploy. "Promise me you'll kill him after he's spilled his guts."

Ryiel's lips lifted in a half smile. "I had no idea your Promise was so bloodthirsty, Gabriel."

"She has her moments."

"I just want him punished."

"And he will be." Gabriel leaned over and kissed my cheek. "But

I will punish him for what he did to you. That way he will know it's personal."

I forced myself to be content with that.

"So, did Kartel say anything about Katja during your unexpected visit?" Gabriel asked Ryiel.

"He made some juvenile remark about hoping I wouldn't be a sore loser." He shifted Jenna to his other arm, and the now wide-awake baby wrapped a chubby fist around his dark hair.

"Did he have any idea what he almost did to you?"

"No, but he does now. I think he sees it as an unexpected bonus—"

"What a prick!"

"—and it might be wise to alert our brothers. I don't like the idea of a mistake giving him some sort of an advantage."

"I'll have Tomas notify them," Gabriel assured him.

"But speaking of advantages, I think we also have one." Looking directly at me, Ryiel said, "Your earlier insight was quite astute."

It's funny how praise can buoy you up, even if you have no idea what you're being complimented about. "Really? What did I say?"

"Kartel is under the impression that I killed the vampires who attacked the village. I don't think he has any idea they disintegrated on their own."

"So his new method of creating vampires is flawed?" Gabriel drummed his fingers on the tabletop, considering the implications.

"So it would appear," Ryiel agreed, "but, as your Promise pointed out, it would be helpful to know how long it takes from creation to collapse."

"Even more reason to find Petrov, then." Gabriel squeezed my hand with the non-drumming one.

Stavros suddenly appeared at Ryiel's side, holding out his hands. With a reluctant sigh, the dark-haired vampire handed over his charge, smiling as he disentangled his hair from Jenna's hold. He had a lovely smile, and I wondered why he didn't use it more often. But living in isolation in a monastery nestled on a slope of the Himalayas would-n't give me much to smile about either.

"What was Kartel doing at my old house?"

"He doesn't have a very high opinion of you." Ryiel watched as the gurgling baby disappeared.

I snorted. "Hah! Tell me something I don't know."

"Very well." Ryiel narrowed his eyes and stared at me. "He came there to kill you, but changed his mind."

"*Why?*" Both Gabriel and I said the word at the same time.

"Why kill you, or why the change of mind?"

I was too busy reconciling myself to the notion that, after one brief meeting, I was on an Original Vampire's hit list, so it was Gabriel who answered. "Both."

"He sincerely believes you'd be better off without her," Ryiel told Gabriel, "and he was fully prepared to dispose of her."

"So how did you dissuade him?"

"I didn't. He'd already decided his intervention was unnecessary."

"Why?"

Ryiel let out a sigh. "He thinks Rowan is incompetent."

"*He thinks I'm what?!*" I bristled with rage.

"In a way, he's not wrong, Rowan."

I hoped Ryiel wasn't trying to be kind because his delivery sucked.

"If you hadn't acted so rashly in asking Gabriel for his protection, your friend wouldn't be plagued with visits from the Dark Realm. Your behavior may not be incompetent, but it was careless, and it has put both you and Gabriel in a precarious position."

"You don't know the half of it," I muttered.

Chapter 20

"Um . . . does anyone know where my daughter is?"

I had been so focused on the conversation at the table, I hadn't noticed the soft pad of feet from the hallway. I was, however, sitting with two beings gifted with extraordinary hearing, and I was sure both of them had heard her.

"Could've given me a heads-up," I told Gabriel in a low voice as I slid back my chair.

"Oh yeah . . . Laycee's awake." He grinned.

Ryiel pulled out the chair next to him and motioned for Laycee to sit. Seeing her hesitate, he said, "Please, I'm tired of the two of them ganging up on me." His outrageous lie worked because she sat down, accepting the cup of coffee he poured for her.

"Jenna?" She looked at me over the rim of her cup.

"Perfectly safe with Tomas and Stavros—"

"Who?"

"Ah, they're um . . ." How to explain a sentinel?

"Tomas functions as my valet and personal assistant," Gabriel told Laycee, "and Stavros works for Ryiel in a similar position."

Laycee put her cup down. "Why am I not surprised you guys both have valets?"

"I don't know . . . why aren't you?"

She laughed. Clearly Ryiel didn't understand about sarcasm. Or perhaps he understood women better.

As if on cue, Tomas appeared with a bundle of pink in his arms. "She heard her mama's voice." All maternal anxiety disappeared the moment Jenna was in her mother's arms. "She's been fed and burped and bathed and changed," Tomas added.

Laycee, completely absorbed by her child, murmured her thanks, and for a few moments we all enjoyed the Madonna-and-child tableau we were given, until it was ruined by the loud grumbling of Laycee's stomach.

"Tch, lass," Tomas fussed in his best Mr. Rogers voice. "When was the last time you ate a proper meal?" Her frown was all the answer he needed, and he began to fill a plate, determined, it seemed, to give her a selection of everything on the table.

"Tomas, you're not feeding one of these guys," I protested.

"Actually, all of this looks great, and I am hungry." She expertly moved her baby to the opposite arm, allowing her to demonstrate a skill all new mothers quickly learn. Eating with one hand. "Did I interrupt something?" Laycee said, watching as Ryiel poured syrup on a waffle for her.

"No, we were just discussing what happened at your house," he said.

Laycee flushed. "I'm sorry about how I treated you, especially after you went, you know." She made an arcing motion with the fork in her hand.

"What did you do?" Gabriel asked, puzzled.

"He tried to cross a threshold uninvited," I told him.

"You did what?"

Ryiel stared at the salt-and-pepper shaker. "What's that phrase humans are fond of using? Ah yes, *it seemed like a good idea at the time.*"

For a moment there was absolute silence, and then Gabriel began to laugh. "Oh my God, I wish I'd been there to see it," he chuckled.

"It was quite impressive," I told him.

"But what on earth compelled you to do such a thing?"

"He was trying to prove a vampire could not come into my house."

"And was quite successful, it would seem, but why would you need to do such a thing, Ryiel?"

"Because I told him a vampire *had* come into my house." Laycee paused, her hand trembling enough to make the scrambled eggs on her fork fall back onto the plate.

"That isn't possible," Gabriel said softly.

"It is if it wasn't a real vampire," I said.

Gabriel whipped his head around and gave me a long, hard look. "It was *him?*"

I nodded. "Can't imagine it being anyone else, can you?"

I could feel the anger as it swirled through his blood. "What the fuck is he playing at?" he muttered on a low hiss of breath.

"I would have thought it was obvious," Ryiel said. "He knows Rowan made a mistake. My guess would be he's trying to goad her into—"

"Doing something else equally stupid and rash and impulsive," I interrupted.

To his credit, Ryiel didn't say "I told you so," and neither did he look smug. But he didn't have to. I was prepared to take full responsibility for my own recklessness.

"So he was telling the truth."

We all looked at Laycee, who in turn looked as if she'd just realized she'd thrown out the winning lottery numbers and the garbage men had already picked up the trash. The piece of bacon held in her fingers fell to the plate. Changing Jenna's position, she now cradled her daughter against her shoulder.

"What did he tell you, Lace?" It was a pointless question because I knew what she'd been told, we all did. It was written all over Laycee's face, but I needed to hear her say the words. To be sure, there was no doubt or misunderstanding. "Tell me what he said." Any doubt on my part vanished the moment I saw how she looked at Gabriel. Her expression was part fear, part not-with-my-daughter-you-don't.

"He said you're going to sleep with her. Her first time would be with a vampire, and it would be Gabriel. He said the only thing giving her his blood had done . . . was save her for himself." Her face suddenly crumpled. "I wanted to keep her away from vampires, not save her for one . . . not save her for you."

"Which distresses you more, Laycee? That it will be a vampire or that it will be Gabriel?"

I was as startled as Laycee at Ryiel's question.

How about the fact Gabriel's gonna look just as hot then as he does right now?

If you can't be more helpful, shut up!

Aw, c'mon! You expect me to believe it hasn't crossed your mind?

"You asked for your child to be protected," Ryiel continued, "and that is what Gabriel has done for you, regardless of what this supposed vampire told you. And, yes, there is a price to be paid for such protection. It is unfortunate the matter was not discussed beforehand, but you cannot take back what has already been given." He sighed as

Laycee began to rock Jenna gently. "Does it make a difference knowing it would happen only once, and your daughter would never know she was with a vampire?"

"It will be her first time," Laycee argued, making it sound like a woman's virginity was the eighth wonder of the world. "It's supposed to be a special moment, magical even. Preferably not a one-night stand." The undisguised bitterness told me more than I ever knew about Laycee's own experience. She hadn't lied to me exactly, but she had definitely been looking through rose-colored glasses when it came to sharing the details.

"It will be special and magical," Ryiel continued. "From what I know of virgins, she will have the advantage of an experienced lover to take her through the process."

"But the choice should still be hers," Laycee said stubbornly.

"Indeed, but you took that away from her the moment you sought Gabriel's help."

"Except I didn't know. The whole thing is . . . creepy."

Ryiel steepled his fingers beneath his chin. "Explain this creepy."

She sighed and moved Jenna back to her original shoulder. Throughout the entire conversation, the baby hadn't burbled once. Laycee looked at Gabriel. "Having Gabriel sleep with Jenna is the same as Rowan sleeping with Jake, and telling me about it beforehand."

"So your problem is with Gabriel."

"Yeah . . . I guess it is."

"What if he wasn't the one?"

Gabriel started to speak. But Ryiel held up a silencing hand.

"But it would still have to be a vampire?"

The dark-haired vampire smiled at her. "No getting around that, I'm afraid."

Laycee stared across the table, first at Gabriel, and then at me. I gave a slight shrug. I had no idea where Ryiel was going with this particular train of thought. I hoped whatever he was going to propose, and it seemed obvious he had something on his mind, it wouldn't push Laycee over the edge.

I recognized the moment she decided to treat the entire conversation as some kind of practical joke. Her smile was slightly off-kilter as she asked, "So who'd you have in mind?"

"Me," Ryiel answered.

"No!" Gabriel exclaimed. "Ryiel, I cannot let you do this."

"The choice has already been made, my friend. I summoned Sinisia when I was in the Void."

"But how did you know?"

Ryiel shrugged. "I didn't. It was an involuntary act on my part, an instinctive reaction, if you will. It wasn't until my conversation with Kartel that I understood why."

"But if you haven't spoken to her, surely she can be sent back?"

Gabriel sounded almost desperate. Obviously, having Ryiel take his place with Jenna twenty-five years from now was about more than deflowering a virgin. I didn't know who this Sinisia was, or how she was connected to the silver-eyed vampire, but I could tell she was a person of some significance.

"I won't send her back," he said, speaking directly to Gabriel. "Don't fight me on this, Gabriel, and besides, the decision is not yours to make. Not anymore." He turned to look at Laycee. "Will you accept me as an alternate and agree to my right to claim your child's blood at the appointed time in return for the protection offered?"

"You can do this?" Laycee asked Gabriel, looking as bewildered as I felt.

"If you agree to it, yes, but the window of time allowed for such a substitution is quite small. You must decide now so the ceremony can be completed right away."

Laycee looked at Ryiel. "Are you going to make her drink your blood too?"

He shook his head. "That won't be necessary."

I hadn't noticed when she had taken Jenna off her shoulder, but she was cradling her once more in her arms. "Sweet little girl." Laycee stroked a soft, downy cheek before giving Ryiel a sharp look. "Will I know when you . . . when it happens?"

"Did you tell your mother?"

Laycee shook her head.

"I can let you know after it is done," he offered.

"No," Laycee's voice was firm. "If she wants me to know she will tell me herself, although I don't think she'll need to say a word." Ryiel's puzzled look was enough to make her laugh and shake her head in mock exasperation. "You have absolutely no idea what we see when we look at you, do you? Don't worry, Ryiel, I'm a mother. I'll know."

Her words did little to clear his confusion, but he wisely chose not to pursue it further. "Do you accept me, Laycee?"

She looked over at Gabriel. "I'm sorry, but I can't have you doing this. It's too . . ."

"Creepy, I know."

"But I still need her to be protected."

"I know that too."

"Then I accept," Laycee said, looking at Ryiel.

He smiled. An absolute stunning, knock-you-straight-into-next-week kind of smile. And suddenly I knew why the people in that village in the Himalayas had been more than willing to befriend him. He looked over at Gabriel.

"Sinisia will need water."

"The pool?"

"Perfect."

It was a balmy night, and if things weren't taking a turn for the seriously weird, I might have suggested to Gabriel we take a dip later. Somehow I didn't think this was going to be the night for it.

"You never told me he had a pool," Laycee said in a low voice as we walked out onto the terrace.

"Oh, yeah . . . he has a pool."

Ryiel said something to Gabriel, but they were talking in a secret language. Tomas and Stavros had come to join us, and from the expression on their faces, it seemed they didn't understand what was being said either. I didn't feel so bad. But the pointed looks being thrown in our direction needed no translation. Whatever was going to happen next, Ryiel was showing some major concern about Laycee's reaction. Whether it was because she was human or a mother I couldn't say, but if I was going to gamble, I'd hedge my bet and say both.

The boys' secret conversation was now over, and Gabriel pulled me to one side. "You're going to have to help with Laycee."

Immediately I was on edge. "Oh shit, Gabriel—what's Ryiel going to do?"

He rubbed my arms, soothing me. "You remember what I did at the hospital?" I nodded. "It won't be like that, not this time, but I need you to trust me."

"I do. You know I do." My faith was rewarded with a brief sweep of his lips over mine.

"You're going to have to make sure Laycee doesn't try to interfere or stop what's happening. It's important that no one but Ryiel and Jenna are in the pool when Sinisia arrives."

"Gabriel." I clutched his arm as I repeated, "What's Ryiel going to do?"

His neon-blue eyes shone so brightly they were dazzling. "You have my word no harm will come to Jenna. No matter how it looks."

I believed him, but even so . . . "Who is this Sinisia, and why does she need water?"

"You should be asking what instead of who," Gabriel said. I made a gesture of impatience. "We need water because Sinisia is a siren."

Chapter 21

A siren? I had to think back to high school and a substitute teacher who spent her allotted time with a class full of teenage malcontents discussing Greek mythology. Sirens, if memory served, were beautiful creatures with voices that made sailors wreck their ships on the rocky coastline. I never quite got why they did this (the sirens, not the sailors), but we're talking Greek mythology. A monopoly on tragedy if ever there was one. And now I was going to see one of the fabulous creatures for myself. I just hoped she wouldn't lure any of us to a rooftop dive.

Ryiel stood before Laycee with his arms held out. I thought for a moment she was going to refuse and tell him she'd changed her mind about having him, instead of Gabriel, protect her child. But though she hesitated for a moment, she willingly placed her baby in the vampire's arms. Quickly Ryiel unsnapped the onesie Jenna wore and handed it back to her mother. The diaper came off next, and then he settled her in the crook of his arm and against his chest. A tiny hand waved in the air. If I didn't know better, I might have said Jenna was fascinated by the tattoos running across his chest. Ryiel leaned forward and, with his free hand, cupped the back of Laycee's head. He whispered something before kissing her chastely on the forehead. The smile he received in return was decidedly wobbly, so I went over to hold her hand. I didn't ask her what Ryiel had said. It was private. If she wanted me to know, she would tell me.

We both watched as Ryiel walked to the edge of the pool. A spark of consternation rose inside me when I noticed we were all gathered at the deep end. Unlike most apartment pools with a maximum depth of maybe six feet, Gabriel's pool made a gradual sloping descent to that number before abruptly dropping to fifteen feet. It was something that had never really bothered me until now, although I couldn't say why. Laycee wrapped her fingers around mine and squeezed my hand. I think she was looking for confirmation she was doing the right thing. I squeezed back.

"I like the tile work," she whispered. I agreed with her. The decorative mix of blues and greens always made the water look inviting, no matter what the air temperature might be.

Out of the corner of my eye I saw Gabriel come and stand on Laycee's other side. Something was about to happen, and whatever it was, he was taking the necessary precautions in case she freaked out. With no idea of what was to come, I couldn't say if his concerns were groundless or not. We all watched the water. Both Laycee and I seemed to suck in a breath at the same time when the still, glassy surface began to move.

It was a gentle wave. The type of movement caused by paddling from one end of the pool to the other on an inflatable lounger while enjoying a tall drink. Only there was no lounger, and even if there were, the pool had been cleaned earlier that day and the pump was still shut off. So what was causing the ripple across the surface? The answer was swimming just below the surface. How she got into the pool was beyond me, because I know I never saw anyone get in the water. At least not from above.

"There's someone in the pool," Laycee said, pulling forward slightly to get a better look. I don't know if it was instinct or seeing Gabriel suddenly stiffen, but I tightened my grip on her hand. "Is that . . . is that a woman?"

If hair length was a true indicator of the difference between the sexes, then I'd have to agree with her. But I live with a guy who uses almost as much shampoo and conditioner as I do, and I was also staring at another whose hair was even longer. I needed more than that to determine gender. As if aware of our quandary, the creature in the pool broke the surface, launching itself a good six or seven feet into the air, arcing its head in such a way the long hair was flung straight up before falling down behind.

That is most definitely female.

Nothing wrong with my inner bitch's eyesight, although the fact our visitor was obligingly naked was more than a little helpful.

"Sinisia, I presume?" I glanced over Laycee's head at Gabriel, who nodded. "And she's a siren?" Another nod. Uh-huh. No wonder sailors wrecked their ships. They probably would have done so regardless of whether or not they were sung to.

At first glance, the siren appeared to be floating in the air, like a magician's assistant performing the amazing levitation trick. Except she wasn't standing on thin air. Water bubbled beneath her foot, connecting her to the pool below in a continuous stream. Tilting her head so her ear touched her shoulder, the siren began to rotate slowly. I confess I thought it was some narcissistic display of vanity, showing the mortals before her a standard of physical beauty they could never hope to emulate. But then I realized I was wrong. The siren was simply enjoying the feel of the warm night air on her skin.

As she spun, the air filtered through the long strands of her hair, wrapping it around her so it covered her perfect breasts and hips. I don't know if this was a conscious act on her part, but it certainly helped me deal with my own feelings of physical inadequacy. I had told myself it was seaweed or some other type of oceanic vegetable matter tangled up in her locks that gave it the odd color, but it truly was green. And it suited her, as did the scales responsible for the pearl-like iridescence of her skin. I was, however, disappointed not to see a strand of seashells around her neck.

Sinisia slowly descended back into the pool, the slender pillar of water beneath her toes lowering her until she was able to reenter the element without a single splash, bubble, or gurgle. To my mind, it seemed as if the water almost parted at will, caressing her form as she sank to the bottom. She swam lazily beneath the surface, rolling and turning with as much grace and poetry as any aquatic mammal. She surfaced in front of Ryiel, tilting her head to one side and looking at both vampire and baby. With a lazy roll, she moved closer to where we were standing, and reaching the pool edge, she raised her head and shoulders out of the water. She beckoned us to approach.

"I won't let go," I whispered, feeling Laycee's hand tremble in my grasp. She gave me a sick-looking smile as I reaffirmed my grip, and together we walked to the edge of the pool.

Sinisia rose on another column of water until we were all eye to eye. Her expression seemed to be one of curiosity, as if she had never seen human women before. Perhaps she hadn't. If the Greeks had it even halfway right, the sirens' only contact with humans had been with males, and seafaring vessels back then didn't exactly enjoy a stellar reputation regarding the character of their crews. She held out a hand, displaying both the palm and the back, as if to prove she held no weapon and her hand was harmless. I was fascinated by the webbing between the siren's fingers, Laycee more the aquamarine color of her nails.

She was without a doubt beautiful. Her face could have easily graced the cover of any beauty magazine. It also told me that at some point along the evolutionary path we had shared a common ancestor, but whereas mine had chosen to remain on land, hers had returned to the water. Though she had scales, they did not cover her body completely, stopping above her elbow. For some unfathomable reason I was delighted to see how smooth and white her forearms were. She reached out her hand and stroked my cheek. I don't know what I was expecting, probably something that felt slimy and wet, but her fingers were smooth, dry, and exceptionally strong. And as she cupped my chin, I had no doubt she could break my jaw with very little effort. So much for harmless.

"Sister," she said in a voice that sounded the way spring rain felt. Light, refreshing, and oh so sweet. I stared back at her, puzzled. Was Sinisia suggesting the evolutionary gap separating us was actually smaller than I realized?

Her curiosity with me apparently sated, the siren turned to Laycee, giving her far more attention than I had received. Her fingers danced over Laycee's cheek and forehead and down her neck. She seemed fascinated by the platinum blond of my friend's hair, threading it through her fingers and pooling it in the palm of her hand. But she made an expression of distaste when she held it to her nose. I imagine the dye Laycee used to keep it that particular shade disagreed with the siren. And then, quite unexpectedly, Sinisia leaned forward and pressed her lips to Laycee's forehead.

"Thank you," the siren said in a singsong whisper.

"For what?" Laycee asked, bewildered, watching as Sinisia slipped back under the water.

Ryiel provided the answer. "For being Jenna's mother, and allowing her to meet you. She has never known a mother before."

"What about her own?"

"She's a siren. She has no mother." Neither one of us knew what to say to that.

Sinisia now rose half out of the water in front of the vampire. Her head tilted to one side, she regarded Ryiel and Jenna curiously. "You have decided?" she asked Ryiel.

"I have." His voice was solemn and grave.

"And you are sure this is what you want? That now is the proper time?"

"I am."

Satisfied with his response she said, "Then I am pleased for you."

"And I am pleased for us both," he murmured. "I know this has been a burden for you."

"Not so much as you might think." She must have seen something reflected in Ryiel's face, a trace of indecision perhaps, because she hesitated. "You're certain you have no regret in summoning me?"

He shook his head, and I watched the ends of his hair brush against the small of his back. "There would always be regrets, Sinisia, no matter when I summoned you, but any I have now are ones I accept."

It seemed to me she did not quite grasp the subtlety of his answer, but after a few moments spent pondering his words, she appeared content. "Trust in yourself, Ryiel," she told him, "for this is as much my destiny as it is yours."

She flipped away from him, disappearing below the surface once more and sinking to the bottom of the pool. Now she began to swim in slow, lazy circles that had her pushing off the opposite walls for added momentum. As she picked up speed, she no longer required the aid of the pool walls; her own strength now provided the necessary impetus. Like the centrifugal force of a washing machine on the spin cycle, Sinisia began to swim faster, moving in an ever-narrowing spiral that drew the water to her. Next to me Laycee gasped, and we stared, mesmerized, at the whirlpool being created. As the surface of the vortex widened, it created the illusion that the swirling base was much deeper than the fifteen-foot bottom of Gabriel's pool.

I'm not sure what happened next, except I think maternal instinct kicked in big-time. Laycee, somehow sensing what was about to happen, made a sound reminiscent of a small animal caught in a trap as she yanked her hand free of my hold and sprinted toward the edge of the pool, where Ryiel was still standing with her baby in his arms. In a blur of motion, Gabriel caught her around the waist. This was the second time in as many days that a vampire had stopped her in mid-stride, but whereas Ryiel had simply held her to him, Gabriel took her down to the ground, pinning himself on top of her to keep her still.

"*NOOOOOOOO!*" she shrieked at the same moment Ryiel flung himself into the maelstrom and disappeared from view.

Immobilized by Gabriel's superior strength, Laycee stopped struggling. Instead she began to weep bitterly, her gaze fixed on the moving pillar of water that was now rising out of the concrete and tile structure. I rushed to her side, glad that Gabriel immediately rolled off her and allowed me to take his place. Sitting on the ground with my legs spread open, I pulled Laycee back against me. My arms wrapped around her, and I began swaying gently as we both scanned the water, searching for any sign of the dark-haired vampire and his precious bundle.

A sudden opening, like a door being held ajar, appeared in the wall of water. "Look!" I pointed, seeing Ryiel in the center of the vortex.

Laycee clutched my arm. "Where's Jenna?" she asked, her voice so full of anxiety she was barely coherent.

"He has her in his arms."

"Oh God—he's going to drown her!"

"No, he won't," Gabriel interjected. "Remember, for nine months the only environment she knew was water. It was her world, and as natural to her as air is to you now." Laycee swiveled her head and stared at him with huge, terrified eyes. "She will not drown, Laycee. She feels no discomfort and will be completely unharmed when Ryiel returns her to you. I give you my word."

She released her hold on me and reached for his hand, the gesture saying more than words could possibly convey. "But how can she breathe in there?" Laycee moaned, her eyes returning to the small figure nestled against Ryiel's bare chest.

"I promise you she can."

The wall of water surrounding the vampire and baby began to undulate as Sinisia continued to move at a frightening pace. I don't think what she was doing could be classified as swimming anymore, and the increase in her revolutions made her nothing but a pale blur of movement. In response to the siren's orbit, the whirlpool began to rise, and Ryiel and Jenna were hidden from us once more. Laycee stiffened against me, and I offered what comfort I could, holding her with equal strength.

The moving wall of water climbed above the surface of the pool.

A foot, then two, then more. When I gauged the wall of water to be almost six feet tall, Sinisia burst up from the center, hovering on the air like a leaf caught on the updraft of a summer breeze, and began to sing. The absolute purity of each cascading note tumbling from her mouth made me feel a connection to the physical world I never knew was possible. I stared at the huge pot of night-blooming jasmine that Tomas and I had planted only a few weeks ago and felt my skin sizzle as one of the blooms opened. I stared at Gabriel, feeling in his gaze the powerful, almost overwhelming, depth of his love for me.

Without warning, the siren's song stopped as Sinisia jackknifed her body in the air and dove straight back down through the center of the vortex. Assuming Ryiel was still standing in the same place, a collision was inevitable. Twisting in my arms, Laycee buried her face in my neck, missing the explosion of light that illuminated the column of water and bounced off the now-dry tiled walls of the pool. A golden aura infused with ribbons of iridescent pearl, seaweed-green, and the blue of a tropical sea washed over Ryiel, bathing the vampire with a dazzling glow so bright I was forced to close my eyes in case my retinas fried.

And then the wall of water that had continued to rise suddenly exploded and drenched everything within fifty feet. I don't know if Tomas and Stavros had been warned about what was going to happen, or if they had witnessed such a spectacle before, but they were prepared. Tomas draped thick towels around our shoulders as Stavros hurried to the opposite end of the pool, waiting for Ryiel to climb out of the shallows. Jenna was immediately swaddled in what looked like a mile of toweling by the sentinel. I made no move to stop Laycee from jumping up and running to her daughter. The lusty wail from the cocoon made us all smile.

Of Sinisia there was no sign.

Picking me up in his arms, Gabriel set me down on a lounger, settling himself behind me and pulling me back to lean against him as he began to dry my hair.

"Where did she go?" I asked, grateful when he didn't pretend he had no idea who I was talking about.

"You won't see her again," he told me in a rough voice. "She has done as Ryiel asked."

Something in his tone sent a chill running through me. One that had nothing to do with getting soaked or the fact I was wearing wet clothing. He paused in mid-wipe, and we both watched Laycee return inside the penthouse, followed by a fussy Stavros.

"I hope she doesn't snap at him." Laycee's temper, normally on simmer, was known to go to a rolling boil if she felt stressed. I didn't see how recent events could be categorized as anything less than stress, and I didn't want to think what might happen if she thought the sentinel was being smothering.

"Don't worry," Ryiel said, joining us. "Stavros is very intuitive about when his help is welcome and when it is not. He will do no more than she will allow." He tilted his head up and looked at the night sky. "There's just enough time for me to drive Laycee home and return before the sun comes up," he commented.

"But Jake isn't back," I protested. "He won't be home until the day after tomorrow. I thought you said it was dangerous for her to be alone, especially after the whole vampire imposter thing."

"As he can no longer use the child to splinter the contract, your demon has no more interest in the mother."

The quiver of excitement fluttering in my belly was enough to override any annoyance I felt at the bane of my existence being referred to as *my* demon.

"Are you saying Gabriel doesn't have to sleep with Jenna?" My voice was suddenly giddy. "That he won't have to be unfaithful to me?"

"Yes, that's exactly—" I launched myself at Ryiel, wrapping my arms around his waist and blubbering unashamedly against his sternum. He patted me awkwardly on the back. Whether it was because he was unused to offering such comfort or his actions were due to Gabriel's watchful eye was difficult to say. Gently he extricated himself from my hold. "Rowan, you really must stop throwing yourself at vampires you're not bonded to."

Through tear-filled eyes, I apologized. "I'm sorry, but you have no idea what a relief it is to know that I won't have to face the Dark Realm in twenty-five years."

Taking the towel Tomas held out to him, Ryiel gave me a sharp look. "You understand this is only a reprieve. The contract you made is still in place—and, I suspect, in full force. You do still have to face the Dark Realm."

The euphoria rushing through me turned into a test-crash dummy hitting a brick wall. "Is that why you want to talk to me?"

His face became shuttered. "Yes, but now is not the time. We will talk later."

I recalled his statement about wanting to deliver his news to me alone, as it would be my decision whether or not to share the information with Gabriel. And also his prediction that I would not. I could feel the curiosity running through my lover as he sat behind me.

"But," Ryiel continued with a weary smile, "I would like to hear about this most recent visit from your demon."

"Gaaaah! He's not my demon!"

Laycee wasn't the only one who'd had a stressful few days. I blew out a breath and re-leashed my temper under the annoyed stares of the two Original Vampires.

"Why do you want to know about the visit?" It was as close to an apology as either of them was going to get. "I don't see what difference it makes now that Gabriel's pledge to Jenna is no longer enforceable." A shadow moved across Ryiel's silvery eyes. "It *is* no longer enforceable . . . right?"

"Gabriel has no tie to the infant," Ryiel confirmed. "His blood no longer protects her." He reached for my hand and dropped something in my cupped palm. The size of a grapefruit seed, the gemstone looked a little like the red diamond in my engagement ring, but darker. Almost like a ruby, but not.

"Where did this come from?" I asked, watching the stone twinkle as it rolled across my palm.

"It's Gabriel's blood. The child cannot carry the protection of two Original Vampires, and my claim now supersedes any other."

"As long as she's protected."

"Of course, and as your connection to me is nothing but academic, there is no reason for the Dark Realm to look at her again." I didn't doubt him, but I was still confused. "Knowing what happened during your last encounter may make a difference in what I tell you as well as how much."

I opened my mouth to protest at the unfairness of that decision, but Gabriel's hand on my shoulder made me close it again. "No more talk or it will be too late for Ryiel to take Laycee home."

Stavros's sudden appearance couldn't have been better timed. Clasping Gabriel by the forearm, the silver-eyed vampire muttered a few words in their secret language before following his sentinel back through the sliding-glass doors.

"Are you okay?" I asked, concerned by the sudden melancholy on Gabriel's face. "What did he say to you?"

"That he would miss me." Pulling me into his arms, he kissed my temple.

"Why would he say that? He's just driving Laycee home." And there was no way I was going to allow this Original Vampire to depart until he and I had had our own heart-to-heart. Even though I was convinced his news was not going to make me do a happy dance, I was determined to hear it. All of it.

"He wasn't talking about right now," Gabriel said, holding me close, "but soon."

"How soon?"

"Too soon."

A chill went through me with enough strength to make me shiver. "What exactly is Sinisia's connection to Ryiel?"

Gabriel gave a weary sigh. The kind you make when you let go of one burden, only to find there's another bigger one waiting to take its place. I looked into his eyes. There was a darkness clouding the neon-blue such as I had never seen before, and it took me a moment to recognize it as grief. He was going to lose Ryiel. I gasped and took a step back, finally understanding what Sinisia had meant when she called me *Sister*. I knew what Ryiel had done, why his claim would supersede all others. And I knew why he would be leaving. Soon equaled twenty-five years.

"Oh my God—he made Jenna his Promise!"

Chapter 22

I thought about the light show in the pool and the siren's sudden disappearance as a wave of nausea rolled through me. "Are you saying she's . . . do you mean she's . . . shit, Gabriel—is Sinisia *inside* Jenna?"

"Yes . . . and no. It's not what you're thinking."

"How do you know what I'm thinking?"

He made a circular gesture in the air with his hand. "I can see it all over your face."

"But that's not how a Promise works . . . is it?" I was suddenly horrified by the idea that I too had hijacked some innocent baby girl's body, making her live a life that wasn't truly her own. Who might she have been without my influence shaping her? What different choices might she have made?

She could be a Taylor Swift fan instead of fantasizing about being a Hinder groupie.

She might prefer red licorice instead of black.

She could—may the football gods preserve us—be a New England Patriots fan.

Okay, let's not get ridiculous.

She most certainly wouldn't be having conversations in her head.

Yeah right, you tell yourself that if it makes you feel better.

Okay, but they'd probably be conversations that were more uplifting.

My inner bitch growled and muttered something highly derogatory as Gabriel put his hands on my shoulders and gave me a little shake to refocus my attention.

"Sinisia is inside Jenna because the human body is roughly sixty-five percent water," he said, pausing to make sure I was following.

"It's the only way to guarantee she can release Ryiel's soul when the time comes." He ran his hands down my arms until he was holding my hands. "She isn't inside Jenna's head, nor will she ever be. She cannot change the way Jenna will grow up, or the way she thinks. Sinisia can't stop her from being the person she is meant to be. She will remain in a dormant state until Ryiel awakens her."

"How's he going to do that? Tap Jenna on the temple with his knuckles and shout *Honey, I'm home?*"

Gabriel smiled. "He'll give Jenna the greatest orgasm of her life."

Now that's my kind of wake-up call.

"So I'm still me . . . ?"

"You always have been. Each Promise is different, Rowan, and the terms set are different for each Original."

"How so?"

He took in a deep breath, and I felt his thumbs stroke over the inside of my wrists. "Ryiel chose a siren because he knew she would remain in the sea until the time came for him to summon her. Keeping her safe was the most important thing to him, but it was also agreed that he would only be able to call her one time. If something happened before she was able to"—he hesitated, searching for the right word—"*implant* herself, there would be no do-over. Ryiel's one chance at redemption would be forever lost."

"But you and I didn't have an agreement like that."

He raised my hands and brushed his lips across the back of my knuckles. "No, we didn't. For one thing, you're not a siren, for which I am eternally grateful."

"Why? Didn't you think Sinisia was beautiful?"

"Of course, but the idea of scrambling over a rocky shoreline hoping for a glimpse of you would be frustrating, to say the least."

"Is that what Ryiel's been doing?"

He shook his head. "No, but then Ryiel was never in love with Sinisia."

I felt as if we were dancing on the cusp of something important. "And you always have been . . . ?"

He smiled. It was a sensuous curve of his mouth that made me clamp my thighs together. "From the first time I saw you. It just took a little longer for you to fall in love with me, I think."

"How much longer?"

The smile became a playful grin. "Almost a full day."

I shook my head. "You're wrong."

"Oh? Then tell me." He tilted my chin up and brushed his lips over my mouth. "When did you know you loved me, Rowan?"

"In my father's tent."

His eyes darkened and glowed with a light I had never seen before. It both unnerved and excited me. I was standing on the precipice of something momentous. Something life-changing. Something awe-inspiring. "Do you remember that moment? Truly?"

I stared at Gabriel, seeing him not as the vampire he was now, but as the angel he had once been.

"I was told it was forbidden to look on you—any of you—because I was a woman, and you despised all women." I let out a short laugh at the absurdity of such a statement. Surely someone, somewhere, had to know this would only make me more determined? "I stole a robe with a hood big enough to cover my hair and hide my face, and I slipped in behind the guards, only . . . you saw me."

Like a closed flower opening to greet the sun, I could feel the memory blooming in my mind.

Pulling the hood of her cloak over her head to cover both her hair and shield her face, the girl slipped into the Warlord's tent. Choosing a place in the back where the glow from the fire pit did not reach, nor the light from the torches, she mingled with the shadows, waiting for them to come. She had been told they despised all women, and the presence of any female would be a great insult. It took all she had not to laugh. Didn't they know such words would only make her more determined to see them for herself? As long as she kept herself covered and stayed where the light was dim, who would ever know?

The abrupt cessation of all conversation heralded their arrival, and she was unable to stop the breath from catching in her throat at her first sight of them. They were more glorious than any of them had imagined. Unfortunately, her gasp was loud enough to draw knowing looks from those closest to her, and even though an unexplained heat flushed her face, she did not look away. She could not. In the moment it took for her to draw a second breath, the girl knew she would never give herself to any mortal man. A fact that did not bode well for the treaty her father had already secured with the promise of her virginity.

Hearing her gasp, the man on her left commented, "Mark my words—we'll all be falling short now."

His companion snorted in disgust. "They have wings! How is an ordinary man expected to compete with such things?"

"I know not, but perhaps it is just as well all eligible maids have been forbidden to gaze upon them." The first man stared pointedly at the cavernous hood that covered her.

Her discovery imminent, the girl made to move farther into the shadows, but the man who had complained about competing with wings caught her by the wrist. "Take care, lady," he warned in a low hiss, "for they are not as mortal men, and you may be disappointed to discover there is much they cannot offer." He paused before adding, "It is said they think women are unworthy of their attention."

She dropped her eyes to the strong fingers wrapped around her arm before looking back up at the man's face, staring pointedly until the hold was released. "Disappointment is not unknown to me," she told him. "To renew our acquaintance would cause no hardship." But deep in the secret part of her heart she knew it for a lie. Surely, if the gods saw fit to grant her prayer, they would not be so cruel.

Moving away from her companions, she looked at the three angels who stood before the Warlord. They had come to offer their strength and skill to help turn the tide in a conflict that had gone on too long. But the Warlord was a cautious man. He would accept no one's help until he understood why it was being offered, and what it would cost him. She continued to stare at the angels, unaware that her heart was now beating faster than normal.

The one to the right had dark glossy hair that shimmered like a raven's wing in the early morning sun. She longed to see his face, for she had been told the color of their wings matched their eyes. If that were true, then he must view the world with eyes of silvery moonlight. The one on the left was blessed with thick locks that reminded her of a sky at twilight. Shades of purple cascaded over his shoulders, enhancing the copper hue of his feathers. But it was the long white hair and bright blue wings of the angel in the center that mesmerized her. She had never seen such colors before. Both were so brilliant she was forced to lower her eyes, unable to decide which she wanted more—to feel the softness of his wings against her skin or run her fingers through the silk of his hair.

The sound of shuffling feet and clanging swords interrupted her fantasy. Their business concluded, the visitors were preparing to depart the Warlord's tent. The girl tried to locate the slit in the tent covering that had offered her entry, but in the sudden press of movement about her she was turned around, and lost sight of it. An unexpected sourness made her stomach churn. Disobedience was a trait her father did not tolerate, and there were many who would be only too glad to see the Warlord's willful daughter punished. The silence that had accompanied the angels' arrival had been laced with a sense of wonder, but the silence that surrounded her now was oppressive and fearful. She had been betrayed. Her presence was a taint on the proceedings. Had it been the man who caught her wrist? Had he wanted a favor to silence his tongue? She clenched her hands tightly to better hide their trembling.

Her eyes were immediately drawn to the tips of the white-haired angel's wings, the long feathers brushing against the ground. The urge to fall to her knees and place her palm between the edge of his wings and the dirt floor was almost overwhelming. Such vibrancy should not risk being dulled by the raised dust of their feet. Knowing all eyes were upon her, those of her Warlord father in particular, she resisted the impulse. She took in a deep breath, but instead of clearing her head, her nose was filled with a scent that reminded her of the icy crispness of the forest in winter. A mix of pine sap and freshly fallen snow that ignited a burn deep in her belly and flushed a heat between her legs. A heat that both terrified and excited her.

Her eyes traveled slowly up his form. The strange leggings protecting his lower limbs were affixed with no binding of any kind that she could see. Next were the soft hide trews that did little to disguise his muscular thighs. Recalling the earlier comment thrown her way, the corner of her mouth twitched to see that he appeared to be fashioned much the same as mortal men, assuming, of course, that the bulge in his pants served the same purpose. A wide belt, decorated with symbols she did not recognize, was wrapped around his waist.

His upper body was bare, but this, she reasoned, had more to do with the accommodation of his wings than the warmth of the day. Her eyes danced with delight over the well-defined abdomen, the heavy musculature of his chest and arms, the wide set of his shoulders. But she couldn't bring herself to look at his face. She had been too bold already, gazing upon him as if she were no better than one of the camp followers, willing to sell her body to any soldier for a few coppers.

Strong fingers cupped her chin and raised her head, forcing her to look at him. The dazzling blue of his eyes, framed by thick dark lashes, was almost more than she could bear. She gasped to see that the rumors were true. The blue of his wings was the same shade as his eyes. But as she continued to gaze, mesmerized by the change from light to dark to light, she was startled to see not condemnation or scorn, as she expected, but humor. A teasing light that not only made his eyes dance, but lifted the corners of his sensuous mouth. His hand reached out toward her and pushed back the hood she had tried to hide in. Her hair fell in a cascade of dark red curls, and he smoothed them back from her face. The touch of his long fingers whispering across her cheek made her heart beat wildly in her chest and the heat in her belly turn to a fireball.

"This," he said, twining a long curl about his finger, "should never be hidden." He continued to look at her, and the intensity of his gaze increased with each stroke of his thumb over the trapped lock of hair. "How does your father call you?"

"Rowan," she answered with trembling lips.

He raised his hand, pressing his lips against the deep chestnut curl. "I am Gabriel."

Then he tilted his head as if hearing a voice no one else could hear, and she saw a sudden weariness fill his eyes. Freeing her from his tenuous hold, he bade her farewell, murmuring her name in such a way that she did not think he would forget it.

And knowing she would never forget his . . .

"Was that when you fell in love with me?" Gabriel asked in a husky whisper.

I shook my head. "No. It was the moment you turned away."

"Ryiel knew." His tone matched the stunned expression on his face. "And he never doubted you."

"Another was with you. An angel with copper-colored wings, I don't remember his name." In truth it was amazing that I even recalled Ryiel was there.

"It was Dariel."

Taking me in his arms, Gabriel kissed me. Long and slow, the kind of kiss that stayed with a woman for an eternity. "I was hiding in the back," I murmured, swaying slightly in his arms. "How did you know I was there?"

"I caught the scent of wildflowers the moment I entered. It was hard to imagine any of your father's formidable warriors perfuming themselves." We both chuckled at the notion before Gabriel said, "And you looked then as you do now."

Suddenly his face began to swim before my eyes, and I felt hot, wet tears spill down my cheeks. "Oh, G-G-Gabriel," I sobbed, clutching his arms and holding onto him. "Your w-w-wings . . . your b-b-beautiful w-wings . . ."

He held me, stroking my hair and making soft shushing sounds until I was all cried out. How could I have forgotten about them? They were magnificent and glorious, and I knew I would probably weep again the next time I felt the thick, ropey scar tissue beneath my fingers. I didn't need to ask why he had chosen me to be his Promise. His reason would be the same as the one I would give if asked why I went to the forest that night. It had been more than a compulsion driving me to respond to the call of the lesser beasts. I had already committed myself to Gabriel, body and soul, that moment in my father's tent. My life was meaningless without him, and I would not allow another to safeguard his soul. Because I loved him.

"So what type of agreement did we have?" I asked once I managed to regain some semblance of control.

"You would live a normal life and if our paths crossed, I would wait to see if you were ready to give yourself to me."

"And how was I supposed to let you know this?" Surely it had to be something more subtle than throwing myself at him.

"You would give me your real name."

"Rowan?"

He nodded and pressed his lips to my forehead. "I had almost given up hope of ever hearing you say it," he confessed.

I was almost too afraid to ask, but I did anyway. "Did our paths cross in all my lives?"

He turned serious. "No, not all of them. Sometimes an unforeseen event stopped us from meeting."

"Unforeseen . . . ?"

"Earthquakes, volcanic eruptions, storms."

"Volcanic eruptions?"

"You were at Pompeii."

"Could have been worse," I said, giving him what had to be the worst smile of my life. "At least I wasn't eaten by lions at the Coliseum."

"Um, that kind of thing actually happened at Circus Maximus, not the Coliseum, and yes, you were."

I felt my stomach roll alarmingly. "Anything else?"

"You mean other than plague and sacrifice?"

"I caught the plague? As in the Black Death?"

He nodded. "It was very common throughout the Middle Ages."

Like that was a big comfort. "And sacrifice?" I kept my fingers crossed, hoping it didn't mean what I thought.

"The Mayans." I uncrossed my fingers. It meant exactly what I thought.

"Well, it's nice to know I'm a walking, talking billboard for reincarnation."

"Yeah . . . you are."

Something in the way he agreed with me didn't sit right. "Okay, hotshot, what am I missing?"

"Not everyone gets to be reincarnated, Rowan." I stared at him, wondering if I had the balls to actually voice the sixty-four-thousand-dollar question. Turns out I didn't have to. "I don't know what happens to them," Gabriel added.

"You were an angel—how could you not know?"

"There was some knowledge, actually a great deal of knowledge, stripped from us when we chose this new life. It was decided our adjustment to the life of a vampire would be easier if we weren't carrying memories of our previous existence."

"How much of your memory did you lose?"

"Most of it," he admitted. "Obviously I retained anything to do with you, which is how I know I was an angel the first time I saw you."

"Do you remember losing your wings?"

He nodded slowly, and the look on his face was a plea for me not to ask. I knew if I did, he would tell me, but I knew he would suffer in reliving the tale.

"Doesn't quite seem like a fair exchange," I told him.

"To have you, Rowan, I would give so much more."

I sighed and pulled the two halves of the thick bathrobe I was wearing closer together. A slight breeze was picking up. One that was strong enough to bring on a chill—

"Hey!" Looking down, I saw my clothes scattered on the ground. I didn't need to check to know I was naked inside the robe. "When did I put this on?"

"While you were talking about our first meeting. You were starting to shiver, so it seemed like the time to get you out of your wet things and into something drier." He came and stood next to me. "Are you upset?"

Upset? No, more like dismayed that Gabriel had been able to undress me without my noticing.

Chapter 23

I stared at what was left of my bed, the brand-new, only-used-once-by-me bed. Aleksei had been nice enough to prop the box springs and mattress against the wall, and to carefully place the splintered bed frame in a neat pile.

"Dahlink, we're really, really sorry."

I'd woken early to find a message on my phone from the lovely Magyar asking if we could meet at my apartment. I'd texted her back with a time. Naturally, I'd informed Tomas of my plans, because with Kartel on the loose and his whereabouts unknown, it would be stupid not to. Also I didn't want Gabriel ripping his sentinel a new one if he had no idea where I was when he woke. On the drive over, I tried to imagine what Anasztaizia might want to talk to me about, especially as she had requested it be a girls-only chat. I crossed my fingers, hoping Aleksei wasn't suffering any aftereffects from the attempt to destroy him.

From the irreparable damage to the bed, I'd say aftereffects were no longer an issue.

"I'm sorry, what did you say?" I turned to look at Anasztaizia. Beautifully turned out, as always, she put her hand on my arm and gave me a look that was more than a little guilty.

"Of course we will replace it."

"Um, I had it specially made."

I'd asked Tomas where the bed in the penthouse had come from, blanching when he told me it was custom-made by an old family firm in Rome. As in Rome, Italy, not Rome, Georgia. With the help of the Internet, e-mails, and Tomas's fluent Italian, the sentinel had guided me through the process of getting the bed of my dreams. Obviously, I wasn't looking for anything as big as the firm's previous effort—the bedroom in my apartment didn't have anywhere near the same square footage—but I did want something equally sturdy. I e-mailed some design ideas and had been delighted with the results. The bed had been shipped in sections, and Tomas had supervised the installation for me.

And now it was broken.

"Perhaps we could contact the company and have another made?"

I nodded, and continued to stare at the carefully laid-out remnants of the shattered frame, wondering if they could be shipped back to see if anything was salvageable. I sighed. There was nothing to be done, and it really wasn't Aleksei's fault, though I was disappointed the bed had not stood up to the physical demands of lusty vampire sex. I was about to turn away when something on the decorative wrought-iron headboard caught my eye. Deciding a closer look was needed, I stepped carefully over the debris.

I immediately recognized the unexpected adornment affixed to the decorative wrought-iron scrollwork topping the heavy maple headboard. A glance revealed its mate on the other end. Judging from the XXL size, it was obvious they had been used by the big guy.

"You handcuffed Aleksei to the bed?" I turned around and stared at Anasztaizia, unable to disguise the look of astonishment on my face. "*Aleksei?*"

The blond head nodded. "Not just his hands," she admitted in a small voice.

A closer examination of the manacles said Anasztaizia's much smaller hands would have fallen out the moment her arms were raised or lowered. No doubt her feet would have had no problem escaping the closed circle of steel either.

"Where did you find cuffs this big?" I asked, intrigued.

"Oh, I had a friend make them for me."

I like her; she's got some interesting friends.

"And he was okay with this?"

"At first . . . he agreed to do it to please me. It was always one of my fantasies."

Ah yes, what woman doesn't want her man shackled to the bed so she can do whatever she wants with him? Especially when it comes to sex. It's the ultimate control trip. Unfortunately, it would appear that the reality hadn't quite been what either of them had expected.

Knowing firsthand what it felt like to be handcuffed, I can say it's not an experience I'm in any hurry to repeat.

"I'm guessing the big guy didn't enjoy being made to feel quite so helpless?"

She nodded. "He loves me, and I know he trusts me, but . . ."

"Vampires have a hard time giving up control in any situation," I said gently, surprised that she would not have realized this. "It's the possessive side of their nature." And it was nice to know I hadn't been given a substandard product. My bed had been made to endure vampire sex, not an enraged vampire attempting to free himself from heavy-duty steel restraints. I decided that perhaps I wouldn't return any of the broken bed to the manufacturers. I was certain seeing the splintered wood and twisted wrought iron would raise both brows and questions.

"You weren't hurt, were you?"

The smile Anasztaizia gave me was answer enough. "I think Aleksei was more scared by his reaction than I was."

"Do you want them back?" It seemed only polite to ask. I mean, what was I going to do with them? I figured Gabriel wanting me naked on the dining room table was pretty wild. Sheesh! I had a lot to learn.

Anasztaizia shook her head. "No, I don't think that particular fantasy is one I'll try again."

I picked up the manacle, feeling the heavy weight in my palm. "Perhaps your friend could make you some that were not quite so strong? Something that Aleksei could free himself from if he needed to?" Without destroying another bed.

Arching a brow, Anasztaizia looked thoughtful. "That's definitely worth considering, dahlink." She paused before giving me a sheepish smile. "Are you very cross with us about the bed?"

If the heartfelt sincerity of her expression hadn't made up my mind, the ring on her finger did. Happy to see she had resumed wearing the enormous diamond engagement ring, I pulled her to me for a hug, saying, "How could I be cross with either of you? Aren't I going to be your bridesmaid?"

"Oh, you're still willing to do it?"

"Absolutely."

"Oh dahlink, you're going to love the dress. I promise!"

Aleksei had mentioned something about me dressed as a pink

meringue, but at this point I didn't much care. If the bride-to-be wanted to have me look like one of those bright pink coconut snowballs, who was I to deny her?

"It's Chanel," she added, squeezing my hand. "A little old-school, but still very romantic."

I didn't just smile, I fairly beamed at her. Chanel, I was certain, had never heard of pink coconut snowballs.

"But don't worry, dahlink, Aleksei is still going to buy you a new bed."

You bet your ass he is.

I followed her out of the bedroom. Stopping by the front door, I adopted a more serious tone and asked, "Everything between you and Aleksei is okay now, right?"

"Of course, dahlink," she paused, "except for him calling me Rowan while we're having sex, everything is fine."

"*Anasztaizia!*"

"I'm just teasing you."

She kissed me on both cheeks before fishing her car keys from her purse. Opening the front door, I was stunned to see Ryiel leaning on the opposite wall with his arms folded. He was, as usual, naked from the waist up, his dark hair reaching almost to his waist.

Anasztaizia gave him a long look before turning and asking, "Is everything all right with you and Gabriel?"

"Uh, what? Oh yeah, of course." I gestured to the dark-haired vampire. "Do you know Ryiel?"

"Only what Aleksei has told me."

At the mention of the big guy's name, Ryiel arched a brow.

"Anasztaizia is Aleksei's fiancée," I told him.

"That must be confusing," he murmured.

"Only if you're a vampire, dahlink." Leaning forward, she kissed me on the cheek. "We'll talk soon."

Both Ryiel and I waited until the sound of the elevator said the lovely Magyar was on her way down.

"Did you actually walk through the lobby like that?" I asked.

Ryiel seemed genuinely puzzled by my question. "Like what?"

I gestured in the general direction of his tattooed pecs. "Do you even know what a shirt is, much less how to wear one?"

He gave me a reproachful look. "I am who I am, Rowan. Accept me or not."

He was right. It made no difference what I thought or said, and if I received a letter from the Tenants' Association about recent visitors to my apartment, I wasn't overly concerned. Wait until they found out how well I knew the owner of the building. I stared at the Original Vampire. He seemed to be taking up far too much space in the hallway.

"How did you know I was here?"

"Tomas told me," he answered.

"And Gabriel? Does he also know you're here?" I certainly didn't want to run the risk of having a pissed-off vampire showing up, fangs bared and snarling.

"Of course. Do you think I would be so foolish as to spend time alone with any Promise?" Not expecting a response, Ryiel went on, "He thought you might be more comfortable if we talked away from the penthouse."

Sometimes it was scary how well Gabriel knew me. And he was right. There was no putting it off now. I was going to hear whatever it was Ryiel had come to tell me. All of it. The bad, the ugly, and the hopeless. Standing to one side, I invited him in.

"I've got coffee, sweet tea, and a whole multitude of alcoholic stuff if you prefer something with a little more kick." My kitchen was still overflowing with bottles.

"Hot water, and honey, if you have it," Ryiel said, producing a small paper bag from somewhere. "It's tea," he added, seeing the questioning look on my face.

"Like English tea?" My aversion to the hot beverage had only been strengthened by my time spent playing the Tea Game with Aleksei.

"Like green tea." He chuckled at my grimace. "I feel the same way about iced tea."

"Heathen," I muttered, trying not to grin too much. I got him a mug and some clover honey that came in a plastic bottle shaped like a teddy bear. "Um, I don't have a teakettle to boil water," I apologized. "Will the microwave do?"

It did, and a few minutes later we were sitting in the living room. Ryiel had his cup of oolong-slap-a-long or some such nonsense, while I settled for a Jack and Coke. I had the feeling I was going to need it.

"Tell me about the last time you saw your—sorry, *the*—demon," Ryiel said, dunking the stainless-steel infusion ball in his mug of hot water.

"Well, I was in the kitchen pouring myself a shot of bourbon—"

"Why?"

"Why what?"

"You were alone, correct?" I nodded. "So what precipitated your need for alcohol?"

"I was upset."

"Why? What had happened?"

I sighed. It was going to be a long conversation, I could tell. "How far back do you want me to go?" I said, taking a sip of my drink.

Ryiel arched a questioning eyebrow. "The beginning?"

"That would mean the night I met Gabriel."

"Ah, well, not quite that far then." Removing the tea infuser from his mug, I watched him put it on the small saucer he'd found in the kitchen. I glanced at the contents of his mug. I've seen ditch water with a more appealing color. "How about if you start with Kartel's visit." He smiled at me as he squeezed a generous helping of honey into the hot liquid. "The abridged version will be fine."

So that's what he got.

It still took me almost twenty minutes to tell, though, and Ryiel only interrupted once to ask about Rat Boy. I don't think I'd mentioned either him or Gus by name during our earlier discussion regarding my abduction. When I was done, I got up to replenish my empty glass. Ryiel refused my offer of more hot water but followed me into the kitchen anyway.

"Where did you say the demon came from?"

I nodded to the sliver of space between the fridge and the wall, a space the vampire now bridged by spanning his hand over the gap. Fingers splayed, he placed his thumb and forefinger on the fridge, and his pinky and third finger on the wall.

"I wasn't imagining it . . . was I?" I was vaguely optimistic, even though I knew it was fruitless.

Ryiel shook his head. "No, he was here, but any portals to you will be sealed when your contract with him is broken."

If it's broken.

I sighed. "You don't need to sugarcoat it for me, Ryiel. I've got a good idea what you're going to tell me. It's why you made Jenna your Promise, right?" He seemed surprised that I knew. "I'm sorry, was it supposed to be a secret?"

"No, I should have known Gabriel would tell you."

"Actually Sinisia told me first. She called me *Sister*." He nodded. If the keeper of his soul was claiming kinship with me, who was he to argue? I leaned against the counter and crossed my arms. "So you'll really be gone in twenty-five years, then?" He responded by giving me a bleak look. I wasn't about to deny him the chance of redemption so he could return to his celestial brothers. I just wished it wasn't going to hurt Gabriel so much to lose him.

"We need to talk, Rowan."

"Why? We both know what you're going to say."

"Do you?" He raised a brow.

"Look, no one appreciates your stepping up to the plate more than me, and I'm grateful that my best friend isn't going to be freaking out at the idea of my boyfriend having sex with her daughter. As for the rest?" I shrugged. "I'll just take however much time I'm allowed with Gabriel, but I really do thank you, Ryiel, for at least trying."

The sound of his fist banging on the counter made me jump. "God, woman, you're impossible! Kartel might not be right in saying you're incompetent, but—damn it!—you are clueless at times."

I stared at him, my mouth falling open. Who the hell was he to call me clueless? Sighing, the big vampire ran his fingers through his thick, dark hair.

"What is it that you think I'm going to tell you, Rowan?"

Jeez, was he really going to make me spell it out for him?

Kinda looks that way . . .

"Okay, it's obvious you haven't had enough time to go through all the papers—or scrolls or whatever—to have found a way to invalidate my contract. If you had," I continued, seeing the question in his eyes, "you would have already told both Gabriel and me. No, it's obvious you haven't found a way out of the contract because there is no way out, and that's what you've found. Proof that the contract can't be broken."

He narrowed his eyes until they were silver slits. "And why do you think I summoned Sinisia?"

"As a gift from you to Gabriel. Let's face it, we both know I screwed up royally when I browbeat Gabriel into giving his protection to Laycee's baby, but you've found a way to give me a second chance. Believe me, no one appreciates it more, and I promise I won't let you down. I'll take whatever time I have left with Gabriel and make every day count. I'll—"

"No, stop it!" he interrupted holding a hand up. "You're starting to sound like a really bad greeting card."

"You don't have to be so rude about it."

He blew out an impatient breath. "You're right, I don't. You're not completely wrong," he conceded. "Making your friend's baby my Promise was a way for me to right a terrible wrong. Had Laycee asked for Gabriel's protection freely, I would not have felt compelled to act, but her request was coerced, and your response, given the circumstances was . . . predictable."

"You're saying I was played?"

"Rowan, he's been playing you from the start."

"So why did you do it?"

"I prefer to think of it as removing a vulnerability that was too easy to use against you. Either of you," he added. "It was my immediate concern."

"And what was your not-so-immediate concern?"

"Kartel is planning something that I fear will have disastrous consequences, and you still have to face your demon."

"He's not—"

"Yes, actually he is."

My jaw snapped shut. I walked into the living room, climbing the two steps that took me up to the raised section of the floor in front of the wall of windows. The lights of the city glowed like Christmas decorations. I could feel Ryiel's liquid silver eyes on me, waiting for me to decide if I wanted him to tell me what he'd found out . . . or not.

"Rowan . . . show me the Bridal Night Chain."

I went to the bookshelf and took down the light blue Tiffany box. "Can you touch it?" I asked, opening the lid to reveal the pool of black opals nestled within. "Gabriel was able to, but I don't know if that's because of his relationship—"

"To you," Ryiel said firmly. "It's because of his relationship to you that he was able to touch the Chain. No intimacy exists between us, so protection is denied me."

"Well, it's going in a safe-deposit box first thing in the morning," I told him.

"No, it isn't." Ryiel shook his head, making his dark hair curl around his bicep and fan out across his chest.

I frowned. "What do you suggest I do with it, then?"

"Wear it."

The floor came up to meet me at frightening speed.

Chapter 24

The shock of his words sent all the blood in my body to a place it wasn't meant to go, making me either black out or have a mini-seizure. I think the end result was pretty much the same. In either case, I was on the floor when I opened my eyes to find Ryiel leaning over me. It was hard to tell if he was concerned or relieved. I put up a hand to push him away, but the feel of my palm pressed against the warm smoothness of his bare skin flustered me. Thankfully, Ryiel overlooked my embarrassment and helped me to my feet, keeping an arm around me until I was seated on the couch.

"That was some sort of a joke, right?" It would be a bad one, but I could forgive his lousy sense of humor.

Ryiel shook his head. "No, it's the only way to guarantee the demon will come to you."

"And what makes you think I'm in a hurry to have that happen?"

"You want to break your contract, don't you?"

"And wearing a string of opals is going to help me do that?"

He nodded.

"Shit, I need a drink."

Taking me at my word, Ryiel went to the kitchen, returning a few moments later with another Jack and Coke for me. I took a big sip. A really big sip. "I think you're the one who needs to start from the beginning," I muttered, giving the vampire a sour look.

"Well, that would mean going back to the first time I met Gabriel . . . in Angel Academy."

"Angel Academy?"

"I'm joking."

"Don't," I said, taking another drink. "I don't think I could stand it." I took his sigh as an apology.

"You're wrong in thinking the reason I made Jenna my Promise was because I'd found proof the contract couldn't be broken," he told me, keeping his expression as solemn as his voice. "It's because I found a way it *could* be broken that I was able to offer myself in Gabriel's stead."

"Then why keep it a secret? Why not tell us both right away?"

"Because I think if Gabriel knows how it has to happen, he will do his best to stop you."

I didn't faint this time, but his words did send a ripple of fear through me. "Shit, if it's that bad, then you better tell me all at once."

"You have to return what was given to you in the exact manner it was given."

"I have to what? Do you mean the opals?" I almost started laughing. I'd been expecting something far worse. I'm not sure what, but possibly a blood sacrifice at the very least. "Give me an address and I'll fucking overnight them to him."

"It's not the Bridal Night Chain—"

"Please don't call it that."

Ryiel looked momentarily perplexed. He might not understand my discomfort, but he would respect it. "The necklace," he continued, "is nothing more than a trinket. It was not a part of your original agreement."

"Then what is it that I'm supposed to return?"

"The piece of himself that you carry within you."

A blood sacrifice would have been easier. What was it about me? It wasn't enough I had my own soul, and Gabriel's soul. Now I also had a piece of a demon too. It was getting a little crowded. I picked up my glass, but somehow it was empty. Ryiel took it from my fingers and returned a few moments later with a fresh one for me. If nothing else, he made a cracking bartender. I took a greedy swallow, feeling the slow, warm burn of bourbon as it contrasted beautifully with the cold snap of cola slipping down my throat.

"And just how am I supposed to do that again?" I asked, staring over the rim of my glass at the vampire sitting opposite me.

"The same way it was given to you . . . with a kiss."

"Yeah . . . I thought that's what you were going to say." In one motion I raised the glass and guzzled down the contents until the glass was empty. "Any idea how I'm supposed to get it in my mouth?" Although I could feel the dark, cold place inside me, I had no idea if it had any type of awareness. Did it know it was inside a different person? Could it feel the wrongness of where it was?

"That won't be a problem. It will fill your mouth of its own volition in order to be returned."

Something in his tone made me ask, "You sure about that?"

"As sure as anyone can be."

Placing my glass carefully on the low coffee table, I gave Ryiel what I hoped was an unshakable look. "That's not good enough."

For a few moments neither of us said anything, and then Ryiel got to his feet. "Don't put it in a safe-deposit box," he said, gesturing to the opal necklace spilling half out of the Tiffany box on the low coffee table. "If he wants it back, let him take it from here. Other people—innocent people—won't be hurt that way." Turning, he walked toward the front door.

"That's it? You've got nothing else?"

Ryiel turned to face me, his silver eyes shining brightly. "I tell you I have a way for a contract with a demon to be nullified, but you have decided it is unacceptable. That is your choice. Despite your lack of maturity in this life, you are an adult, and as such, I expect any decision you make to have been reached after considering all eventual outcomes and possibilities. I will not insult you by telling you the choice you have made is the wrong one."

"Perhaps I was a little hasty," I said. "I'm still trying to work around the idea of having to wear the damn necklace."

He stared at me for a moment, a very long moment, before saying, "Kartel wasn't entirely wrong about you."

The mention of Vampire Smurf's name put me on the defense. "What's *that* supposed to mean?" I bristled.

"You're not incompetent, Rowan. Incompetence means not having the skill to do something successfully. It's not the skill you lack, but the belief in your own ability to succeed. You have already decided you cannot defeat the demon. He's too strong, too big, too sexy in all his black feathered array!" He made a noise that seemed to be a mix of frustration and disgust. "Yes, he is all those things, Rowan, so you must find a way to use that to your advantage. If you think you cannot defeat him, no doubt he thinks it too." He smiled at me. "And that has already given you an edge."

I began to chew on my lower lip, shaking my head. It wasn't that

I failed to appreciate the pep talk or want to believe it, but I wondered when Ryiel had last seen my demon in his sexy, black-feathered array.

"Of course," he continued, watching my face closely, "if your desire to break the contract is false, then you do Gabriel a grave disservice by not telling him."

That pissed me off. "How can you say such a thing?" I snarled. "If I didn't want to break the contract, why am I still here? It would have been easier to just give myself to Satan-in-Waiting when he told me I'd consented to Gabriel's adultery."

"Satan-in-Waiting?"

"He won't tell me his name," I snapped, "so what else am I supposed to call him?"

For a moment we looked at each other. A very large vampire doing his best to look stern and forbidding, and one terrified me, failing miserably at looking as brave as he expected me to be. The panicky feeling inside me was on a massive roller-coaster ride, but it began to subside when Ryiel moved away from the door and sat in the chair opposite me. His arched brow I took as my invitation to resume our conversation. Presumably from a point where I felt comfortable. Trouble was, there was no comfort zone in this topic.

"You say in order to break the contract I have to return the piece of him that's still inside me, and the only way to do this is by kissing him. So does that mean I'd get back the piece of me he stole?"

"He cannot keep it once he has accepted his own back. Yours will return to you of its own accord."

"So then the only difficulty I see is in getting him to kiss me."

"I don't think that's going to be a problem, Rowan. He has already stated his carnal desire for you by gifting you with the Chain. Wearing it will be your declaration of your willingness to capitulate."

"That's all well and good, but wearing the Chain is only half of it. None of this will work if I can't convince him I want him more than Gabriel."

"No, it won't," Ryiel agreed. "Are you a skilled enough seductress to do this?" He sounded hopeful.

I thought back to the only time I'd performed a striptease for Gabriel. Somehow hopping around on one foot while I tried to disentangle my thong from the heel of the stiletto I was still wearing wasn't anywhere near as sexy as I'd thought it would be. Especially not when I fell over, giving Gabriel the kind of view I usually reserved for my gynecologist. All in all, it was a memorable experience, though not for the reason I had hoped. But I did come away with a newfound respect for women who pole dance wearing six-inch heels. In light of that experience, I thought it better if I came clean regarding my limitations as a femme fatale.

"I don't want to do anything that's going to make him suspicious," I told the vampire across from me. "If I'm going to play him, then I'll be more convincing if I keep it as close to the truth as possible."

"How are you going to get him to believe you don't love Gabriel anymore?"

"I'm not. This isn't about love. It's about one-upmanship. I just have to make him believe I want to fuck him more than Gabriel. If he knows anything about the female mind, he'll know all about the need for revenge sex."

"Revenge sex?" Ryiel clearly had no clue how a woman might extract payback if she felt she'd been wronged. Just found out your boyfriend's been cheating on you with that slut in accounting? Go sleep with his best friend. "And you think this will work?" he asked dubiously.

"It better, 'cause I've got nothing else to go with." I blew out a breath. "Of course, the plan is to get him to kiss me and not actually have sex."

"What if he decides to force you?"

I shook my head. "He won't. He could have done that already. It's important to him that I give myself freely, or at least appear to."

"Why?"

"Ego? Bragging rights? Who knows?" I shrugged. "You're male, you tell me."

Wisely, he kept his mouth shut. We both stared at the opals spilling onto the low table between us.

"So you have decided to do this?" Ryiel asked softly.

"You sure there's no other way?"

He put his elbows on the arms of the chair and steepled his fingers beneath his chin. "I truly cannot say, but this solution does seem the best fit for the situation."

I sighed. Then yeah, I was going to do it. For a moment I was tempted to ask him if it really had been his intention to walk out the door and leave me, but then I decided not to. Some questions were better left unanswered. Although he'd been right about one thing. I definitely couldn't tell Gabriel what I was going to do, which meant the sooner I went ahead with this, the better. One look at my face and my lover would know I was going to do something he really wouldn't like.

"And you're certain I actually have to wear that thing?"

Ryiel nodded. "Unless you know of a better way to bring him to you . . . ?"

Guess an e-vite isn't going to work, huh?

"And I have to be completely naked?"

"Of course."

I could feel the heat creep up from below my neck as I asked, "Who's going to help me put it on?"

For the first time since he'd walked through the door, Ryiel looked uncomfortable. He shifted in his seat, sliding toward the edge and putting his chin in his hand. A little like that famous statue of the guy who's thinking.

Betcha he wasn't trying to decide the best way to put an opal the size of a small plum up some girl's whazoo.

"Um . . . I could instruct you . . ."

"I'm going to be naked, Ryiel, and isn't the chain supposed to tie my hands behind my back?"

Ryiel got to his feet and ran his fingers through his hair. He looked very much like a man who had been asked to explain the workings of the Large Hadron Collider to a class of first-graders.

"I cannot touch it," he said, giving me a bleak look.

Fair enough. "Is the victim usually expected to put this on by herself?" He shook his head. "Then who helps her?"

"Another female."

"Does she have to be intimate with the other female too?" Now really didn't seem like the best moment to satisfy any curiosity I might have about girl-on-girl sex. It was a relief to be told no. "Okay, but I'm guessing this other female also isn't human?"

"Probably not."

Well, that put both Laycee and Anasztaizia out of the picture. "Do you know of anyone who could help me?"

You would have thought I'd just asked him to put on a pink tutu and dance the role of a sugar plum fairy in *The Nutcracker*. "I live in an abandoned monastery in the Himalayas," he said in a dazed voice. "How do you suppose I would know anyone who could help you?"

"I don't know, aren't there like vampire bars or something? I mean places where real vampires can hang out with other vampires?" I might as well have been speaking Swahili, except he probably understood that. "So you're telling me you haven't been out or hooked up with anyone since you got to town?"

He made a snarly sound and ran his fingers through his hair in frustration. "In case you hadn't noticed," he muttered, "I've been occupied."

"Hey, don't blame me for asking." I sighed.

"What about the boyfriend? Does he know anyone?" For a moment I thought he'd lost his mind, until I realized he was talking about Aleksei. Trying to come up with a plausible reason would be the problem. I always went to Anasztaizia for help. To exclude her now would send up a red flag. "You couldn't tell her? See if she would ask him?"

I adored Anasztaizia, but I also didn't want anyone I cared about to be on the receiving end of Gabriel's temper when he found out about what I had done. And he would find out. Even the two sentinels were out of the question. Tomas for obvious reasons and Stavros because I'd already seen what the necklace could do. I certainly wasn't about to ask him to put himself at risk for me.

"There has to be someone," Ryiel muttered.

"Yeah, well, I don't think there is. You're just going to have to help me as best you can, and we need to get this done—or else."

He pulled his brows together and gave me a worried look. "Or else . . . what?"

"Or else I'm gonna lose my nerve." I had a feeling if I put this off much longer, finding someone to help adorn me with a ridiculously long piece of jewelry wasn't going to be a problem. I'd just hand myself over to the Dark Realm and be done with it.

"Do you want another drink?" Ryiel asked, picking up my empty glass. I couldn't recall the last time I'd downed three Jack and Cokes in such a short space of time and still been stone-cold sober.

"Yeah, but forget the Coke," I told him. "Actually, you can forget the glass too. Just bring me the bottle." I took two good swigs, spluttered a little, and then waited as the fiery warmth tripped happily down the middle of my chest and pooled in a spot not too far below my navel. I thought about the piece of Satan-in-Waiting that had taken up residency inside me. If he liked bourbon, he'd better make the most of it. I was toying with the idea of taking another mouthful when the doorbell rang.

"You expecting company?" Ryiel asked.

I shook my head. "If we ignore it, perhaps they'll go away." The last thing I needed right now was company. I strained my ears, listening for sounds of movement from out in the hallway. Hearing nothing, I shrugged. "Must've got the wrong apartment," I said.

"No," Ryiel told me, "your visitor is still out there. I can hear movement."

My unknown visitor rang the bell again. Only instead of just ringing the bell, whoever it was decided to annoy the piss out of me by using the chimes to play a mini symphony.

"I hope to God you sprain your finger," I muttered, yanking open the door.

The bell pusher leaned against the wall, a forefinger still depressing the lighted button. I didn't know whether to laugh or cry, but I was certain of one thing. When the Cosmic Wheel of Fate decides to fuck you over, it doesn't hold back.

"Hello, Little One," Katja said, giving me a sickly smile. "Have you missed me?"

Chapter 25

It's funny how the body will have an unexpected reaction to certain things. I know certain smells can bring back a specific memory, transporting you to an exact moment in the past. Sometimes this can be a good thing, especially if the recollection is a good one. Reliving the instant is like slipping on a favorite coat, one that promises to always keep you warm. Other times the memories aren't so great. Being forced to step back into an agonizing freeze-frame of time can be even more excruciating than the original event. Then you had no idea what was coming. Now all bets are off.

I stared at the violet-eyed vampire bitch leaning against the wall, able to feel once more the prick of her sharp nails digging into my upper arms as she held me, and the sting of her fangs puncturing the side of my neck. But the very worst thing was the burning sensation as she tore her mouth across my shoulder, hoping to make me bleed out. If I lost too much blood before Gabriel could get to me, well, that was just too bad. She just hadn't counted on Sebastian coming to my aid. Truth be told, no one had.

"What the fuck are you doing here?"

I should have been on my guard and wary about finding her on my doorstep, but all I felt was a cauldron of bubbling anger set to spill over. There was a ton of stuff I still didn't know about vampires, but I knew a lot more than I had when I'd first met Katja in the Greenley Heights multiplex parking lot. And I was a damn sight more confident of my relationship with Gabriel than I had been then. Playing mind games wasn't going to work this time.

"You might find this hard to believe," she said in a raspy whisper, "but you're not who I'm looking for." I was actually glad to see the flash of animosity that sparked in her eyes. It would have been too awful if she'd suddenly gone all goody-two-shoes on me.

"Then stop hanging on my damn doorbell," I snarled.

I knew Ryiel had moved up behind me when I saw Katja's eyes shift to a spot above my head. "Ah . . . you are here."

I can say in all honesty that Katja was the very last person I ever expected to see again in my lifetime. Even when Stavros first told us she had escaped the monastery, I never thought she'd be so colossally stupid as to come within a hundred miles of either me or Gabriel. I couldn't imagine she thought we were going to forgive and forget. I leaned against the open door and folded my arms.

"How did you know he was here? With me," I added out of spite.

She sighed, peeved at having to explain. "I've been following his scent."

Well, that is what a bitch does, isn't it?

"And where's Vampire Smurf?" I asked.

She gave me a blank stare. "Who?"

Absolutely fucking clueless.

"Your boyfriend. Where's Kartel?"

Her narrow shoulders lifted, and it suddenly became apparent that her slouch against the wall had nothing to do with an insolent attitude on her part. She needed the support.

"I don't know. He left me in Madrid."

"Why?" There was more anger than curiosity in Ryiel's voice.

"Maybe he got tired of me, yes?"

That, I decided, was probably the most honest thing I'd ever heard Katja say. The pencil-thin female vampire shuddered slightly, and I looked at her. She was shivering. I frowned because generally vampires didn't feel the cold. Arctic tundra temperatures maybe, but the sixty-eight degrees in the hallway should have been positively balmy to her. Her behavior warranted a second look. A long second look.

The black hair that I had envied for its glossy sheen had lost its luster. It hung dull and lifeless, still reaching her hips, but the bounce and swing was no longer there. A cloudiness in her eyes dimmed the sparkling purple irises, making them appear washed-out. She wore no lipstick, and her mouth, which I had once almost been tempted to kiss, was now a pale slash in a ghostly face. I glanced at her hands, mimicking mine by being folded across her chest, and saw her nails were devoid of any polish. As I recalled, Katja had been extraordinarily proud of her long manicured nails. Her fashion sense appeared as edgy as ever, but the fringed miniskirt and matching midriff-baring top seemed to hang on her frame. Even the short bolero jacket looked a few sizes too big.

She looks different . . . weak . . . if I didn't know better, I'd say she was sick . . .

I did know better, but even I had to agree with my inner bitch. Katja definitely looked more than a little worse for wear. Her pallor reminded me of another vampire I'd seen recently, though she wasn't quite as bad off. "When was the last time you fed?" I asked.

"Why? Are you offering, Little One?"

"Not if you were the last vampire on the planet," I huffed.

Ryiel put his hand on my shoulder, and—it was bitchy of me, I know—but I smiled seeing the quick flash of distress on her face.

"I am mistaken in coming here," Katja muttered, pushing off the wall and turning away from my door. She managed a few feet, wobbling unsteadily on her high heels, before pitching over. Ryiel was beside me and caught her in his arms before she hit the ground. It was an Oscar-worthy performance.

He turned, concern written all over his face. "Rowan?"

I stared back at him, unable to believe what I was reading in his face. "Oh, come on—you can't be serious? You want me to invite her inside?" Appalled didn't even begin to cover what I was feeling. "You do remember she tried to kill me, right? I mean you actually saw that, right?"

"But now she's the one who's dying."

Oh, puh-leeze!

This was nothing more than vampire theatrics. I was about to ask why I should care, but he saved me from sounding vindictive by pointing out it might not be in my best interest to turn her away.

"She could help you," he said. "She's female and a vampire, and you need the help of both with the Bridal Night Chain."

"She's more likely to strangle me with it."

"I doubt she's got the strength," Ryiel observed.

Do you think it's possible she actually got fucked over by Vampire Smurf?

"Can't think of anyone nicer for it to happen to," I muttered under my breath. Ryiel pretended not to hear me, but the arch of his brow told a different story. "Um, doesn't she have to be able to be awake to be invited in? How else will she know?"

"As long as the incapacitation isn't an overt act of subterfuge—"

"Why don't you just say faking it?"

"I just did," he snapped irritably. Seemed like I wasn't the only one affected by Katja's sudden reappearance.

"And you're sure she'll help me? Any doubts and I'll make you leave her on the goddamn mat."

"She'll help you," Ryiel said confidently, coming toward the door.

"What makes you so sure?"

"Because she came here to ask forgiveness." I was impressed. I never thought Katja would be sorry for what she did to me, much less feel the need to actually apologize. "She came looking for me, Rowan," he reminded. "Not you."

I narrowed my eyes. "And how does apologizing to you translate into helping me?"

I wasn't trying to be difficult, though the expression on Ryiel's face said he thought otherwise. I absolutely did not trust the bitch and wanted to have all my ducks in a row before letting her inside my apartment. It was bad enough I had a demon that could come and go as he pleased. A psychotic vampire bitch was really pushing it.

"Because I won't forgive her unless she does."

I can live with that. Can you live with that?

Yeah, I could. Besides, I really didn't have a choice. I stood on the other side of the open doorway and issued my invitation through gritted teeth, telling myself that if—no, when—I got through this ordeal, Gabriel was definitely moving me to a new apartment.

Ryiel laid Katja down on the couch, and to prove I wasn't a paid-up member in the Bitch-of-the-Year club, I brought him a basin of warm water, a washcloth, and a towel. Kneeling by her side, he carefully wiped the unconscious vampire's face. She looked smaller somehow, kind of shrunken in on herself, and the comment about not having the strength to strangle me didn't seem quite so outlandish.

Bet she'd give it a good try, though . . .

"She looks fucking awful," I muttered.

"You're not so hot yourself." Ah, not quite as unconscious as we thought.

Just hearing the rasp of her voice made my own throat hurt, so I went to the kitchen and got a large glass of water. When I returned, she was sitting up, her arms around Ryiel's neck as he knelt before her. He was murmuring to her in a low voice in a different language—probably her native tongue, if I had to guess. His large hand was rubbing soothing circles over her back. If I didn't know better, I'd say she was crying into his neck. I think Ryiel must have told her I was standing there because she suddenly jerked up and turned her head away from me. The movement of her hands said she was fussing with her face.

"Here, drink this," I said, holding the glass out to her when she turned back around.

Katja's too-bright eyes looked startled, surprised that I was actually addressing her. She stared suspiciously at the glass in my hand. "Yeah, you're right," I told her, "I spit in it." The purity of the contents proved me a liar. Taking the glass from me, she muttered something that sounded an awful lot like *how fucking childish* before drinking down half the glass.

"Whoa," Ryiel said, taking the glass from her hand. "You'll just bring it back up if you drink too quickly." He blotted the corner of her mouth where she hadn't been able to swallow quite fast enough.

"Are you really dying?" I asked.

She gave me a humorless grin. "You must feel like you won the lottery knowing that."

"Not with the kind of day I've had," I snapped back.

Truth be told, I didn't really know how I felt about it. The nightmare of Katja's human childhood seemed to have polluted every aspect of her life as a vampire. Unable to let go of her past, she had allowed it to warp and contaminate every choice she ever made. I didn't feel sad for her—she was five hundred years old, for God's sake!—but how she had lived her life was a conscious determination on her part. Was I happy she was dying? No. It's not like we were ever going to be friends, but I did think to have been used by Kartel was a fucking waste.

"What happened with Kartel? Is he going to show up on my doorstep looking for you?"

"He wouldn't be able to find me even if he wanted to. I'm dying because I'm no longer bonded to him." She paused. "I'm not bonded to anyone."

Okay, but that didn't explain—

"Why haven't you fed?"

"Can't. Is side effect of Kartel's cocktail. Blood won't stay in my body long enough." I saw her reach for Ryiel's hand and squeeze it hard enough to make her already pale knuckles turn skeletal. "You should be happy, Little One. I'm going to starve to death."

"Oh shit." It's true I had wanted her to suffer the same horrible agony she had put Oscar through when she starved him, but now that it was a reality, I felt . . . well, I actually felt kind of shitty. "Can't you have some sort of transfusion or something?"

Katja gave a sharp laugh to stop herself from calling me an idiot. "I am vampire. They don't work with us."

"Oh . . . so what happened? With Kartel, I mean."

Briefly, Katja gave us the rundown on the blue-haired vampire's visit to the monastery. I'll give her credit—she didn't throw any apologetic glances Ryiel's way. If she wanted his forgiveness, I assume it had already been asked for in their private tête-à-tête. She owned up to everything she had done.

"So what went wrong?"

"Why do you think anything went wrong?" Her eyes sparked with a flash of the old fire.

"Because you're here looking like hammered shit. Something didn't go according to plan. What made Kartel break his bond with you?"

God, I hope the bastard suffered like Ryiel had.

"Nothing," she said, slowly draining the glass of water. "The drug's effect is temporary."

"How long does it last?"

"Two days, maybe a little longer." She tried to snap her fingers, but the pad of her thumb couldn't quite make a strong enough connection with her finger to produce any sound. "That's how long it lasted with me. I don't know about the others."

"Others? There were others?"

"You think I was the first Kartel tried it on?"

No, actually that might have been me, and if it wasn't that exact drug, it was definitely some variant.

Looking at Ryiel, Katja said, "You should contact the other Originals. See if there are unexplained disappearances . . . vampires who vanish mysteriously."

"Wouldn't they feel it?" I asked. "Like Ryiel did?"

"Not necessarily," he answered. "Part of the reason I was affected so badly was due to proximity. Katja was practically standing right next to me when the bond broke. Although we have a connection to every vampire we turn, geography and time will weaken the link."

"So if you turned a vampire and never saw him again, you might not know something bad had happened unless you specifically tried to contact him?"

"Something like that."

"Not even if he died?"

"Vampires can and do die, Rowan. Nothing lives forever. And not every vampire who dies is killed by an Original." He shrugged his wide shoulders. "Would you be surprised to know there are vampires who commit suicide? Longevity can be a terrible burden."

Especially if you're facing it alone. I thought of Aleksei and his wish to have Gabriel take his life when his beloved Anasztaizia died. "So Kartel's drug was able to terminate the bond between you and Ryiel, but it only kept you bonded to him for a couple of days?" I picked up her empty glass and went into the kitchen, replenishing it from the filter on the kitchen faucet. "Did it give him enough time?" I asked, returning with a full glass for her.

"For what?"

"To do whatever it was he needed. Didn't he ask you to do something for him?"

"No. He took me clothes shopping," Katja said, making a gesture to her outfit. For some reason, I assumed what she was wearing were clothes she'd had in the monastery. Ryiel made a strange scoffing noise, muttering something in a different language. "He's never heard of Pro Bass Outfitters, that's why," Katja said disdainfully.

"It's Stavros's favorite store." Ryiel smirked.

"And you wonder why I went to his bed with a knife?"

"Children!" I clapped my hands together, making both vampires look at me. "Let's get back on track, shall we?" I turned to Katja. "So you have no idea if the drug you were given lasted long enough for Kartel to accomplish his goal?"

She shook her head. "No, but I don't think it did, because he flew into a terrible rage when he felt me slipping away from him."

"And that's when he left you in Madrid to fend for yourself?" Ryiel murmured more to himself than either of us. "With no money? No resources? No one to reach out to?"

I was going to ask how she had gotten from Europe to the U.S.

but decided I really didn't want to know. "And you have no idea where Vampire Smurf is?"

"Why do you keep calling him that?"

"It's a reference to his hair and a cartoon from her childhood," Ryiel told her, making my mouth drop open. I had no idea he knew. He shrugged nonchalantly. "Tomas told Stavros, Stavros told me."

Katja dismissed the explanation. "No, I have no idea where Kartel went after he left me."

She grabbed for the towel as a fit of coughing suddenly overtook her. The effort to clear the irritant in her throat and airway was exhausting, and I saw blood on the towel when she was finally done. It seemed to me she was growing weaker by the minute. I looked at Ryiel, but his expression was shuttered and told me nothing. If he cared for her—and on some level I knew he did—he was keeping it to himself. Or perhaps this was his way of showing his affection. There was too much about the silver-eyed vampire that was a mystery. One thing I was sure of, however; if Katja was going to help me, it had to be now. She wasn't going to do me any good if she collapsed trying to tie me up.

"Did Ryiel tell you what I need you to do?" Her glance, coupled with the sudden tightening of his jaw, told me he had not. I waited until the prolonged silence forced him to look at me. "Did you forgive her?" At least he had the decency to look somewhat abashed as he nodded. "Of course you did," I murmured softly.

"What do you want from me, Little One?"

"To help me put on a Bridal Night Chain," I said as calmly as I could.

"Me?"

A part of me was expecting a flat-out no because, well, it was me asking. Another part thought she might fall into hysterical laughter that I would think she'd even consider helping me. What I hadn't expected was the grave consideration with which she pondered my request before asking to see the Chain. I fetched the jewelry box and opened the lid. She didn't try to touch the necklace as any other woman would have; instead, she deliberately put her hands behind her. She looked at me, then at Ryiel, then back at me.

"Gabriel didn't give you that," she stated in a flat voice.

"No, of course not," I told her. "Why would you think this was from him?"

She glanced at Ryiel, and something passed between them. Some warning, I think. "If you think I will help, then first I need to know where this came from . . . and what you are planning."

"Is that absolutely necessary?" I was of the opinion that the fewer people who knew, the better.

"If you want my help . . ." She shrugged and spread her hands. "Let me save you the trouble of lying to me, Little One." Cautiously she touched the box with a forefinger, almost as if she thought it might be alive, waiting to uncoil itself and strike anyone foolish enough to come close. "This has come from the Dark Realm, which means you are playing with fire. I need to know what will happen when everything goes wrong."

"Why do you think that's going to happen?"

"You and the Dark Realm are not a good mix," she said, giving me a weary smile. "Now, will you tell me, or should I leave?"

It took surprisingly less time than it had taken her to tell us about Kartel. But then I wasn't doing a bang-up impersonation of a consumptive on her deathbed. She stared at me for a long time after I was done, and when she finally spoke, it was to Ryiel.

"You approve of this plan?"

"Can you think of another?"

Please say yes, please say yes—and please let it not involve me being naked with a large opal placed in my vagina.

Using Ryiel's arm for support, Katja slowly got to her feet, not bothering with her shoes.

"Come," she said, holding out a hand to me.

"What are you going to do?"

"If you're hoping to keep your head attached to your neck for longer than five minutes, then you have to look like you want to sleep with him." She gave me a disdainful look. "We need to do something with your hair and—do you have makeup?"

"What do you need me to do?" Ryiel asked, sounding relieved to have the matter taken out of his hands. At least temporarily.

"Find another bottle of liquor," Katja told him, gesturing to the bourbon on the table. "That's not going to be enough."

Chapter 26

"Do you have any idea what you are doing?"

"Kinda, sorta."

Katja snorted. "So in other words, no." She stared at me as I sat on the closed lid of the toilet. "What do you think is going to happen when the demon finds out you're lying?"

"What makes you think he'll find out?"

She rolled her eyes. "You're not that good a liar, and he's a demon—they *always* find out."

I shrugged. "Well, in that case, I guess he's gonna be pissed."

Her laugh was a watered-down version of what I'd heard before. "You have no idea," she told me. Moving to the counter, Katja began sorting through the makeup I'd provided. She discarded all of it save for a kohl pencil, eyeliner, and a small pot of dark-green glittery eyeshadow I'd bought for Halloween. "No false lashes?" she asked.

"Um, no. I don't wear them."

"You should. They would make a big difference." Blowing out a breath, she pulled some mascara from the discard pile. "Well, I suppose this will have to do," she muttered irritably.

"Look, I don't need any lectures," I snapped. We'd only been in the bathroom a few minutes and she was already pissing me off. One more word or eyeball roll and I would march out and tell Ryiel his choice of helper sucked.

A sharp line appeared between Katja's brows as she frowned. "You're scared." From the tone of her voice, it was clear this had never occurred to her.

I shook my head. "I went beyond scared some time ago. I'm now fucking terrified. Does that make you feel better?"

Picking up my hairbrush, she shrugged. "You're scared and I'm dying. We make a perfect couple."

She gestured for me to turn around, and even though I was loath to do it, I complied. At least I could watch her reflection in the glass wall of the shower unit. Katja was quick and efficient, brushing my hair free of tangles. I was surprised, however, when she separated it into three parts and made a loose braid. From her disparaging remark about needing to do *something* with my hair, I had expected it to be more imaginative.

"How is me looking like a Viking princess going to get a demon all hot and bothered?" I murmured, as Katja tied a length of ribbon below the nape of my neck but above the start of the braid.

"This isn't for him," she said, fastening more ribbon to the end of my hair. "This is for Gabriel . . . to remember you by."

"I . . . what . . . ?"

I never saw where she got the scissors from. There was just the flash of steel glinting in the glass in front of me as Katja pulled the braid with one hand and cut through the hair above the top ribbon.

"Oh, you fucking bitch!" I yelled, feeling the unexpected hot prick of tears behind my eyes. Whirling to my feet, I shoved her, completely ignoring the fact she was holding a very large pair of shears in her hand. A thrust in any one of a half-dozen places would have easily incapacitated me, only she didn't attack me or even try to defend herself. Instead, she stumbled back, her shoulder striking the corner of the towel rack, making her suck in a breath and wince in pain. Seeing the length of braid still in her hand, I yanked it from her grasp. "What the fuck have you done?" I snarled.

This was my hair, truly my best feature, but one I'm ashamed to say I never really gave much thought to until I knew how much it pleased Gabriel. He would wrap it around his hands during sex or drape it over his arm when I lay next to him. Every time we showered he would wash it, comb conditioner through it, and make sure it was rinsed squeaky clean. And he loved brushing it. I'd never known anyone before who could make the act of separating tangles a truly erotic experience. And now it would be a long time before he ever did it again.

I stared at the thick, chestnut-colored skein in my hands, truly appreciating for the first time the glorious shade of deep brown highlighted with just enough burgundy to add depth and warmth. My God, how could you not want to run your fingers through it? No wonder Gabriel always preferred I wear it down. He was forever twisting a curl around his finger, wanting to bury his face in it—Christ! I wanted to do the same thing, but now . . . now . . .

"It will grow back if you survive," Katja croaked from her semi-slumped position against the bathroom wall.

Even though what she said was true, it would never be quite the same. I sneered at her own hip-length mane, the braid in my fist twitching as my hand shook with anger. "You ever had this done to you?"

Ignoring my glare, she got wearily to her feet. "When I was thirteen, I was dressed up and taken to a nobleman's house. I don't know why, but two princes were visiting. I was given to them to play with. They were not so much younger than me, and the smaller of them wasn't so bad. Of course he did everything his older brother told him to do. And this one, the firstborn, he already understood he could do whatever he wanted to me and not have to answer for it. They stripped me naked, tied me up, and cut off my hair. It took them a while because the knife they used wasn't very sharp, which was a good thing for me, and it's probably more accurate to say they pulled out more of my hair than they actually cut."

I could see the memory burning brightly behind her eyes. The fear and terror at having been abused, and anger at knowing she'd been unable to prevent it.

"When they were done with my hair," Katja continued, "the older one forced my mouth open so his brother could piss in it. I suppose I should be grateful his aim was bad. Of course the younger boy already knew he could not do the same for his big brother. Not without losing a finger." Seeing the look on my face, she smiled. "Don't worry, Little One. I went back to see them not long after I was made vampire. I made certain they both died slowly and horribly. And that is the only time I can remember having my hair cut," she added with a frown.

She was seized by another coughing fit—one that was violent enough to make her double over and wrap an arm around her midriff. I put the braid on the counter and grabbed a hand towel from near the sink, giving it to her in exchange for the scissors. Now it was my turn to escort her to the toilet so she could sit down. High spots of color stained her cheeks, and she hawked up something phlegmy and spit it into the towel.

I caught sight of myself in the mirror and, startled, took a step back. My hand trembled as I put it on the nape of my neck, feeling the cool blow of air across my skin. My entire head felt strange, lighter.

"You can thank me later," Katja said, watching me.

"Don't hold your breath," I told her. Folding my arms across my chest, I made a decision. "I think you've done enough, Katja. Perhaps it would be better if you left."

"Don't be ridiculous. You can't put the Chain on by yourself."

"I'll find a way."

She pounded her fist on the counter. "Stop being such a fucking baby—it's only *hair*." She pulled in a deep breath, struggling to maintain control. "You want to go to the Dark Realm and tell a demon you'd rather fuck him than Gabriel, then you'd better *look* like you mean it. You think he doesn't know the hold Gabriel has on you? That he won't be able to smell Gabriel on your skin, taste him in your mouth. You think this demon won't notice the way your body responds to him and know the difference?"

She got up from the toilet seat and grabbed me by the upper arms. And I knew, if I really needed to, I could shake her off with very little effort.

"If you want him to believe the lie," Katja continued, "and want any chance of coming back, then you have to look the part. Become something he's not expecting. If you go to him, looking the way you look for Gabriel, you're telling this demon that all he's getting is sloppy seconds. Not quite the message you want to send, I'm thinking. At least let him think you've made some effort to put Gabriel behind you."

Her words made sense, and I understood what she was saying. But I still wished she hadn't cut off my hair.

"It's your decision, Little One. Are you going to go through with this . . . or not?" The scissors magically appeared in her hand again.

I shuddered, closed my eyes for a moment and took in a deep breath. "Yeah, I'm in."

"Good. Let us finish this then."

Katja wasn't as skilled as Laycee, but then I doubt my best friend would have been able to distance herself and do what was needed. I was going to catch hell from her when she saw my new do.

If she sees it . . .

"Okay . . . shower," Katja said, putting down the scissors.

This was where I assumed she would leave me, but she simply leaned against the sink.

"You want to wash me too?" I asked.

"I'm going to see you naked soon enough, Little One. Let's get this over with so there won't be any surprises."

"What are you expecting? An extra boob or something?"

"You better hope not. It is my understanding that a Bridal Night Chain is a most precise piece of jewelry. I need to see if there will be any difficulties putting it on."

I took *difficulties* to mean any cellulite in my hips and thighs. My resentment simmered as I turned my back and stripped. I reached for the shower door, but her voice told me to turn around. The way I was clenching my jaw, I was in danger of cracking a molar. I could feel her eyes scanning me from head to toe, taking note of every freckle as she did so. And I have a lot of freckles.

"A heart, really?" She smirked, pointing to my groin. I wasn't about to tell her it had been Gabriel's idea, or that it had been his hand shaving me. "Razor or cream?"

"What?"

She put a hand on her hip and gave me a withering look. "Get rid of all body hair, and I do mean all of it. Arms, legs, pits, everywhere."

"What, you don't want me to turn this into a skull?" I gestured to the heart.

"Not if you expect me to insert a jewel inside you."

When I emerged from the shower, Katja handed me a shot of bourbon, which I knocked back without any hesitation. "No wonder Aleksei likes you," she said, giving me what was possibly the first genuine smile I'd ever received from her. "You would have made a good Russian."

"Maybe I was, in a previous life."

"Not in the past five hundred years, Little One. I would have known."

I had no idea what to say to that, so I said nothing. Katja sat me back down on the toilet and busied herself with my makeup. She frowned and pouted as she applied powder and eyeliner, not allowing me to see until she proclaimed herself satisfied. I turned around and my mouth dropped open.

The inside of my eyelids were rimmed with kohl, while a liberal sweep of eyeliner went all the way from each inner corner to the outer edge of my eyebrows. These too had been heavily shaded and arched in a way I would have considered cartoonish, but somehow looked . . . okay. With the amount of eye shadow she'd used, I needed exaggerated brows. Katja had covered my entire lid with the dark-green glittery shadow, using it alongside my nose so it now looked thinner and more patrician. My cheekbones were highlighted, and more clever shading in the hollow and along my jaw made my face look hungry in a completely immoral way. My mouth was now a ver-million pout, thanks to an extended outline and lip gloss that was not mine. Bourbon wasn't the only thing Katja had brought back with her while I was taking a shower.

"False lashes would have been easier," she murmured, giving me a critical look.

I don't know what she was worrying about. With the amount of mascara I was wearing, there was a good probability my own lashes would simply snap off when it came time for me to clean my face. But the crowning glory—with no pun intended—had to be my hair. After another go-round with the scissors, followed by some drying and gelling, the end result rivaled a porcupine on steroids.

"Holy fuck," I muttered, slightly shell-shocked at my transformation.

"Good fuck or bad fuck?" Katja asked, putting another shot of Jack in my hand.

"I don't know," I admitted, tossing down the drink and feeling a fire explode in my chest. "I've never . . . I didn't know I could look . . ."

"Let's go see what something with a cock and balls thinks."

She was out the door before I could register my disapproval of her disrespect. Making sure the end of my towel was tucked tightly between my breasts, I followed my stylist into the living room. Ryiel said nothing, but his eyes narrowed and his nostrils flared. I had no idea if his reaction was good or bad. Katja's shrug was all *he's-male-so-what-does-he-know* and told me nothing. But it really made no difference. Nothing to be done about it now.

"I want you to promise me something, Ryiel," I said, looking at him. He seemed astounded to hear my voice emerging from such an unfamiliar face.

"What is it?"

"Nu-huh. You have to promise me first that you'll do it." I watched as he considered the possible ramifications of making such an agreement with me. I really couldn't blame him. We wouldn't be here now if I had been more careful with words and promises. God knows my track record would have made any other vampire refuse me without so much as a second thought. "It doesn't involve the Dark Realm or babies or your Promise," I assured him.

"Your Promise?" Katja seemed surprised. "You have summoned Sinisia to you?" The big vampire nodded, and her expression became one of disappointment. I wondered what had happened between them to cause such a reaction.

"It was time, Katja," he told her in a gentle voice.

"Of course it was. I just . . ." Her voice trailed off as she became lost in her own thoughts.

"Very well, Rowan," Ryiel said, turning to me. "I give you my word."

I took a deep breath and hoped both my heart and voice would let me say what was necessary.

"Don't let Gabriel come after me, no matter what happens. If I do not come back by myself, then it's because I cannot . . . because whatever is left of me should not come back. Do you understand?" I walked over and placed the skein of hair that Katja had cut off in his hands. "Give this to him . . . and tell him I love him, very much."

He started to say something, but I turned away. He'd already given me his word. I didn't need anything else.

The necklace box was on the low coffee table. I picked it up and looked at Katja. "Okay, where are we going to do this?"

"The bedroom? You might feel more comfortable there."

Suddenly I was glad that Aleksei and Anasztaizia had broken my bed. I might not be able to go through with what I needed to do if I was reminded of Gabriel holding onto the headboard as he thrust into me. Didn't stop me from hesitating at the door, though. A large hand came from behind me and pushed it open. My hesitation turned to alarm when I realized Ryiel was following me into the room.

"Wasn't Katja going to do this?" I asked, clutching the towel between my breasts a little tighter.

"She is," he rumbled, "but Katja doesn't know how to put it on, so I will instruct her."

Oh goody. Now I got to have two vampires seeing me in my birthday suit.

Chapter 27

R yiel told me there was a method to putting on this particular piece of jewelry. I nodded, hearing him but not really hearing. All I could think of was how he seemed to dwarf the room. Sensing my sudden apprehension, he stepped forward and cradled my face in his large hands.

"Don't be embarrassed, Rowan. When I see you I feel nothing but admiration for your courage." He tilted my head so I was now looking up at him. His eyes were a starburst of silver and black. "Look deep inside you. This is not the first time you have shown such resolve. Find that memory, Rowan. Use its strength to help you do whatever is necessary."

I had absolutely no idea what he was talking about. I couldn't imagine ever being in a situation that would require the grit and determination I was going to need if I had any hope of pulling this off. Leaning down, Ryiel pressed his lips against my forehead, and his kiss felt like a blessing, a benediction.

"By the way," he murmured gently, "I love what you've done with your hair."

I laughed and dropped the towel. It was no use pretending either vampire was somehow not going to look at me naked. The sooner we all got used to it, the better. Especially for me. "What now?" I asked, trying my best not to sound anxious.

"Hand Katja the necklace," Ryiel said. "It's important that it comes from your hands to hers."

I hesitated. "Are you sure it won't burn her?" I had assumed she would be able to handle the opals, but no one had actually *said* she could. It would be pointless if she couldn't hold the gems.

"It won't as long as the necklace is passed from your hand to hers. You are giving your permission for her to help you," Ryiel said.

"And I couldn't do this with you?"

"Absolutely not." He looked shocked that I would even consider such a thing. "No intimacy exists between us and even if I had your permission, I am male. It is forbidden."

Cupping Katja's outstretched hand I pooled the necklace into her palm, watching as it overspilled her fingers. I sighed with relief as she appeared to suffer no adverse reaction.

"Now, go stand over there," Ryiel instructed, pointing his finger.

"Why there?"

"It's the center of the room."

"Is that important?"

"Well, it means Katja will be able to move around you."

"You really don't want me falling over, Little One," she smirked. "With a length of Chain in my hand I might accidentally choke you."

I knew it—accidentally my ass!

"Oh, I'm sure Ryiel will keep an eye on you," I told her.

I went to the spot Ryiel had pointed to and stood, trying to resist the urge to cover my pink and freshly shaved mons with my hands. Trust me, it wasn't easy. The carpet beneath my feet was a thick pile, and the padding far more generous than what was normally laid, but I could still feel the hard floor beneath the balls of my feet.

"Now," Ryiel continued, "I'm going to instruct Katja, but it's better that I do so in her own language. You're only going to have one chance of getting this right, and I need to make sure there is no misunderstanding."

He rattled off a long string of words that sounded like he was in desperate need of something to relieve indigestion. Katja nodded, appearing to agree with his preference for Pepto-Bismol over Maalox.

"Try to relax," Katja murmured, "and stop looking so ashamed. Your body is . . . okay. Not great, but okay."

Well, I'll be . . . was that an actual compliment?

I wasn't ashamed per se, but I did feel uncomfortable having two complete strangers see me naked. I think the reason vampires don't have any insecurities about being naked around us is because they know how perfect their bodies appear to humans. That kind of edge does wonders for the ego. I don't know what Ryiel felt as he looked at me. Hopefully, it was nothing more than a mild clinical interest. He might gaze at the inking in the small of my back, admiring the dexterity of the tattoo artist who unknowingly marked me with Gabriel's name. Katja, however, was different. I could feel her eyes scrutinizing and cataloging every flaw and blemish she found.

"You know I still don't like you, right?" I said, looking her in the eye.

"Of course." She returned my look with one that was puzzled. "Why? Did you think we would go shopping?"

I snorted. "God, I hope not."

"Little One, I've seen your wardrobe. Trust me, you could only wish I wanted to take you shopping." Seen my wardrobe? Like hell she had. I'd caught her admiring my La Perla undies in the bathroom. "By the way, it's a shame Gabriel has to restrain himself with you."

"Restrain?" I arched a brow.

"All that excess energy has to be released somehow." She stared at the shattered pieces of the bed frame, piled neatly on the floor.

"That was Aleksei and Anasztaizia." I leaned forward and put my lips next to her ear. "I let them use my apartment. I'm sure if you sniff the mattress you could still pick up Aleksei's scent, unless of course your sense of smell has gone."

"Did you know I was his first," she said, ignoring my invitation. "Aleksei was quite a memorable lover."

It seemed to take the wind right out of her sails when I mentioned Aleksei had told me the same thing. Not the memorable lover part, but about Katja being his first.

"Enough," Ryiel interrupted. "No more talking." He snapped something at Katja in her own tongue, and she gave him an exaggerated sigh. He was intuitive enough to sense that whatever détente Katja and I had agreed to, it could unravel in a heartbeat with one wrong word. I watched Katja smirk behind his back, so I stuck out my tongue. Childish? You bet, but it made me feel better.

I wasn't fooling myself about the female vampire. Katja was unstable, unpredictable, and I didn't believe for one minute she was over her obsession with Gabriel. Her willingness to help me now was only because her run-in with Kartel had gone unexpectedly awry. The chance to see me naked and on my knees was just too good to pass up. Life, I decided, really was filled with the most amazing twists and turns.

I felt pressure against my throat and realized the necklace was around my neck, much like a choker would be. Katja gave a little tug, enjoying my discomfort before a low growl had her backing off. Following Ryiel's directives, she moved with a quiet efficiency, winding the long string of dark opals around each shoulder blade before coming back under my arms. I'd like to say the few traces of sympathy I saw on her face were genuine concern for me, but I knew better. Making Ryiel believe she was capable of compassion was more like it. And it was a lie. The chain of smooth stones now circled each breast before crossing over my stomach to go behind my back once more.

"Hands," she murmured in my ear. I hesitated, waiting for Ryiel's nod before complying. "Palms together." When most people put their hands behind their back in order to be restrained, they usually put them side by side, palms facing outward. The awkward position Katja had requested put an immediate strain on my shoulders. From the complicated looping and crossing over that was happening behind me, it was going to be impossible for me to free my hands.

I think that's the idea, let's not forget this is all about submission . . .

I jerked when I felt Katja touch the cheek of my ass. The cool feel of her fingers coupled with the unexpectedness of the touch made my pulse quicken and my heart rate boom.

"It has to go between your legs and come out in front."

I don't know why she was whispering; it wasn't as if Ryiel couldn't hear her. But perhaps she finally got what I was doing and was trying to make me feel better. Or not. I parted my legs slightly, enabling her to pass the chain between them. The process of securing my hands had reduced the chain to a single strand of opals, with the largest stone fastened to the last link. I stared down at the dark, apricot-sized gem now looped over Katja's fingers. The red and green striations seemed to glow, making the damn thing look as if it was winking lasciviously at me.

Katja drew in a breath—one deep enough to make her nostrils flare. She had a hole pierced in her left naris, something I realized must have been done before she was turned. I don't know why I found it so extraordinary. People have been piercing various body parts for well over a thousand years. Having her nose pierced sometime in the sixteenth century would not have been so strange.

"You understand what this means," she said, turning the opal over so it lay in her palm. "Once this is inside you, it can only be removed in one way . . . by one person."

"Yeah . . . I know." Trepidation made my voice husky. "I'm just worried it might fall out when I move."

"It won't," Ryiel said. "It's charmed."

I snorted. "Charmed? That's not exactly what I'd call it." I looked down at Katja, who was looking back up at me with a steady, un-flinching gaze. "Go ahead," I told her. "Put it in."

She actually didn't have to touch me, which was a godsend as far as I was concerned. The moment the edge of the opal made contact with my skin, it kind of jumped out of her fingers and slid inside me almost as if it had a mind of its own. There was no real pain. Just an uncomfortable feeling of *fullness* in a way that was totally different from having Gabriel inside me.

"Are you okay?" Katja asked.

Whether real or as a way of appeasing Ryiel, she did look con-cerned.

I nodded. "Yeah . . . I'm okay."

I clenched my inner muscles to see how the stone would react and was mildly disgusted to feel it move with me. There was nothing at all sexually exciting or stimulating about it. I inhaled deeply and then ex-haled slowly. My heart was still beating like a Triple Crown winner.

That's a good thing. If you're thinking about having hot sex with a demon, it should be racing. I decided not to chastise my inner bitch. She would be my only companion on this descent to the Dark Realm, so I wasn't about to alienate her. God knows I needed all the friendly voices in my head I could find.

"What now?" I stared at the silver-eyed vampire, doing my best to swallow down the fear that was trying to claw its way out through my throat.

"He should find you kneeling," Ryiel said. With his hand on my elbow and being careful not to let his fingers touch any of the opals, Ryiel helped lower me to the carpet. If I thought it had been a chore standing on it, I could already tell it was going to be murder on my knees. He dropped to my side, gracing me with one of his special-moment smiles. "Now you wait."

The sound of Katja inhaling a breath told me she was going to say something, but I really wasn't in the mood. Seeing the look in my eye, Ryiel said something that had her making a smart about-face and exiting the room without sparing me as much as a glance over her shoulder.

"How long do I have to wait?" I could feel the panic starting to rise. What if Gabriel came before the demon? There was no way I could keep him out.

"Don't worry," Ryiel assured me. "The Chain is calling to him. He knows you are waiting."

I swallowed and forced myself to be calm. "Then you had better leave and make sure Katja leaves with you."

He stood, and I tried to look up at him, but the configuration of the chain would only let me raise my head so far. "Keep your promise to me, Ryiel."

He nodded, his dark hair flowing around him like a cape. "I will."

I didn't see him leave because I closed my eyes, but he left the bedroom door open so I could hear the latch of the apartment door click when he closed it firmly behind him.

I had never felt so alone. Or so terrified.

Chapter 28

I had no idea how much time had passed since Ryiel left. It might have been ten minutes or five hours.

If it was five hours your muscles would have seized up!

Good point. And it was nice to know my inner bitch had not abandoned me.

There was a part of me that kept clinging to the foolish notion that Ryiel was going to suddenly appear in the open doorway yelling "Gotcha!" and applaud me for being such a good sport and playing along. Of course, the reality of my situation said no way in hell would any prank pulled by a vampire involve getting me naked. Or include Katja in the planning.

This was no prank.

I took a couple of deep breaths. Inhaling deeply, exhaling slowly. If I didn't do something to restore my heartbeat to a more normal rhythm, I was going to keel over before I had a chance to fix anything.

Um, just so I'm sure I understand . . . why are we doing this again?

Because I refuse to live the rest of my life with the Sword of Damocles hanging over my head. It's enough I know the Dark Realm exists, but allowing this demon the freedom to interfere in my life—and the lives of those I love—is completely unacceptable to me. He crossed a line using Laycee, and if I have the chance to right this, I will.

But Laycee is not in danger anymore, and neither is her baby.

True, but the weak link in this entire scenario is me. The only way to be sure he can't hurt anyone else I care about is to deny him access to me, and the only way to do that is to break the contract between us.

This plan isn't foolproof, you know.

Nothing ever is, but it's all I have, and I will make it enough.

Good. As long as you understand . . .

If my inner bitch was able to manifest herself into a real person, I would have wrapped her up in a big Aleksei-style bear hug. Just as fear was about to overwhelm me, she brought me back into focus, reminding me of why I needed to do this.

And one last thing . . . why are you decked out like some sort of expensively wrapped sacrificial offering?

Because I have it on good authority that demons love receiving gifts. Especially the bright shiny kind. Now go rest up. If I have any hope at all of being convincing, I'm going to need your help.

Piece of advice?

Sure. I'll take all the help I can get.

Don't try to seduce him. That's not what he's looking for, and besides, with that hairdo, you'll never pull it off.

Gee, thanks.

My heartbeat had returned to a more normal rhythm, and although I fully expected it to explode into racing cheetah speed the moment he appeared, I was hopeful my demon would be vain enough to assume he was the cause. It's not like I was going to be able to hide it from him. The ache in my shoulders was starting to really bother me, and my thigh muscles were flirting with the notion of cramping. Unfortunately, because of my unique necklace, there was no way I could reposition myself.

You're supposed to be submissive, and that nearly always includes kneeling.

Good reminder.

"Oh my God—what the hell are you doing?"

I turned my head and groaned to see Gabriel standing in the doorway, his hands clutching either side of the doorjamb. I could see the strain on his biceps as he looked at me in horror. I shouldn't have been that surprised, and yet I was. Since he knew Ryiel wanted to talk to me in private, I would have expected Gabriel to remain at the penthouse until he heard from me. And Ryiel had given me his word he would say nothing. It seemed that someone hadn't been able to keep his promise.

"Gabriel . . . go away. You're not supposed to be here."

"Ahhh, sweetheart, no. I can't let you do this."

I've never seen him look more hopeless, more filled with despair. What I had done, what I was doing, was far worse than any other mistake I'd made with him.

"Gabriel . . . you have to go."

He crossed the room and dropped to his knees before me. Reaching out with his hand, he cupped my chin and raised my head so I could look at him. "You don't have to do this, Rowan. Not for me. I promise we'll find a way to get through this. We still have almost twenty-five years to find a way out—"

"Stop!" I snapped.

I stared at him, narrowed my eyes, and took a long, hard look. He stared back. The devil, as they say, is in the details.

Or the demon is in making a mistake . . .

Something about this whole scenario was off. It felt slippery and wrong. I was looking at Gabriel, but my sense of him was fractured. It was as if I was only being allowed to see a part of him, which didn't make sense unless . . .

"God, you're so fucking arrogant," I sneered. "You really think I would go to all this trouble for you?"

"What are you saying?"

His voice dropped to a husky whisper that was almost right, but not quite. Just as his eyes were almost the perfect shade of neon-blue, but were now darker at the edges—something I'd never seen before. Praying I wasn't making a mistake, I swept my eyes over him, taking in his customary all-black wardrobe of shirt, pants, and boots. Boots I couldn't help but notice as he'd crossed the room because the silver tips glinted at me. Gabriel wore biker boots. He wouldn't be caught dead in cowboy boots. Slowly, I let my eyes travel up to the hand that was now resting on his thigh. The hand that bore no wedding ring. The circle of mahogany between twin bands of platinum had stayed on his finger since the day I'd put it on. Gabriel never took it off, but he wasn't wearing it now. And then there was his comment about still having twenty-five years. How could that be when Ryiel had already negated Gabriel's obligation to take Jenna's virginity?

With a jerk of my head, I pulled my chin from his grasp. "Okay, if you want to stay and watch, be my guest. But don't say I didn't warn you."

"You're not seriously going to go through with this?"

Another mistake. Where was the outrage? The man I loved would not be pleading with me. He'd be all kinds of pissed and making sure I knew it.

"You're not listening to me, Gabriel." I made a noise of disgust. "That's the problem, you never do. Look, the sex is great, but I need something more, and if you'd been paying any attention to me, you would know that."

"What do mean *something more?* What more? I've given you everything—"

"Have you? Have you really?" I prayed my eyes weren't deceiving me. "You had that bitch in here, *in my bed!* Did you think I couldn't smell her?"

He stared at me, and the look of horror he'd worn on first seeing me was nothing compared to the expression on his face now. It was all the confirmation I needed. I tossed back my head and smiled at him. "Why do you think I had Aleksei break the bed for me?"

He got to his feet and took a few staggering steps toward the door. "If you go through with this, Rowan, you know there's no coming back. I won't be able to look at you again, not after you've been with him."

"Don't let the door hit you on the ass on the way out," I mumbled under my breath, knowing he would hear each word clearly. A few seconds later there came a loud retort as the front door banged shut, and even though I knew in my heart it had not been Gabriel kneeling before me, I still had to fight down the urge to weep.

At least you know Ryiel didn't break his promise to you.

Yeah . . .

I swallowed and felt a mild scratchiness in the back of my throat. My mouth was dry, and I suddenly noticed how warm the air was, but more than that, it felt heavy and thick. Fine time for my thermostat to go on the fritz!

I don't think it's your thermostat . . .

I tried to pull a breath into my lungs, but whereas it hadn't been a problem a few moments ago, now I couldn't seem to manage a normal inhale. Reduced to taking short half-breaths, I began to pant like one of those dogs with a smooshed-in nose and a tongue constantly lolling out the side of its mouth. Perspiration began to bead on my forehead and upper lip. There was a clammy feeling at the back of my neck. If this kept up, I was in serious danger of sweating off Katja's carefully designed makeover.

I closed my eyes, straining to hear any sounds coming from beyond the bedroom door, but all I could hear were my own increased wheezing and the rush of blood filling my ears. A drop of moisture rolled between my brows and took the direct route to the end of my nose, where it hung perilously, trembling and quivering, before letting go and splashing on my thigh. Like lemmings throwing themselves off the edge of a cliff, once one had taken the plunge, others followed. In a matter of only seconds, I'd gone from perspiring and leapfrogged into full-fledged sweating. I pulled on my lower lip. The sticky feeling on my teeth told me I was scraping off the bright-red lip gloss. I was more upset that Katja had declared deodorant a no-no.

"No lotion, no powder, no perfume or deodorant," she told me as I dried off after my shower.

"Seriously?"

Turning my head I sniffed. I was still odor-free, but for how long was anyone's guess. It seemed to me that the temperature was climbing. Was it just here in the bedroom, or was the entire apartment getting toasty? I was pretty sure the air around me had now cranked up to sauna level. My scalp began to prickle, and the hair at the back of my neck was wet. I could feel my spiky new do beginning to wilt. Gel and hairspray can only withstand so much. Droplets of moisture trickled between my shoulder blades, heading down my back. I pressed my bound hands against my skin. The last thing I wanted was a salty sting in the crack of my ass. Unfortunately, I couldn't do anything about my face.

Wetness pooled at my temples and streaked a rivulet down the side of my face and along my jaw. In a matter of moments I was wet all over. And not, in my opinion, in a good way.

I let out a moan. The ache in my shoulders from having my hands tied behind me was getting unbearable, and my muscles began to spasm from the constrained position. I looked down and saw my thigh begin to flutter and jump in a way I'd never seen it do before.

"Awww shit!" I yelled. "If you're coming, would you goddamn get your ass here!"

"Your wish," said a voice from the doorway, "is my command."

I shook my head and blinked back the salty sweat that was stinging my eyes. "What did you do? Stop for pizza?"

He chuckled. "I do like a woman who can make me laugh."

My demon was in his Armani suit persona, and I couldn't help but notice that everything was exactly the same. Too much the same to be a coincidence. It occurred to me that perhaps he didn't actually get dressed or put on clothing the way humans and vampires did. If so, surely he would change the tie or his jewelry or his shoes. Perhaps all he had to do was simply picture the image he wanted to present in his mind, and—*presto chango*—he became it. Certainly would explain a lot.

"Sold any cars lately?" I wheezed, sounding more like an asthmatic pug with every passing minute.

He looked at me, his gaze dark and penetrating as it lingered on every glistening curve of my body. I didn't care. He could look all he wanted. The sooner he was done, the sooner I could get to my feet. Hopefully.

"You look different," he commented.

No shit, Sherlock! "Yeah . . . I got my hair done."

"Your face looks different too."

"New lipstick," I told him. Without the benefit of a mirror or any other reflective surface close at hand, I could only imagine the mess I looked. All the sweating, which showed no signs of slowing down, must have done a real number on my makeup. Still, there was no accounting for what some men find attractive. From the slow smile that lifted his mouth, the train wreck look was obviously a favorite of his.

"You're wearing my gift," he said, stepping closer to me. "And I was so sure I'd have to wait a little longer before I saw it on you. Like twenty-five years longer."

"What can I say? I'm a girl who likes to open all her presents at once and try them on to make sure they fit."

"And do they?" He stared pointedly at my groin.

"Hard to tell from this angle," I told him. "Why don't you see for yourself?"

"Oh, I fully intend to, Rowan." He gave me a flash of his teeth as he smiled. I couldn't believe how cool he looked. Not in a polished, urbane way, although he was all that too, but more of a completely non-sweaty kind of way. He wasn't even shiny, damn him!

I groaned, feeling a spasm in my side. "Any chance of loosening this up a little?"

Oooh, that's good, make him think you want to keep wearing it.

"I don't think you quite grasp the implications that come with wearing such an item," he said walking slowly around me. "You're supposed to be submissive, offering yourself to my will." Having satisfied himself that I was properly bound and secured as per the current demonic handbook regulations, he now dropped to his haunches before me. It was eerily reminiscent of the pose Gabriel had just taken before me.

"I assumed the whole meek and dutiful thing was more a suggestion than an actual requirement."

"Really? Why ever would you think that?"

"Are you telling me this Bridal Night Chain is more than symbolic? Sorry to disappoint you, but I'm really not into marriage. If I was, I'd already be married to Gabriel." I couldn't be sure, but I swear I heard a hiss at the mention of his name. "He did ask me first."

"And if I insist on a ceremony?" His smile was sensuous, producing a different kind of heat that pooled around the jewel inside my body.

"Well, if it means that much to you . . . but I get to choose my dress." I had visions of a Vegas showgirl running through my head. Something with lots of sequins, rhinestones, and masses of feathers.

"And here I was thinking it was every little girl's dream to get married."

"Yeah, and the focus word in that statement is *little*. As in young, prepubescent. Have you seen the divorce rate these days? Why would anyone ever get hitched?"

"Well, I don't do divorce."

No. I didn't imagine he did.

The moisture on my face was making my eyelashes stick together. Without the use of my hands, I had no choice but to open my eyes really wide in order to un-stick the uppers from the lowers. This also meant my mouth popped open in a comical "O" shape.

"Are you trying to summon up some sort of demigod in the vain hope of counteracting the Chain's enchantment?" he asked, making his brows arch quizzically.

"Oh, for God's sake!" I blew out a breath and watched as droplets danced in the air. "If you won't untie my hands, then could you at least get a towel and wipe my face so I don't suffer any permanent vision loss from eye irritation."

He paused and seemed to be looking for trickery in my request. "No," he said, "but I will take you somewhere that's more comfortable."

Chapter 29

There was a sizzle, and the pungent smell of sulfur filled the air. Nothing like the fragrance of rotting eggs to exacerbate my breathing issues. Thankfully, I realized what was happening a split second before it occurred, and turned my head to my shoulder and closed my eyes before he transformed.

"Rowan? Look at me, Rowan."

Shaking my porcupine quill hair was answer enough. I felt the ground vibrate as he came toward me, and something hard reached beneath my chin. I resisted, but I felt a sting as a sharp edge sliced my skin. I was already too wet to feel the blood running down my neck, but I could smell it. The bastard had used his nails to cut me! I jerked my head around, almost going cross-eyed at what was in front of me. It hadn't been his nails. In fact, his hands were fisted firmly on his hips. Waving in front of my face was the pointed tip of his tail, dripping with my blood.

I stared at him, raking in everything from the obscene corkscrew horns erupting out of his forehead to the disturbing cloven hooves on which he stood. He'd adopted his man-beast form with the smooth, well-defined human upper body, and the heavy, dark pelt of fur that covered him from the waist down protecting his strangely formed lower limbs. Strange only because there was no disguising the animalistic formation of bone and muscle.

Oh, and let's not forget the cock he was so proud of, although what he ever expected to fuck with it was beyond me. I think even Catherine the Great would have declined.

"Just so you know," I said, doing my best not to gag on the smell, "this is not my favorite look for you."

His grin was startlingly white against the blackened lips and skin of his face. "Ah, but it's the only skin I can wear for this."

"For what?"

The idea that he might want to have sex with me in this manifestation was more terrifying than anything I could ever imagine. He'd split me open for sure. Reaching down, he picked me up in his arms and held me to his chest. The chain, pulled tight by the movement, cut into my flesh, making me wince.

"You'll feel better soon," he said.

I wasn't convinced that his idea of better and mine were necessarily the same. I looked up at him, seeing the scars that pitted his face and neck, spilling over his shoulders and across his chest. Reminders of trials he had overcome? His eyes glittered red and gold, and his long earlobes brushed the tops of his shoulders.

"Where are you taking me?"

His grin widened. The close-up view of the razor-sharp teeth crowding his mouth was more than I wanted to see. "As you've already destroyed the furniture, I have no choice but to find another bed. One better able to accommodate me."

"So I'm guessing it's not the Waldorf?"

"No, somewhere a lot more private."

I lay on my stomach, holding my breath as the length of Bridal Night Chain securing my hands was removed. The chain had cut into my flesh, requiring each gem to be pulled free from my swollen skin. It hurt like a son of a bitch, and I didn't even try to stop the tears that flowed. Strong fingers rubbed my wrists, restoring blood flow and feeling to my numb hands. Ignoring the stinging pain in my muscles, I yanked my hands away, clasping them together and sliding them beneath me between my breasts. I snarled and snapped with bared teeth when the other hands tried to take them back. A low rumble sounded, and it took me a moment to recognize it as laughter.

"Very well, we'll get to the rest later," he whispered in my ear, "but come, you need to sleep."

Whatever was supporting me moved suddenly, throwing me off-balance and rolling me into arms waiting to embrace me. He pulled me close, molding me to fit the contours of chest and hip and thigh. Fear and anxiety had left me too exhausted to offer anything in the way of resistance. It had also dropped my body temperature, and my survival instinct arched me toward the warmth emanating from his body. With a will of its own, my hand reached up and tangled itself in the long silk of his hair, and then I heard the faint sound of rustling. Rustling accompanied by the pleasingly familiar scent of anise, which carried with it the spicy tang of danger. A light touch across my shoulder made me crack open an eye. I was covered in feathers. Black as sin, each glossy length was tipped blood red.

"Sleep, Rowan," his voice commanded.

And closing my eye, I snuggled deeper inside my cocoon and did just that.

When I opened my eyes again, I stretched. It was an automatic reflex that caught me by surprise because it meant my hands were no longer bound. Quickly I closed my eyes and performed an inventory with my fingers. No chain around my neck, nothing pressing into my back. I rolled up on one hip—no mildly uncomfortable feeling between my cheeks. Ah, but not quite everything was gone. Though no longer attached to the chain, I could still feel the large opal nestled within me.

"Once this is inside you, it can only be removed in one way . . . by one person."

Katja's voice echoed dully inside my head. Yeah, getting that baby out wasn't going to be quite as easy as I'd hoped it would be.

I sat up and looked about me. The bed itself was high, covered with a sea of ornately embroidered pillows and cushions, and instead of traditional sheets or blankets, I was enveloped in bolts of silk and satin and velvet, all in varying shades of red and black, which came as no surprise. Swinging my legs over the edge of the bed, I hopped down, not noticing the small stepstool provided for that purpose until my feet were already on the floor. I pushed aside the sheer panels hanging from the ceiling and stepped into the room. Everywhere I looked, the black-and-red color scheme had been continued. Black walls splashed with what I hoped was red paint and not actual blood. The bed was the dominant piece of furniture, making the occupier's proclivities somewhat predictable. But, to be fair, there were also two chairs in front of a fireplace, both black with red seats, and between them a black lacquer table with a red pitcher and two glasses.

Oh my God, a pitcher—and I'm dying of thirst! I sniffed the liquid cautiously but could smell nothing. I poured a small amount into one of the glasses. It looked like water, it smelled like water, it even—I dipped a finger in the glass and put it to my tongue—tasted like water.

What if it's poisoned?

If he wanted to kill me, why go to all this trouble? He could have easily done it back in the apartment and saved himself the bother of dragging my corpse down here.

Yeah, leaving you in the apartment would have given you top spot in the unsolved kinky-sex-gone-wrong police blotter.

It took two very large glasses of water before my thirst was slaked. And then I had to pee. I looked around for entry to another room and spotted an open archway. It led to what appeared to be a fully equipped bathroom. I used the toilet, hoping that it was functional and not just for decoration. It appeared to operate normally when I flushed it, and I figured if the toilet worked, then so would the shower. Although there was a chance my demon would return while I was washing, I decided it was a chance worth taking. Somehow it felt better to face him looking like myself.

Removing all the goop from my hair was a challenge, and I cleaned my face at least four times just to be sure every scrap of makeup was gone. I was surprised to find I'd kept most of my lashes. Finished, I returned to the bedroom wrapped in one towel while rubbing my now much shorter hair with another. It had occurred to someone that I might be hungry because plates of food were set on the table next to the pitcher. There was fruit, bread and cheese, and a covered dish. And the pitcher had been replenished. Cautiously, I raised the lid on the covered dish. Who thought stew could be so appetizing? A fire now blazed in the hearth, giving the cavernous room a kind of cheery glow I wouldn't have thought possible. Someone had straightened up the bed and left a robe for my use. That made me almost as happy as the stew. I looked around, staring hard at the darkness beyond the light's reach. I couldn't be sure, but I told myself no one was there.

I was in the bathroom, cleaning my teeth with a washcloth, when the prickle between my shoulder blades said I wasn't alone. Considering the bathroom had no door, I was lucky he hadn't seen me using the toilet.

"Couldn't find a toothbrush," I said, explaining the need for the washcloth wrapped around my finger. It wasn't great, but better than nothing at all.

"I knew I'd forgotten something," he told me, watching as I scooped a handful of water and swooshed it around in my mouth before spitting in the sink.

"Guess you don't worry about cavities, huh?"

He answered with a chuckle.

"Did you remember lotion?" I asked.

He pointed to a jar on the counter that held an aromatic cream. I put a generous dollop on my hands and rubbed it in, getting a nice tingle in return.

"Shall we talk?" he asked, stepping to one side and waving a hand back toward the bedroom.

I was happy to move past him. In my experience, conversations held in bathrooms usually involve a lot of anger and/or crying. Perhaps it's the underlying knowledge of the room's function that allows people to unburden themselves more freely with a toilet and sink in view.

I took one of the chairs by the fire; he took the other. "So," I began, rearranging the robe I was wearing so it covered my legs, "what shall we talk about?"

"Your reason for accepting my gift."

I gave him a puzzled look. "Wasn't that what you wanted?"

"Of course." He leaned forward and, with a flick of his finger, parted my robe, exposing my legs to mid-thigh. "And I couldn't have been more thrilled to see you wearing it, but . . . why now?"

I stared at him. He was in a more relaxed version of Armani. No suit, but tailored slacks and a crisp red shirt that was open at the throat. No jewelry either, I noticed. Not even the pinkie ring. He was also barefoot.

"I'm a woman," I said, tilting my head to one side. "I'm allowed to change my mind."

"Did the broken bed in your apartment factor into your decision?"

I tried not to show my delight at his use of information I'd shared with the fake Gabriel. "Perhaps," I admitted.

"And the Russian broke it?"

It was nice to know he'd been paying attention. "Aleksei owed me a favor."

"Yes, but why destroy the bed in the first place? Was it because of Katja? I know she was there, I could smell her scent. It was faint, but I recognized it."

OMG—not only had he taken the wrong path, he was skipping

ahead of me. "Can you blame me?" I asked. "A possessive nature isn't the exclusive province of vampires, you know."

"But Gabriel didn't fuck her"—he frowned—"surely you realized that?"

"Just because he didn't doesn't mean he wouldn't have. It was enough she was in *my* apartment—in *my* bedroom—with him. What he did or didn't do with her makes no difference. She shouldn't have been there."

"What if she came to apologize for what she did to you?"

I couldn't decide if he was taking the side of the faux Gabriel or was trying to confuse me. "Flowers and a note would have been just fine. Better even." I blew out an irritated breath. "Look, I don't give a damn why she was there. He says he loves me. He had no business giving the time of day to a woman who nearly killed me."

Dear God, please let the women are from Venus, men are from Mars confusion apply to demons as well as vampires.

I gripped the arms of the chair—just enough for him to see my anger, but I had to be careful not to overplay my hand. My anger over the imaginary rendezvous would be normal; wanting to rip Katja's head off and mount it on the wall might be considered excessive. "And he wonders why I'm pissed at him," I muttered.

"So how did you know she had been there? Surely Gabriel wasn't so foolish as to tell you?"

Although I had told the fake Gabriel I'd been able to smell Katja's presence, the demon would know it to be a lie. Human noses weren't that good. "Aleksei told me," I confessed, hoping my fib would be forgiven. "So he broke the bed." At least that was the truth.

I held my breath, my mind racing as I tried to anticipate his next question in an effort to stay a step ahead. I had dangled the mental carrot in front of him; now all I needed was for him to take a bite.

"So what you're really after is . . . revenge sex."

Hallelujah!

"Do you know any other kind that's better?" I leaned forward, making sure the front of the robe gaped open, giving him a nice view. Of course he'd already seen me completely naked, but it's different when it's being offered because someone wants you to have it.

He rested his chin on folded hands. "That's not why I gave you the Bridal Night Chain."

"Ah, yeah, I know, and I'm sorry if I've misused it, but does it really

make that much of a difference?" I decided to take advantage of his ignorance about Ryiel's making Jenna his Promise, hoping he hadn't
been brought up to speed. "Look at it this way, we'll each get a taste of
what's to come, and, as I'm sure you know"—I dropped my voice to
a throaty purr—"anticipation can be quite an aphrodisiac."

He tapped a forefinger against his chin, looking at me with a stud-
ied air. "So you're proposing we have sex now, I return you to Gabriel,
and then do what? Reclaim you, as promised, in twenty-five years?"

I nodded slowly, wearing what I hoped was a sultry smile. "Something like that."

"Don't lie to me, Rowan."

Oh fuck. The smile on my face froze. "What do you mean?"

He got to his feet and shook his head, making his dark hair fall
rakishly across his forehead while his eyes glowed red. He held out a
hand, and I suddenly realized this might be my opportunity. I might
never have a better moment than right now. He wanted me. It was in
the way his eyes kept roaming over me, the barely discernible tremble in his fingers, the surreptitious slide of his tongue across his lips.
I placed my hand in his, and let him pull me to my feet.

Long fingers ran through my hair, then trailed down my neck,
across my shoulders, and along each side of my rib cage. Just the
right amount of pressure to make me gasp instead of giggle. His hand
cupped my breast, stroking it through the silky fabric of the robe before lightly pinching the nipple, which hardened immediately at his
touch. His smile was wolfish. I waited until he looked into my eyes
before running the tip of my tongue over my lips.

"Mmmm . . . feels nice," I murmured, pressing myself against him.

His kiss was a fast, unexpected swipe of his lips across my mouth.
For a moment, I was stunned, thinking I'd missed my chance, but then
I realized it was the perfect opportunity to make him think there was
no danger in kissing me. I returned the pressure of his lips, allowing
the tip of my tongue to dance at the corner of his mouth.

I wish I could say that it felt awful and I wanted to be sick, but
that would be a lie. The truth is, I *was* attracted to him on a physical
level. We'd both known it since our first encounter. He appealed to
me in a way that was dangerously explosive. I just didn't know how
far my unpredictable lust for him could be used against me.

Chapter 30

"Will you tell me something?" I asked, looking up at him from beneath my lashes. My coquettish behavior was purely accidental. I have no idea how to be flirtatious. But it seemed to work because he leaned into me, rubbing his hands along my arms.

"Ah . . . you want to know my name, don't you?"

"But you've already promised to tell me that," I reminded, recalling all too clearly the specific set of circumstances he required. He smiled, but I didn't know if it was because I remembered or because he could keep it secret a while longer. "No, this is something else," I told him.

"What do you want to know?"

"Do you know what Kartel is up to?" I have no idea why I asked such a thing, except my intuition suggested that, whatever grand scheme Vampire Smurf was planning, he was getting help from somewhere.

"You think I am helping him?"

So much for thinking I could be subtle. "Are you?" I asked. "He bragged about having a power in his hands. Something so great it was going to change the world." It was nonsense, of course. I had no idea if Kartel had ever said anything like that, but it wasn't hard to imagine him doing so.

"A power so great it will change the world . . ." He mulled the words over before smiling down at me. "I suppose it will make no difference to tell you."

His arm circled my waist as he shared the blue-haired vampire's plans. Plans he had helped form, plans he would help execute. The words spilled out of him, chilling me with their detail. Though I tried my best, I couldn't help the tremble that swept through me.

"Does it excite you?" he asked, mistaking the reason for my shaking limbs.

I didn't answer him. Instead I took his face in my hands and pulled it down to me. He kissed me deeper this time, swiping his tongue across my own, licking and tasting, exploring the warmth of my mouth. And that's when I felt a sudden stirring deep inside me as something anchored struggled to break free. Recognizing the feel of its master, it began rushing through me. Wanting to be reconnected, to become once more a part of the whole. Ryiel had warned me it would find its way into my mouth of its own volition, and he hadn't been wrong. There was a fullness in my throat and the back of my mouth, and something slimy now coated my teeth.

Taking my courage in both hands, I thrust my tongue into the dark recess of the demon's mouth. He stiffened slightly, surprised by my forwardness, but then, like all vain males, assumed my lust for him had got the better of me. I pushed up to the roof of his mouth and scraped the vile piece of him off me. His eyes flew open, burning with fury, and the arm around my waist pulled even tighter. I could feel him trying to dislodge the piece of himself so it would once more return to my mouth. Desperately, I tried to pull my tongue back, retreat from his mouth so I could press my lips together and deny him access, but he tangled with me. Vicious barbs stabbed at the underside of my tongue, and the taste of my own blood suddenly washed back into my mouth. I resisted the urge to swallow, unsure whether I would take his scrap of evil back into my body if I did so. And just when I was certain I had surely failed, that he was going to keep my soul and ensure that the contract between us remained intact, I felt the pull of something that was intrinsically mine.

Immediately, I dropped my hands from his face, becoming limp in his arms and giving myself up to receive the precious piece of me I'd thought was lost forever. It slammed into me with the violence of a racecar hitting a wall at two hundred miles an hour. He pulled his mouth from mine with such ferocity, I'm surprised I didn't lose a tooth in the process.

"Bitch!" he snarled, twisting the front of my robe in his fist.

I could see something dark and slimy behind his teeth, but he had changed the configuration of his mouth, and the multitude of razor-sharp teeth prevented whatever was now on his tongue from escaping. I turned my head, burying my face in the crook of my arm, holding it tight with my other hand so I could cover my mouth.

Unfortunately, I hadn't reckoned on being picked up and flung across the room. The millisecond it took for my brain to tell my body what was about to happen was way too long. I felt something crunch as my back hit the wall, and fell forward to the floor. I was in agony, the pain so intense I was barely able to register the vibrations in the floor as he came for me. Looming over me, terrible in his rage, he wrapped his hands around my throat, pulling me up and squeezing.

"You dare to deceive me?" he screamed, spittle flying from his mouth and landing on my cheeks. "You dare to offer yourself and then refuse me? Not here, not in my realm. I am no vampire to be trifled with."

He brought his face close to mine.

Close enough that I could see the flames that fanned the vertical slit in each eye.

Close enough that I could see the maggots crawling in the fibrous tissue of his corkscrewed horns.

Close enough that I could smell the decay and corruption of his soul.

He opened his mouth, and I struggled against him, knowing he wanted to make me take back that part of him. But our contract was broken. I could feel it, and I knew he could as well. Unless I willingly gave him a piece of my soul, the terms could not be reinstated. I saw in his eyes the moment he realized I understood the termination of our contract far better than he had anticipated. In frustration, he pushed his hips against me, his threat blatant. I panicked. I wanted no other part of him inside me, and most certainly not that. I could feel the burn of his fingers as they tightened. I could only hold on for a few seconds more, and then he would be able to do whatever he wanted. Some things can be taken without consent. I stopped struggling and forced myself to look into his eyes, letting him see the contempt and utter loathing in mine.

And then suddenly he released his hold on me, dropping me to the floor, where the back of my head struck the ground hard enough to make it bounce. His hands were gone from around my throat. I put my own in their place as a shield should he resume his attack, feeling the terrible scalding blisters that were erupting on my skin. I tried to move, wanting to crawl to the shadows and hide myself in the darkness, but excruciating pain radiated out from my hips and shot down my legs when I tried to move. The agony was so intense I screamed—out loud or in my head I couldn't tell.

I was under no illusions . . . I was going to die at the hands of a demon. No doubt the Grim Reaper was already scurrying along labyrinthine passageways cut deep in the earth, delighted at the chance to tell me to fuck off.

But you can't die unless Gabriel does.

I hated to crush my inner bitch's optimism, but now that my contract was broken, I didn't think that part was still in effect, if it ever had been, here in the Dark Realm.

Well . . . shit!

She was taking it a lot better than I thought she would.

I lay with my cheek pressed against the stone floor, fighting against the wave of oblivion trying to claim me. Someone once said how we die is just as important as how we live. I was determined to look my demon in the eye one last time so he would know he'd been bested by a mere human.

The hand that covered my mouth muffled my scream as I was rolled onto my back. I squeezed my eyes shut as a jillion jolts of pain fried nerve endings, decimated muscles, and shattered my bones.

"Rowan, sweetheart, I'm here."

My eyes flew open to see a familiar curtain of white blond hair pooling on my chest as Gabriel leaned over me. He held a finger to his lips, urging silence while he slowly removed his hand from my mouth. I stared at him, wanting to believe he was real, but not trusting myself to do so. I'd thought he'd been real before, but that had been a lie, and I was in so much pain, I couldn't trust my senses.

"How . . . ?" It was all I could manage.

"Katja told me."

Now I knew the image was a lie. The psycho-bitch vampire would never do anything so unselfish. Anger rose in me, strong enough to blanket the pain coursing through me. If my life was going to be forfeit, then the bastard should have the decency to wear his own face as he led me to the edge of the abyss and threw me in.

"You insulting prick," I said, gritting my teeth. "You didn't fool me before by pretending to be Gabriel. It's not going to work now."

"Fool you . . . before?" He had the nerve to actually look baffled before asking, "When did I come to you before?"

He wants to play games? My inner bitch seemed perturbed.

Okay, I'd play.

"In my apartment . . . while I was waiting for *you.*" I tried snarling my reply, but I was back to the asthmatic pug imitation.

The smooth forehead creased, and a heavy, vertical line formed between dark brows. I could almost read the sequence of events, real and imagined, that were going through his mind. "Rowan, the last time I saw you, you were leaving to meet Anasztaizia at your apartment."

Oh, he's really good.

Yeah, but how would the demon know that?

"I sent Ryiel to talk to you, but if I'd known . . ."

He trailed off, and instead of seeing sorrow or sadness at my predicament, his eyes flashed with unmistakable fury that I had been hurt. A seed of doubt rooted in my brain and began sending out shoots, struggling toward the truth. His fingers traced a path down the side of my face, stroking my jaw. I'd known it hadn't been him in my apartment, but how could I know if what I was seeing now was really Gabriel? I might be closer to death than I knew, and my imagination was simply conjuring up the last image I wanted to see. There was only one way to be sure.

"What did you say to me . . . the first time you ever saw me?"

His smile was a thing of beauty, and if I was close to death, then I could not have asked for anything more glorious to be the last thing my eyes beheld. Long, elegant fingers moved to my head, and I felt them thread through my spiky hair.

"*This should never be hidden,*" Gabriel murmured, leaning forward to press his lips against mine. "And had we been anywhere but your father's tent, I would have kissed you just like that."

The floodgates opened as I tried to throw my arms around his neck, but as my anger diminished, the searing pain fracturing my body returned. Endorphins have their limitations. Pulling off his shirt, Gabriel wadded it up and placed it under my head. The sight of his muscles flexing in the low light made me catch my breath. Even then.

We both turned our heads as the sound of slow hand clapping bounced off the walls of the chamber, echoing with a strange resonance. I felt Gabriel stiffen as he rose to his feet, standing protectively in front of me.

"You realize I've taken her many times over already," the demon sneered. Though he wore his Armani persona, he had not changed his eyes. Even from where I lay, I could see the red glow and black vertical pupils. A way of reminding Gabriel of what he truly was. As if Gabriel had ever forgotten.

"And yet you still have both eyes, so your words are nothing but an idle boast," Gabriel declared.

"You think she would have the strength to disfigure me in the process?"

"I know she would," Gabriel responded with pride.

The demon made a scornful sound. "Nevertheless, she was willing to give herself to me."

"To break the contract between you. For no other reason."

"Tell yourself that if it soothes your pride."

He came across the floor, his movement reminding me of a large predator stalking his prey. I watched as Gabriel repositioned himself, balancing his weight more evenly on the balls of his feet, relaxing his body. With arms hanging loose at his sides, he curled his hands into light fists. It was simply a matter of waiting to see who threw the first punch. And that would depend on which of them lost his temper.

Ordinarily, I would put my money on Gabriel remaining calm and clearheaded, but this was no ordinary opponent he was facing. And I didn't mean because he was a demon. That was not nearly as significant as the fact he'd been created from the same orb of celestial light as Gabriel. Formed in pairs, angels were given free will to choose whether to walk in the Light or the Dark. And while not twins in the truest sense, they did retain a certain awareness of one another.

"My pride has no need of soothing," Gabriel said. "Perhaps you should look to yourself. It will not go well for you once it is known that you failed to maintain a pact initiated at the behest of the Dark Realm—" He paused. "Assuming that it ever was," he added softly.

My eardrums were in danger of being perforated by the roar that buffeted me like a gale-force wind. The structure of the chamber was such that it amplified sound, returning it in a wave that physically pushed me until I was flattened against the wall. I couldn't have said which hurt more, my back or my ears.

The fight, such as it was, was over before I even registered that it had begun—a blur of movement happening too fast for me to follow—and the outcome had already been decided. Despite the ringing in my ears, I was able to recognize the sounds of conflict, the sickening crunch my brain associated with breaking bones, something I had become all too familiar with recently, and the odd splattering that indicated a pummeling of flesh. And then there was silence. As loud and painful as the roar was, I could still hear echoing inside my head. I doubt the altercation had taken more than a few heartbeats, and it was over. I just didn't know who had won.

Pulling myself from the shadows, my ragged nails finding whatever purchase they could, I dragged myself away from the wall. Ignoring the agony in the small of my back, I reached the center of the room, where I pushed myself up on my hands as I searched for Gabriel. I saw nothing. Neither Gabriel nor the demon. Had the unthinkable happened? Were they both dead? Were they so evenly matched there had been no advantage on either side? Or had they simply disintegrated like one of Kartel's vampires?

"No-no-no-no-no!" I sobbed before strong arms picked me up, and the scent of everything winter filled my nose.

Gabriel's mouth found mine, and I welcomed the feel of his tongue sweeping over my lips, even though the salty taste of tears filled my mouth as I welcomed him in. When he finally released me, I stared up at him, seeing the abrasions and contusions already starting to heal.

"Is he dead?" I asked in a low voice.

Gabriel shook his head, closing his eyes briefly. "I cannot take his life, even if I wanted to," he told me. "Not here, not in his own realm."

I don't know why, but I was glad. I did not want Gabriel to have to shoulder the weight of that burden.

"Then where is he?" I asked, fearful the demon might leap from the shadows and attack us once more.

"I don't know," Gabriel murmured, resting his forehead against mine, "but he is gone."

It took me a few moments before I realized the fiery pain in my lower back and hips was also gone. There was no hot-poker ache infusing my limbs with a scorching heat. In fact, I couldn't feel anything at all. The muscles of my chest, arms, and shoulders throbbed with a dull, pounding ache, but I was numb from the waist down.

My demon might not have killed me, but he'd done something far worse. He'd paralyzed me. I didn't need to tell Gabriel; he could see the fear in my eyes, and I think he could tell from the lack of movement, or perhaps the sudden unnatural dead weight of my lower body, what had happened.

"We need to leave here," he said.

"Are you taking me home?"

"Eventually."

Chapter 31

I should not have been surprised to learn that *eventually* was code for a pit stop in the Void. I don't know why Gabriel didn't tell me. Perhaps he thought I would resist, but I no longer feared the Void. It welcomed me like a prodigal daughter, healing my broken back, and my bruised and blistered skin. It even went so far as to ask if I wanted a certain foreign object removed from my—you better believe I did. And as I swirled in the dark embrace of the only true power in the Dark Realm, I asked why I was being shown such favor. The Void, unused to having someone listen, told me. The answer was not unexpected.

I was returned to Gabriel by way of the penthouse terrace, and sadly, there was no disguising where I had been. I looked as if I'd just stepped out of a pool of septic waste. Smelled like it too. Gabriel immediately picked me up and jumped into the pool. I can only guess his first instinct was to wash me clean, and it worked, although I later learned Tomas had to have the pool drained, sanitized—probably exorcized—before declaring it fit to be used again.

Wrapping me in a big towel, Gabriel took me straight to bed, holding me while I slept. I was surprised when I awoke to learn I'd been unconscious for almost three days.

It was Tomas who told me there had been a somewhat contentious discussion between Gabriel and Ryiel regarding the silver-eyed vampire's part in my excursion to the Dark Realm. Recognizing the emotional impact of continuing to defend his actions, Ryiel chose to leave. Abruptly.

"He should have told me," Gabriel said, still hurt by the actions of the vampire he regarded as so much more than a friend.

I propped myself up on the pillow and looked at my lover. A light sheen of perspiration, a result of our lovemaking, made his skin glow. "Telling you was the choice he gave to me, and I made him promise to keep my decision a secret." The neon-blue of his eyes darkened suddenly, a sign that told me he felt as if he'd been betrayed twice. I grasped his hand, kissing each finger before asking, "Would you have tried to stop me, if you had known?"

He snorted. "Of course I would."

"Then don't blame Ryiel for keeping his word to me." Turning his hand over, I pressed my lips against his palm and continued to look at him. I didn't need him to tell me what he wanted to do. I could read it in his face. "Go find Ryiel. Apologize and make peace. Don't waste what time you have left with each other."

"I don't know what to say."

"Admitting you acted like an asshole would be a good start," I volunteered.

"I don't like the thought of leaving you."

"I need to spend some time with Laycee."

I leaned forward and gave him a long, lingering kiss, which turned into a demonstration of other uses for my tongue.

Laycee welcomed me with open arms, then gave me the expected ration of shit about my hair. Professional pride made her tidy it up for me so I looked more cute, loveable hedgehog and less angry porcupine. It was a great improvement, and I couldn't believe how much time I was now saving in the shower. I managed to last two weeks before the craving for peace, quiet, and a bathroom without a diaper genie in the corner got to me.

As always, Laycee understood. "Is everything all right with you and Eye Candy?"

"Yes. He and Ryiel had a misunderstanding. He's gone to apologize."

We were sitting on the porch swing, and Laycee immediately jumped up to make sure Jake was still seated at the kitchen table, reading the newspaper funnies to his infant daughter.

"It's nothing to do with him and Jenna, is it?" she asked in a whisper.

"No," I assured her, smiling at the way she avoided using Ryiel's name. "It's strictly a vampire guy thing."

"Ahhh." A knowledgeable lift of an expertly penciled brow put the matter to rest.

Instead of returning to the penthouse, I decided it was time to face my apartment. Naturally, I told Tomas where I would be, just in case anything happened to me while Gabriel was still in absentia. The sentinel offered to meet me, so I wouldn't have to go through the process alone, but I told him that rather defeated the purpose. He agreed with my decision, but made me promise to call him if anything felt wrong.

I was met at my apartment door by a certain amount of fear, but I forced myself to move past it. If I could tell the Grim Reaper to take a hike, then I could walk through this door. Besides, Ryiel had assured me my demon couldn't come after me again once the contract was broken, unless I gave him cause to. My apartment had been cleaned and my bed replaced. According to his note, Tomas had passed on the hefty fee for a rush delivery to Aleksei, who hadn't so much as whimpered on receiving the bill.

I spent the next couple of days unpacking boxes that had been in storage, and trying to decide what to keep and what to send to Goodwill. Four twenty-something CPAs moved into the apartment down the hall, and being neighborly, they invited me to their housewarming. I was elevated to the status of a goddess when I showed up with all of Aleksei's leftover booze. I returned home to find a spray of freesias on my pillow with a note. Gabriel was back from his trip and wanted to take me on a date. I took that as a good sign that he and Ryiel had reached an understanding.

Someone had made a valiant effort to replace at least most of the burned-out or missing lightbulbs from the sign at Rosie's Bar. I wondered if they might take a stab at the gravel parking lot next, but it was going to take more than a couple of boxes of 100 watts to help the one lone light. I parked my Charger between two pickup trucks, both of which had seen better days. I didn't see anything that belonged in Gabriel's garage.

There had been a few changes inside Rosie's since the night I'd first met Gabriel there. The trophy deer head on the wall was sporting a Santa hat. Whatever enterprising soul had put it up there had been disinclined to remove it. I wondered if it might be replaced with a green derby come St. Patrick's Day. The other changes consisted mainly of new signs promoting different makes of beer, but it was going to take more than the offer of a few imports to put Rosie's on the map.

It was a weeknight, so the place wasn't exactly jumping. I took a seat in a booth, and when the waitress came by, I ordered a Jack and Coke, and asked for a clean glass. Puzzled by my request, she nonetheless returned with my order almost immediately.

"Do you have any vodka?" I asked.

"Yeah, of course."

"Stoli Elit?" The blank look on her face was answer enough. I reached in the tote bag I was using as a purse and pulled out a bottle. The waitress watched as I cracked open the seal and then filled the empty glass she'd brought me. "I want you to give that to the blond guy sitting two booths behind me," I told her.

"Uh, you're not s'posed to bring your own liquor," the waitress admonished me.

I put the bottle of vodka on her tray, next to the glass I'd poured. "Keep it behind the bar," I told her. "In case someone else asks for it."

Problem solved, she gave me a toothy grin and went to deliver the drink. Less than thirty seconds later, she was back, looking slightly flushed. Both drink and bottle were still on her tray.

"What did he say?" I asked.

"He said to tell you if you wanted to buy him a drink, the least you could do was deliver it yourself."

"He said that, did he?"

The waitress nodded. I could see the cogs turning in her head as she wondered if perhaps she ought to have been a little more diplomatic. Too late to do anything about it now. She shrugged and put the glass of vodka down in front of me. And the bottle too. "Just in case," she said, before turning and walking back to the bar.

With my tote bag over my shoulder, I scooted out of the booth, pausing to pick up the glass and the bottle of Stoli. I could feel stares coming from the bar. The waitress had shared the incident with her regulars, and curious to see the outcome, heads were now turned.

Gabriel sat wedged up against the back of the booth with one leg spread along the seat. I guessed there wasn't enough space for him to sit with both legs beneath the table and be comfortable.

"Buy you a drink?" I asked.

"Is it really buying if you're providing your own bottle?" he asked.

"I'll make sure I tip the waitress a C-note before I leave."

"Wow, you must really want to buy me a drink."

I slid in opposite him, managing to get both my legs under the table without any problem. "How's Ryiel?" I asked, pushing the tumbler of vodka across the table to him.

"Good. He sends you his best." The upturn at the corners of his mouth told me he and the dark-haired vampire had parted on better than good terms. I was glad. Picking up his glass, Gabriel downed the vodka in one go. "Katja died," he said suddenly, losing all traces of good humor.

"Oh . . . I'm sorry."

"Are you?" He arched a brow in surprise at my response before refilling his glass from the bottle sitting between us.

I decided that yes, I was sorry. I could afford to be magnanimous because I was the one who was alive. For a few moments, we sat and said nothing. The wail of a love gone wrong poured out of the juke-box, and I thought it sounded similar to the one I'd heard the night Laycee had called me from this same bar. But then I think most country songs sound alike, given enough time and alcohol.

I stared across the table at my lover. His hair shimmered in the low light, and his eyes were darkening. Something was bothering him.

"Ask me, Gabriel, whatever you want to know. I won't lie to you."

He sighed, hesitating a moment before saying, "Is the contract truly broken?"

Ah, so that was it. He'd not asked me outright, and knowing the power of words when dealing with supernatural beings, I understood why he needed to hear the confirmation from my lips.

"Yes," I said gravely. "The contract is truly broken."

I didn't know it was possible to look relieved and worried at the same time, but Gabriel managed it. "Is there anything I need to know?" he asked in a low voice.

"Kartel is going to start a war between vampires and humans," I said, deliberately misinterpreting what he was asking me. "And the Dark Realm is going to help him."

Deciding to let me have my way, Gabriel crossed his arms and nodded. "Ah, so that's what he was up to." The ripple of his biceps said they missed my touch. "It will be a difficult accomplishment without a way to create his army."

"How so?"

"We didn't find Petrov at the location the informant gave us, but we did find a notebook he seemed to have left behind. It contained a detailed account of the whereabouts of every drug stockpile Kartel had amassed. It's all been destroyed."

"That was a stroke of luck." My tone clearly demonstrated my disbelief. Gabriel just shrugged. "But what's to stop Kartel from getting Petrov to just make more of the same drug?" Even though his disappearing act suggested Petrov was aware that Kartel had no further use for him, the blue-haired vampire was still his maker. Petrov could always be compelled.

Gabriel emptied his glass. "Petrov is dead."

"Did you . . . ?"

He shook his head. "No. He took his own life. I can only assume he realized any sanctuary I offered would be temporary in nature, and with no other Original to protect him, he took the only option available."

"How did he do it?" I don't know why I asked. Morbid curiosity perhaps?

"The Sahara desert is quite lethal, or so I am told."

Our waitress stopped by, bringing me another Jack and Coke. I thanked her, enjoying the shocked look in her eyes when I placed the hundred-dollar bill on her tray and told her to keep the change. Being rich had its moments.

"So Kartel's plans have been derailed?"

"For the time being," Gabriel agreed.

"You don't seem very concerned," I observed.

"You are my only concern." He paused, giving me a look that promised nothing but a lifetime of devotion. Reaching for my hand, he turned it over and rubbed his thumb gently across my inner wrist. "Is there anything we need to talk about?"

This time I wasn't mulish. I knew what he was asking, what he needed to know. Had I surrendered any of myself in order to break my pact with the Dark Realm, and if so, how much? And he wasn't asking because of anything so foolish as male ego. He was asking as much for my sake as his own. Gabriel didn't want me thinking I couldn't come to him because of choices I might have made.

"Why did you ask the Void to heal me?"

My question wasn't what he expected, and surprise flared in his eyes. "The Void and I have an . . . understanding."

I knew as much because the Void had told me so. It was on the tip of my tongue to ask him what such an understanding had cost him, but I didn't. There are some things better left unsaid.

Even between lovers.

"It was the Void that removed the opal . . . not him." Gabriel's relief at my words was palpable, and I covered the hand holding mine with my free one. "Is there anything *you* want to ask *me?*"

He narrowed his eyes. "Are you going to grow your hair back?"

Still self-conscious about my shorter look, I put a hand to the nape of my neck. "I haven't decided. Do you want me to?"

"Only if it pleases you to do so." He raised my hand to his mouth and brushed his lips over my knuckles.

I looked at the hand that held mine, seeing the platinum-and-mahogany ring on his finger as it caught the light and shone. The ring he hadn't taken off since the day I'd put it on him. The ring I knew he would never take off. Gabriel would keep me safe, and if he couldn't, then the Void would. Because he had asked it to.

I had no idea what had happened to us before, and I accepted that I might never know. Had I hurt Gabriel in the past? Yes, I could feel it somewhere deep inside me, though the details were lost. But I couldn't live my life worrying about things I couldn't change. I was in love with a vampire, and he loved me. Always had. Body and soul.

"Do you still want to take me to see the Northern Lights?" I asked.

He grinned. "Of course. Just tell me when."

"What's the name of the place again?"

"Kangerlussuaq."

"Do you suppose we could find a priest in Gang-er-loose-sue-arc?"

"I'm sure we could." He hesitated. "Why do you need a priest?"

"I think I'd like to be married under the Northern Lights."

His smile was pure seduction. "So is this your way of telling me we're going to be okay?"

I smiled. It was such a human thing to say. I felt, as well as heard, the collective sigh from the bar area as I leaned across the table and kissed him on the mouth.

"We're going to be better than okay," I promised.

Go back to where it all started with Carla Susan Smith's *A Vampire's Promise,* available wherever digital books are sold!

TRUST YOUR INSTINCTS

Rowan Harper is nothing but a smart-mouthed bookstore clerk with a crappy love life on the night she walks into Rosie's Bar. Most of the drama in her life is borrowed from her best friend's adventures. But when she meets Gabriel—tall and movie-star gorgeous— everything changes. Never mind that she turns down the drink he offers, or that he brims with secrets she can't begin to guess at. He ignites a desire in her she never suspected—and shows a fascination with her she can't explain.

He has no family, no job, no bank account; he knows where she lives and her favorite flower. An aura of mystery cloaks him, even as Rowan grasps for facts, even as she fears an answer that could destroy her happiness. Gabriel can guide her through a wonderland of new sensations. But only if Rowan trusts him enough to follow . . .

Winner of the OKRWA "Finally a Bride" contest.

Visit us at www.kensingtonbooks.com

CARLA SUSAN SMITH

A VAMPIRE'S PROMISE

A Vampire's Promise Novel

Carla Susan Smith owes her love of literature to her mother, who, after catching her pre-teen daughter reading by flashlight beneath the bed covers, calmly replaced the romance book she had "borrowed" with one that was far less risqué, and much more appropriate! Though she was encouraged to include different genres in her reading tastes, romance—paranormal romance in particular—has always been her first love.

Born and raised in England, Carla now calls South Carolina home, where she lives with her wonderfully supportive husband, awesome son, and a canine critique group (if tails aren't wagging, then the story isn't working!). When not writing, she can usually be found in the kitchen trying out any recipe that calls for rhubarb, working on her latest tapestry project, or playing catch-up with her reading list. Please visit her at www.CarlaSmithauthor.com.